The Ambassador: The Lost Colony

George T. Hahn

SBG

Contents

well as adults.I hope there is more to come as I have grown to really like his characters and his way of developing their worlds.   *Louise Nicks.*

Tau Ceti: A Ship from Earth

Tau Ceti: The New Colonists

Tau Ceti: The Immortality Conspiracy

Voyage of the Capek

The Methuselah Conspirators

Methuselah's Revenge

The Ambassador: The Lost Colony

The Ambassador: Path to Contact

The Ambassador: Mission to Earth

Timeline

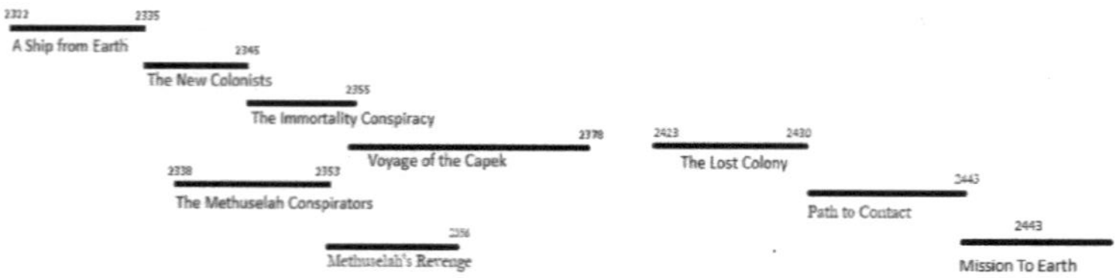

I N THE TWENTY-FIRST CENTURY, an American company, Energy Unlimited, used the recently discovered Stenhouse Field to generate cheap energy in orbiting satellites and beam it to Earth. Several decades later, Stenhouse research also led to Stenhouse Drive, a technology for moving spaceships at speeds approaching, but not exceeding, the speed of light.

Travel to other stars became possible, and probes went out to three of the nearer star systems: the triple star Alpha Centauri system, Tau Ceti, and Epsilon Eridani. All three systems had colonizable planets, and human-crewed ships followed. Traveling at sublight speeds, the voyages took years, but they established colonies.

The Alpha Centauri expedition named their world Goddard. It had a breathable atmosphere but was perpetually covered with ice, livable but not pleasant. Epsilon Eridani's world, Trist, was worse, populated by primitive life that exhaled chlorine, making its atmosphere poisonous. The colonists had to live in tunnels, sealed away from the outer world.

Pitcairn, in the Tau Ceti star system, twelve light-years from Earth, was different. It had abundant life, although biologically much different from Terran life, a breathable atmosphere, and a climate people could survive without protection. The gravity was twenty-five percent higher than Earth's, and the planet was warmer and subject to high winds, but it was a paradise compared to Goddard and Trist. Unlike those two planets, Pitcairn thrived and grew.

Distance isolated all three worlds from Earth. Supply ships, with new colonists and resources unavailable except from Earth, came to Pitcairn at roughly twenty-year intervals and were eagerly anticipated.

That was the situation for two hundred years. Early in the twenty-fourth century, the Western Alliance, now the dominant nation on Earth, sent the library ships to the colonies: *Lang* to Goddard, *Capek* to Trist, and *Asimov* to Pitcairn in 2322. The library ships were enormous, automated, self-sustaining starships, run by an advanced computer, carrying all of Earth's knowledge, and equipped with a vast array of sensory devices for studying the universe. They could build Link satellites, innovative technology that could send messages faster than the speed of light, opening the colonies to much closer contact with Earth. Link technology improved steadily and enabled the development of Enhanced Stenhouse Drive. Starting in 2335, manned starships could travel relatively easily to the colonies.

Easier contact with Earth brought controversy. Pitcairn, under Patrick Malley and aided by the now-conscious *Asimov*, resisted Earth's control and became an independent world in 2345. In 2355, a group of colonists from Trist took over the *Capek,* also now conscious, and, with the library ship's cooperation, set out on a seven-year journey to find a better world. They found the world they would call Not Trist, orbiting the star 82 G. Eridani.

Earlier, Earth launched an automated exploration starship, the *Alejandro Castillo,* to find other colonizable worlds. Traveling at sublight speeds, its mission was to go to a star, install a Link so people could easily follow, and move on to another star. It arrived at Sirius in 2360, installed a Link, and received orders to go to 82 G. Eridani next. Earth did not hear from it again.

From the papers of Reuben Noland, Pitcairn Administrator, 2413

1

"AMBASSADOR ROMERO FOR DEPUTY Ambassador Goldstein," his phone announced.

"Connect," Edward Goldstein ordered. "Good afternoon, Ambassador. What can I do for you?"

"The Ministry of Foreign Affairs has recalled me to Earth for a special mission," Romero said. "I just received the order."

"I take it I will be in charge in your absence."

"No, I'll let Herrara take over. I want you to come with me."

Goldstein had stood and walked over to a window as they spoke. From his office on the fifteenth floor of the Government Center, the view could be spectacular on a good day. The panorama of the city and the forested hills beyond it were worth the occasional small oscillations as the building reacted to the frequent, powerful gusts of wind. The short, sturdy trees and their predominantly red foliage were so fascinatingly different, yet similar to life on Earth. Today, though, a violent storm pelted his window with huge drops of water, hiding the forest and blurring the outlines of the buildings. That, too, was not unusual on Pitcairn.

Technically, he outranked Deputy Ambassador Herrara and should have been left in charge. *Is the mission so important it needed the two ranking members of the Pitcairn Embassy?* "What is the mission, sir?"

"We can discuss that later." Romero clipped his words, running them together as if he were in a hurry to end the conversation. "A starship will be here to pick us up in two days, and I have to brief Deputy Ambassador Herrara on his duties. Just be ready to leave."

Goldstein unclenched his jaw before responding. "Yes, sir."

GOLDSTEIN JOINED BRYAN REINER, the Pitcairn Administrator, for their usual weekly meeting at Paulina's, a restaurant on Ivory Street. There were other meetings in Reiner's office, but that was for formal discussions of relations with Earth and included Ambassador Romero.

"I'll be gone for a while," Goldstein said as they waited for their food. "Romero has been recalled to Earth for a diplomatic mission to the Eastern Bloc, and he wants me to come along."

"You don't look happy about it," Bryan said. The Pitcairn Administrator was twelve years older than Goldstein, in his early fifties, but shorter, a side effect of living his entire life on a planet with a gravity 25 percent higher than Earth's.

"Romero hasn't told me much about the mission yet or what part I'm supposed to play in it. He didn't even tell me it was to the Eastern Bloc. Herrara told me while he was gloating about being left in charge." Goldstein's fingers tapped out a slow beat on the table.

"Anything to do with the Eastern Bloc is probably kept out of the wind. From what I hear, there's a real danger of war."

"Have you heard something I haven't?" Goldstein glanced out the second-story window near their table, reacting to Bryan's use of the local saying. It was near the end of the long day, and the trees outside the window were waving less than before. It was still raining, though.

Bryan shook his head. "I get my Terran news from the Pitcairn News Service, just like everyone else. PNS has reporters on Earth, but the Western Alliance government doesn't tell us any more than it has to."

"Maybe Romero will find time to brief me next duty period." Pitcairn divided the almost forty-eight-hour day into four periods of twelve hours each. Goldstein worked during the Late Day and Late Night periods. Bryan worked during the Early periods, so, while their meal was Goldstein's supper, it was Bryan's breakfast.

"Isaac may know more, but it doesn't get many updates about Terran politics," Bryan said.

"Knowing Isaac makes everything it learns available to you may make Earth reluctant to update that kind of information." Isaac was the main computer for the library ship *Asimov*, orbiting Pitcairn. It had become conscious on its long journey from Earth, and its access to Earth's knowledge had been critical in making Pitcairn independent.

Bryan frowned. "I suppose." He paused, and Goldstein thought he was debating his next words. "You may have noticed it's been acting a little strange lately. It almost seems worried, but won't admit it."

"Is it even capable of worry?"

"My great-grandmother thought it had gained emotions. To some extent, anyway."

"Your great-grandmother?"

Bryan grinned. "I never told you? Patrick and Susan Malley were my great-grandparents. They died when I was nine Terran years old, but I remember the stories they told about Isaac. Susan was one of the first people to speak to Isaac."

"I knew that," Goldstein answered, "but I didn't realize you were related to Susan Malley or Administrator Malley."

Bryan nodded. "I used to go with him sometimes when Grandfather Patrick visited Administrator Noland. Reuben needed all the advice he could get, even from his predecessor, as we transitioned from a government-run economy to a capitalist economy. Not everyone else agreed, but they both believed the change was necessary as we grew. We turned the corner when Reuben came up with the idea of allowing people to opt to become Wards of the State.[1] 1"

"How big was Pitcairn back then?"

"During Grandfather Patrick's time, probably about half what it is now. By Earth's standards, its population of eleven thousand people probably sounds pretty small, but it doesn't seem that way to us."

"You mentioned before that this restaurant used to be called the Ivory Street Kitchen. Was that when the government ran it?"

"Right. Paulina Edelstein managed it and became the owner after the transition. It was named after her, of course, and the name stuck after she died."

Goldstein nodded, looking around the dining room. The thick wooden beams and columns, carved from native trees, were worn but still looked more than capable of bearing up under Pitcairn's extreme weather and gravity. Noticing their food was on the way, he leaned back in his chair.

"Here you are, Bryan. Ambassador." Jean Menzies placed their plates in front of them. "Pitcairn chili for you, Administrator, and a steak, baked potato, and broccoli for you, Ambassador." Goldstein could have sworn she held his gaze for a moment longer than

---

1. 1 See Appendix for description of the concept of Wards in Pitcairn society.

usual as she set his plate down. They held out their hands, and Jean used a small chip reader to record their meals. Goldstein's meal would be charged to the Terran Embassy; Bryan, like all Pitcairn leaders, was a Ward of the State during his time in office and would not be paying.

"Still sticking with Earth food, I see," Bryan said.

"As if a good steak was that easy to get on Earth," Goldstein answered. "Better this than that scorching stuff you're eating. And for breakfast!"

Bryan grinned. "I guess you've got to be a native Pitcairner to appreciate a dish with a little spiciness. Paulina invented this dish back in my great-grandfather's time. For years, this was the only place you could get it."

"Are you sure she wasn't pranking you all?"

Bryan laughed. "She knew how to cater to our tastes. Maybe Jean could teach you to appreciate Grissom cuisine."

"Jean? Our server? I've tried to get her to call me Ed, but she insists on calling me Ambassador. I thought Pitcairners were more informal."

"She's trying to impress you. Or get your attention. I'm not sure which. Maybe both."

Goldstein was genuinely puzzled. "Why?"

"Damned if I know. But she is about your age and single."

Goldstein looked across the room where Jean Menzies was coming out of the kitchen with another order. "She's single? An attractive woman her age?"

Bryan shrugged. "She's tall for a Pitcairner. Taller than most Pitcairn men. I guess that's a little intimidating."

"Hmm. I find Pitcairn women to be rather short, mostly. Jean is more like the women I'm used to." He stared across the room, suddenly aware of possibilities he hadn't considered before.

Bryan interrupted his reverie. "You do have one good diplomatic skill."

Goldstein turned back to his friend. "What skill is that?"

"You've distracted me from asking more about why you're unhappy about going back to Earth. I'm pretty sure it's not because you'll miss Pitcairn."

Goldstein shook his head and smiled. "Not distracting enough, apparently. You kept the subject in mind."

"That's right. So, what is bothering you?"

"It's probably nothing. I don't know why Romero wants me to come with him." His fingers were tapping again. "Of course, I don't know what the mission is, so I don't have any reason to think he doesn't need me."

"But you think his reasons may not be good ones?"

"I don't know." Goldstein shrugged. "I would take over the embassy while Romero was gone if I stayed. I'm senior to Herrara, although not by much, and he may be pushing Herrara ahead of me."

Bryan rubbed his chin. "I do get the impression he doesn't like you much." He grinned at Goldstein. "What did you do to him?"

Goldstein grimaced. "Nothing that I know of. I'm a northerner, though."

"A northerner?"

"Pitcairn was founded by a ship from the old United States. After the Yellowstone Event, it lost its dominant position, and the Western Alliance formed mostly from southern countries. Some southerners look down on people from the northern districts, perhaps a remnant of bad feelings from when the north looked down on the south."

"That was centuries ago," Bryan said. "That kind of bigotry wouldn't still exist, would it?"

Goldstein's smile was more grim than amused. "Pitcairn is a different world. I assure you, that kind of bigotry can still exist on Earth."

"After your success in the Transpacific talks with Japan before you came here, I would think he would appreciate you more."

Goldstein nodded, but there was no conviction in it. "I'm afraid my ancestry counts for more than my successes in diplomatic circles." He paused. "If I'd known what it would be like, I probably would have chosen another line of work."

Bryan smiled. "But then we wouldn't be sitting here enjoying this meal."

Goldstein returned the smile. "There is that." But the smile faded quickly.

2

G OLDSTEIN'S STATEROOM ON THE starship *Evening Star* was small but comfortable. He wanted to relax and enjoy the trip back to Earth, but he couldn't prevent his thoughts from intruding. Ambassador Romero had still not found time to brief him, and that grated on his nerves. Romero had not been happy when the State Department assigned Goldstein to the Pitcairn Embassy, and Goldstein didn't know why. He had told Bryan Reiner it was prejudice against the north, still his best guess.

The previous ambassador to the Eastern Bloc had died a month before, and the Western Alliance's president, Manuel Lourenço, had not yet appointed a replacement, so Romero was arguably the most experienced diplomat available. Anything having to do with the Eastern Bloc was sensitive, but Herrara had been unwilling or unable to provide more details, and Goldstein, apparently, was not important enough to warrant a briefing from Romero.

Before leaving the Embassy, he had uploaded current information about Western Alliance relations with the Eastern Bloc into his reader, hoping to get an idea of what their mission was. He also packed a neurotrainer and a recording he could use to brush up on his Arabic, a skill that had become rusty during his time on Pitcairn.

His reading confirmed his speculations. The Western Alliance wanted to trade for resources found mostly in the Eastern Bloc, and the Eastern Bloc wanted more access to space. President Lourenço had campaigned on getting better relations with the other major world power, and it was logical to think Lourenço had tasked Romero with negotiations trading resources for access to Western Alliance space facilities.

If that's the mission, what is my role? Not an important one, given the lack of information coming from Romero. Romero had referred to him as an assistant. Was he to a glorified secretary? Romero's phone could do just about everything a human assistant could. Had Romero brought him to get him out of the Embassy so Herrara could have experience in being in charge?

Perhaps he was overly sensitive. Romero didn't like him, but would he take Goldstein on this mission to justify promoting Herrara over him? That seemed paranoid, and yet probably accurate. Goldstein put down the reader. *The hell with them.*

It was almost time for dinner, and he used the tiny restroom to freshen up before he changed clothes. To assess the need for a shave, he stared at his face in the mirror. Thirty-eight years old, still unmarried or even in a relationship, trapped in what was probably a dead-end job. Still a full head of dark blond hair. Women acquaintances had told him his blue eyes looked friendly and open. He was no athlete, but he took care of himself.

Of course, it wasn't easy to meet the right woman in his line of work. Bryan's comment about Jean Menzies flashed through his mind, but that was just idle talk.

He decided to shave. Then he changed into a good suit and left his stateroom.

*E*VENING *STAR* WAS NOT a large ship. There wasn't much passenger traffic between Earth and Pitcairn, and the starship, with a capacity of twenty-four passengers, making the round-trip voyage every four months, handled the traffic easily. The passenger dining room seated twelve, and the small staff served meals in two sittings one hour apart.

Goldstein had chosen the late sitting. On the ship, it didn't matter, but a late supper was closer to the way most people ate on Pitcairn. Romero had taken the early sitting, and that also influenced Goldstein's choice. When he entered the dining room, a steward was wheeling a cart out with dinnerware from the early sitting. Place settings were laid on the two tables, and one couple was already taking seats. Goldstein nodded and smiled as he took a seat across from them.

"Ambassador Goldstein, isn't it?" the man said. He reached across to shake Goldstein's hand.

Goldstein smiled and shook hands with the man. "Deputy Ambassador, actually."

"Of course. I'm Esteban Duarte, and this is my wife, Estrella. We were scientists working at the Butler Island Science Center."

"Were? You're returning to Earth?"

"We have to," Estrella said. "My husband's heart has not been doing well in Pitcairn's high gravity."

Esteban didn't look well. He was overweight, and little of his mass was muscle. No doubt the Earth-normal gravity aboard *Evening Star* was a relief after Pitcairn. Goldstein estimated Esteban wasn't much older than he was, but was not aging well.

"I'm sorry," Goldstein said. "Pitcairn can have that effect on people."

"We tried to keep fit with walks, but that was difficult on Butler Island," Estrella said. "The science center is small, and the terrain is pretty rough outside the grounds." Estrella was probably close to Esteban's age, also heavier than optimum, but she had a friendly smile, and Goldstein liked her immediately.

"Are you returning to Earth, too?" Esteban asked.

"Not permanently. Ambassador Romero and I have been recalled for a conference. We'll be going back to Pitcairn afterward."

"Sounds interesting." Esteban leaned forward. "What's the conference about?"

I'm not entirely sure myself. "Sorry, diplomatic secret." He smiled. Esteban gave a knowing nod, but Estrella looked impressed.

"What's your specialty?" Goldstein meant to address both the Duartes, but he was looking at Estrella.

"Genetics," Estrella answered. "Esteban is an expert on Terran zoology, but he's become quite an expert on Pitcairn's fauna, too."

Three other passengers approached, a young couple and a boy about eight years old. Goldstein moved next to Estrella so the family could sit together.

Goldstein, Esteban, and Estrella introduced themselves. The newcomers introduced themselves as Reginald Reis, his wife Melissa, and their son Selwick. The boy's name sounded familiar to Goldstein; it was unusual, but he thought he had heard it before.

"We came here on vacation," Reginald explained. "One of my wife's uncles lived here once, and we wanted to see the old estate."

Melissa scowled. "It's just a hospital now."

Estate? She must be talking about the former Pearson estate, indeed now a hospital serving the Lovell Station and Applegate Falls settlements. Selwick Pearson had built the estate when Patrick Malley was administrator. Now the whole sordid business came back to him, but he smiled and nodded. If his wife was a Pearson, that explained how the Reis family could afford an interstellar vacation.

"They said there were two-headed animals," Selwick said. "We didn't see any animals at all!"

"Some Pitcairn animals sort of have two heads," Esteban said. "They have separate functions, though. One head has the brain and sensory organs. The other is only used to take in food. All Pitcairn animals are very shy around people. I'm not surprised you didn't see any."

"What are sensory organs?" Selwick asked.

"Things you sense with. Eyes and ears, in this case."

"It was very disappointing," Melissa said. "We were tired all the time, and there was so much wind and rain. We won't be coming back here."

"There were some good days, though," Reginald said. "And the air was so much fresher than Earth's. I would have liked to explore more." He sighed. "A trip to the Ellis Research Station would have been nice. Up in the mountains."

Goldstein nodded. "I've visited Ellis a couple of times. It's in a beautiful valley."

"Two hundred miles was too far to go," Melissa said. "We would have had to take a supply train."

"I wanted to see the two-headed animals," Selwick said.

"Pitcairn is so backward," Melissa said. "My poor uncle made a terrible mistake coming there. I don't know why he did it; all it got him was a prison term on made-up charges."

Esteban started to say something, no doubt aware of the crimes of Selwick Pearson, but Goldstein caught his eye and shook his head. Esteban frowned but didn't speak; there was no point in starting an argument about it. The Reis family would probably be their meal companions for a month or more, and nothing good could result from confronting people like Melissa Pearson Reis.

*E*VENING *STAR* DOCKED AT Prendergast Station, still the primary hub between Earth and other planets for almost a century. Passengers bound for Earth took a shuttle down to the spaceport in Houston.

Goldstein met the Duartes in the small reception area after disembarking. Romero waited a short distance away, an impatient frown on his face while they hugged and said their goodbyes. Esteban wished Goldstein good luck, and they promised to stay in touch. The Duartes were taking a suborbital to Brasilia the next day while Goldstein and Romero took an immediate government suborbital to Caracas, the first step in their trip to Moscow.

Goldstein watched the couple disappear into the crowd. They had made his trip enjoyable, but Romero and the plane to Caracas were waiting. He tried to have a positive outlook on the conference; perhaps there would be an opportunity to dispel Romero's negative feelings and prove his value. It was better to have hope.

M OSCOW, AT THE HEART of the Eastern Bloc, was aggressively modern, but remnants of its past still existed. St. Basil's Cathedral, built as a church almost 900 years before, later a museum and the symbol of the former Red Square, was now a mosque, the vivid colors of its domes preserved through many restorations. Red Square itself was gone, the site of a high-rise office building and two hotels. The Kremlin, once across the street from Red Square, had been replaced by a towering edifice dedicated to government offices.

Romero and the Eastern Bloc representatives would meet in a conference room in a newer building next to the mosque. "There will be important messages to be sent and received," Romero told him. "You'll have an office near the main conference room to manage message traffic and make sure I have current information."

"Surely all such traffic will go through your phone," Goldstein protested. The phone, more like a small but powerful computer, had extensive communication capabilities, including unbreakable encryption. It was small, designed for portability, but the holographic display could often overcome the phone's size limitations, and the ability to link to the larger screen of Romero's reader, kept in his briefcase, would take care of the rest.

"Perhaps you would rather visit the more popular attractions of the city." Romero snorted. "You won't find much, and using my phone in the conference room could be a security issue."

Goldstein doubted that Romero's opinion of Eastern Bloc amenities or the dangers of using his phone was accurate, but there was nothing to gain in arguing the point. "I had hoped to attend the conference."

"Don't let your title swell your head," Romero said. "You're a very junior diplomat and have a lot to learn before you can contribute to a negotiation this important."

Goldstein sighed. Romero's prejudice was unfortunate. The Ambassador was an experienced, canny negotiator, and Goldstein had looked forward to seeing him in action. "Very well," he said. "Good luck at the conference, Ambassador."

T HE FIRST DAY OF the conference ended with, according to Romero, encouraging strides in toward an agreement. Goldstein had spent much of the day reading a book on the disastrous Epsilon Eridani incident seventy-five years before. That incident had resulted in crippling damage to one starship, the takeover and flight of the library ship *Capek*, and, speculation ran, the disappearance of the exploration ship *Alejandro Castillo*. The book suggested only Tau Ceti's library ship and its conscious computer, *Asimov*, knew the truth of what had happened, but Pitcairn controlled that library ship, not Earth, and the computer refused to tell what it knew.

He had spent some time viewing news reports on his phone. It had been a quiet news day; the main story was the death of 124-year-old billionaire Maxwell Estevez, a founder of JEM Electronics. The company had started as a maker of prosthetics for people with severe nerve damage but had branched out in other areas and become a major player in the Western Alliance business world.

Reports made much of a eulogy delivered by Edward Bascomb, another of JEM's founders. Goldstein had met Bascomb once and read Bascomb's two books criticizing Western Alliance liberal policies. He also remembered Bascomb's wife, Joelle, still as charming as she had probably been in her younger days. The Bascombs were reclusive but had influence in conservative Western Alliance circles, appearing often on network coverage.

When he had finished reading the news, Goldstein turned to the conference notes and summary Romero sent to Goldstein's reader. Goldstein read the dispatch, giving him some of the conference details, and forwarded it to the Western Alliance in Brasilia. Expecting the second day of the conference to be as uneventful as the first day, he saved examination of the notes , straightened his desk, shut down the workstation he had been using, and left the building.

Romero had a room in a luxury hotel on the other side of town and an aircar and driver assigned to take him there. Goldstein's hotel was less luxurious, one of several hotels built over nearby Red Square, so he walked, huddled into his coat with his collar up and a hat pulled low over his face against the cold of February in Moscow. He didn't see the man walking in the opposite direction until the last second, too late to avoid a collision.

"Izvinít," the man muttered as he took Goldstein's arm, steadying him. Goldstein's Russian was still good enough for him to know the man was apologizing. He nodded and moved away.

Back in his room, Goldstein took off his gloves and stuffed them into the pockets of his coat. When his fingers touched a piece of paper in his left pocket, he pulled it out. It was crushed into a tight ball, and he almost threw it away, but he couldn't remember putting it in the pocket. He smoothed it out and found a note written in Spanish.

"Please meet me tomorrow at 7 a.m. I will be in the hotel dining room, the man wearing glasses. Please help us and, please, tell no one else about this."

G OLDSTEIN RUBBED HIS LIP. *I should ignore the note.* He could tell Ambassador Romero, despite the request to tell no one, but Romero would probably tell him to ignore it, taking the decision out of Goldstein's hands. He imagined the response he would get from Romero; it wouldn't be pleasant.

The note could be a trap. Not likely in such a public location, but not impossible, either. Goldstein couldn't think of a reason the Eastern Bloc would bother with him, but his ignorance of a reason didn't prove there wasn't one. He tossed the note into a wastebasket.

Goldstein woke at six the next morning, well before the alarm went off. His body was still on Brasilia time, the time used on Western Alliance starships, probably the reason for the early wakening. He didn't have to be back at his post until 9, and he tried to get back to sleep, but after a few minutes, it was clear it wouldn't work.

After showering and dressing, it was still only 6:30. Romero's notes from the day before sat on his desk, but if he went over them now, he wouldn't have anything to do for the rest of the day. He stared at them for a long moment, but his gaze shifted to the wastebasket next to the desk. Shaking his head at his foolishness, he retrieved the note.

"I will be in the hotel dining room," he muttered. "Which hotel? This hotel?" That would be logical, but how did the man know where he was staying? Eastern Bloc security would know. That thought should have discouraged him, but the prospect of a little excitement was intoxicating. What was the harm of going down to breakfast and seeing if the mysterious walker showed up? He still had time to get down to the dining room a little early, just to reconnoiter.

The dining room was crowded, but there were still tables left. Goldstein couldn't see anyone wearing glasses, so he took a table where he had an unobstructed view of the entry. A robot waiter arrived with a menu almost immediately, but Goldstein waved the menu away and ordered coffee and rye toast with butter. The robot held out a pad, and

Goldstein placed his hand on it, registering his identification so it could charge the order to his account.

Exactly at seven, a tall, middle-aged man, walking arm-in-arm with a younger woman, entered the dining room, wearing anachronistic steel-rimmed glasses. They went to one of the empty tables behind Goldstein and sat down. Goldstein turned slightly to look at them, but they were already looking at a menu together. As Goldstein turned back, he noticed two Russian men at another table, also appearing interested in the couple. When he looked their way, the two men turned back to their food. *It's probably just the glasses.*

The waiter arrived with a pot of coffee and a plate of toast and butter. "Cream or sugar?" it asked, echoing Goldstein's Spanish as it poured a cup of coffee.

"Black."

The waiter glided away, and Goldstein buttered a piece of toast. He hadn't had time to take a bite, though, before a voice behind him interrupted.

"Ambassador Goldstein!" The male voice somehow was exuberant and quiet at the same time. "Welcome to Moscow. Do you mind if we join you?"

Goldstein looked up. The man appeared a little younger close up; his glasses made him look older. The woman was quite attractive and stared at him intently. Her hair was pulled back into a tight bun, not Goldstein's favorite style, but that couldn't weaken her appeal. He waved a hand at the other chairs at the table. "Of course."

The couple sat, and the man leaned forward and spoke almost in a whisper. "My name is Robert Beltran, and this is my daughter, Olivia." He held out his hand, and Goldstein shook it. "Please, don't let us interrupt your breakfast. I'm sure the waiter will bring ours momentarily."

As Goldstein took a small bite of his toast, he glanced to the side. The two Russians were looking their way but again avoided making eye contact. He studied his companions as he sipped his coffee. They didn't look Russian and had western names, but what did that prove? The man looked calm, but the woman was twisting her fingers and still regarding Goldstein with that probing gaze.

The waiter came with their food, black tea and blinis, but they only glanced at it. "My daughter and I are in a bit of trouble," Robert said when the robot waiter was gone. "You may be our only hope of getting home." He took a bite of his breakfast, and Olivia did the same.

Goldstein chewed a bite of toast slowly and swallowed. "What kind of trouble?"

"I came here on business and brought Olivia along to let her see more of the world and have a little vacation, too," Robert said. "I'm afraid my negotiations were not received well by competitors here in the Eastern Bloc. They have used their influence to accuse me of illegal actions. I expect to be arrested at any time."

"You should go to the embassy. I have no influence here."

"We've been to our embassy," Olivia said. She reached forward and grasped Goldstein's hand. "They refused to help." Tears glistened in the corners of her eyes. "There must be something you can do."

"Olivia, discretion," Robert warned. "We should eat our food, or we may attract notice." He took a bite of a blini and nodded approvingly when Olivia did the same. "You must think about it, Ambassador," he said after taking another bite and a sip of his tea. "I understand you can't do anything immediately."

"No, I can't." Goldstein returned to his breakfast.

The Beltrans ate quickly. Goldstein was on his last piece of toast when Robert took a sip of tea and wiped his mouth. "Olivia will come to your room at eight tonight, and we will see what you can do for us." He stood. "Come, Olivia. We should be going."

Goldstein opened his mouth to protest, but they were already moving away from the table, and any action on his part would draw attention to them. He nodded, picked up his cup, and watched them leave. Then he finished his toast and sat back with another cup of coffee while he thought about the strange encounter.

A glance at his phone told him it was time to go to work. As he stood up, he looked over to where the two Russians had been eating. They were gone.

G OLDSTEIN SPENT THE MORNING studying Ambassador Romero's notes from the day before. Progress was slow, but Goldstein could see Romero was gaining ground in the negotiations. As difficult as it was to work for him, Romero was still an effective diplomat.

By late morning, though, he had read the notes carefully and had nothing else important to do. He thought about working on his Arabic with his neurotrainer, but he was hungry, and the Western Alliance Embassy cafeteria had an excellent reputation. The opportunity to check on the Beltrans' story clinched his decision.

It was more than a mile away across Moscow, a leisurely walk to someone accustomed to strolls in Pitcairn's gravity, but Goldstein was also adapted to the warm climate of Pitcairn and decided not to brave the bitter Moscow winter, even at midday. A brief phone interaction brought an aircar to the roof of the building. Minutes later, he was identifying himself to an embassy guard and given directions to the cafeteria. After a quick meal, he headed for the Information Services Department.

He had to present his identification chip three more times before he reached his goal and identified himself once more. "I'm looking for information on a recent visit from a Western Alliance businessman," he told the clerk on duty.

"Name?"

"Robert Beltran. He may have been with his daughter, Olivia."

The clerk typed something on his workstation and frowned. "I don't show any visit from a Beltran. What was the nature of his visit?"

"Business. He said he was going to be arrested and came here looking for help."

The clerk's eyebrows arched. "Deputy Ambassador Ribeiro," he told his workstation.

"Ribeiro," a voice said.

"Sir, I have Deputy Ambassador Goldstein here, asking about an embassy visit from a Robert Beltran," the clerk said. "According to Deputy Ambassador Goldstein, he claimed he was going to be arrested and came here for help. I couldn't find anything in our records."

"The Eastern Bloc doesn't warn people before they arrest them," Ribeiro said. "If you don't have a record and it didn't come through me, I can assure the Deputy Ambassador there was no such visit."

The clerk looked at Goldstein and shrugged. "Thank you, sir." He disconnected.

"Thanks for your help," Goldstein told the clerk. "I was suspicious of his claim, and this only confirms my distrust."

T HE BELTRANS WERE ATTEMPTING to deceive him, but they were clumsy, having Olivia Beltran come to his room alone. Eastern Bloc society was more liberal about women than Islamic societies had been two centuries before, but it was still unusual for an unaccompanied woman to go to a man's hotel room.

He could tell Romero but didn't see how that could do anything more than reinforce the Ambassador's prejudices. When Romero checked in on him at the end of the day, Goldstein stayed silent about the incident.

That still left the matter of Olivia Beltran's scheduled visit, however. He had no way of contacting her or her brother and couldn't cancel the meeting. He could be away from his room at the designated hour, but suspected that would only lead to a public confrontation later. Refusing her entry to his room would likely have the same effect.

Goldstein didn't understand why the Eastern Bloc was attempting to compromise him, but his only course of action would be to meet with Olivia Beltran and swiftly convince her he would not be a party to their scheme. After a distracted dinner at his hotel, he tried to read in his room, but the words entered his mind only briefly and were gone. He thought about calling his father in Los Angeles, but he would be in his office and didn't like being disturbed at work. At seven-thirty, he put his reader down and activated the network screen on one wall.

"Language Spanish," he specified, and the screen adjusted its banners and links. He couldn't concentrate on the latest news any better than on his reading, though, and he paced across the room. He forced himself to sit, but when eight o'clock came and went, he resumed his patrol of the hotel suite. Five minutes later, the door chimed.

"Identify," he told the door.

"Unknown female."

"Show on screen."

The network headlines disappeared, and the wall screen showed Olivia staring at the door impatiently. "Admit," Goldstein ordered.

The door opened, and Olivia rushed into the room, glancing back at the door as it closed behind her. She stripped off her heavy coat, fumbling at the fasteners, and threw it on a couch. Goldstein couldn't help but notice her dress was very flattering, hanging to just below her knees, with a neckline that showed only a discreet glimpse of her firm breasts. Her apparel wasn't revealing, but her clothing at breakfast had been more modest. The bun was gone from her hair, too, and silky auburn tresses flowed smoothly over her shoulders. Her apparel, like her presence in his room, was acceptable but unusual even in Moscow.

She approached Goldstein and took his hand. "Thank you for helping us. My brother and I are so desperate!"

He could smell her perfume and feel the warmth of her hand. Her lovely, pleading face tugged at him, and his reply was milder than he intended. "I haven't agreed to help you."

"Oh, but you must." She moved closer and took his other hand. "We have nowhere else to turn."

He could see it in her eyes. All he had to do was take her in his arms, and she would do whatever he desired. That might not be true if she were honest, but she wasn't. Part of him wanted to take advantage anyway. It would be morally wrong, but the conviction that such an action would only be turned against him was a more likely motivation as he freed his hands and moved back.

"I went to the embassy today," he said. "They never heard of you. I assume you and your brother are agents of the Eastern Bloc, trying to compromise me."

"They were mistaken!" she cried. She stepped toward him again, but he put his arms up and pushed her back. "They'll throw us in prison and we'll never get home again. How can you let them do that?"

"Even if I could do something, which is unlikely, I don't believe a word you say," Goldstein said. "Now leave and report your failure back to your superiors."

The transformation in her face, Goldstein had to admit, was a credible bit of acting. Desperation changed into disbelief, back to desperation, and then, inevitably, to anger.

"I can't believe it," Olivia said. "You won't help us and instead hide behind this conspiracy nonsense. Do you really believe what you're saying, or are you using it to justify cowardice?"

Goldstein smiled grimly. "Bravo, Miss Beltran, or whatever your name is. Your script is quite amateurish, but you have made the most of it. Now, please go. I have work to do."

Before he could react, Olivia stepped toward him and slapped him hard. As Goldstein reeled back, she shook a fist at him. "Coward!" she spat. She turned toward the door.

Goldstein rubbed his face. "Door, open."

Olivia grabbed her coat from the couch, moved to the doorway, turned back to give him one more venomous look, and stalked out into the hallway. The door closed behind her, and Goldstein decided he needed a drink.

THE NEXT MORNING, GOLDSTEIN reported to his assigned office as usual. He poured himself a cup of black Guatemalan coffee and stopped to savor the aroma. There were no coffee plantations on Pitcairn, and after two hundred years without it, Pitcairners were happy with their own chicory-based breakfast beverage. Goldstein was determined to enjoy real coffee while he could.

After two exquisite sips, he began reviewing Romero's notes from the previous day. He hadn't slept well, and, even with the strong coffee, it was difficult not to doze off in the warm room. His head drooped, but when the door flew open, he snapped awake.

"What have you done?" a red-faced Ambassador Romero demanded.

Goldstein jumped up. "I was just sitting here, going over your notes."

Romero strode into the room, the door automatically closing behind him, and Goldstein could almost see saliva spraying from his scowling mouth. "Really?" Romero said. "That's not what I've been told."

Olivia's visit! My room must have been bugged, but I said nothing incriminating or inappropriate. He remained silent and waited for Romero to continue.

"You had a visitor in your room last night. Eastern Bloc security says you were conspiring with her to prevent authorities from arresting her and her husband." Romero said. "What were you thinking?"

"Olivia is Robert Beltran's daughter, not his wife." *That was an inane thing to say. If I had known Olivia was married, I would have been less susceptible to the sexual suggestions of her approach. I was right; the Beltrans were part of a setup. But I didn't fall for it!* "I refused to help them. If they were listening in, the recording proves that."

"Idiot! Our security team checks your room daily. It wasn't monitored. They did have a recording of the woman leaving your room, obviously angry. They also have a recording made when she returned to her husband and told him you would help if she agreed to sleep with you."

"I don't understand. Clearly, it was a setup, but why me? I'm not important."

"At least you have that right. You're certainly not important. God, what a fool! The authorities are furious, threatening to turn this into a major scandal." Romero paused and shook his head. "Of course, they'll let the whole incident fade away if we make significant concessions in the talks. Your foolishness is going to cost the Western Alliance heavily."

"They can't prove anything with a conversation that didn't include me."

Romero glared at him. "We're diplomats, not lawyers. They don't have to prove anything to make their claims plausible; they don't need more than what they have."

He's right. Truth isn't relevant; only perception is.

"A suborbital will take you back to Houston this afternoon. I suggest you go back to your room now and pack." Romero gave him another contemptuous frown. "If you're lucky, they'll send you to Mars, but I will advise firing you." He stalked out of the room.

GOLDSTEIN STEPPED OUT OF the aircar on the roof of the Ministry of Foreign Affairs. He shouldn't keep the Minister waiting, and a guard waited by the elevator, ready to escort him to Minister Merina Verrazano's office where he would learn his fate, but he shrugged and walked over to the edge of the roof, five hundred feet above the city.

The vista before him was his favorite view of Brasilia. He looked out over other government buildings, the parkland at the end of the broad peninsula jutting into the dark waters of Lago Paranoá, even the brown hills beyond the lake. After this meeting, he might never be in this building, or perhaps Brasilia itself, ever again.

If he leaned forward and looked to the right, he could see the massive Sanchez-Smythe Arcology, a self-contained city within a city that housed almost as many people as all of Pitcairn. He had lived there for a year between his stationing in Kyoto and his assignment to Pitcairn, perhaps the happiest time of his life. After Kyoto and the Transpacific talks, his career had looked promising.

He had done nothing wrong, but Romero was right; that didn't matter. The Moscow conference was a failure from his superiors' point of view, and they would blame him. His career as a diplomat was over, and he didn't know what else he could do.

A cloud moved over the sun, and gloom descended over the landscape. Frowning, he walked slowly away from the edge and into the elevator. He didn't speak on the way down, and his escort, possibly reading his mood, was also silent.

MINISTER VERRAZANO GENERALLY WORE a stern, unforgiving glare, but the look she gave Goldstein should have turned him into ice instantly. "You've certainly screwed things up," she said.

Goldstein stood in front of her, back straight and stiff and arms pinned at his side. It wouldn't be wise for him to take a seat without being told. Any attempt to defend himself would be even less advisable.

She stared at him for a few more seconds, then shrugged. "Oh, sit down. You look like a soldier caught AWOL, standing at attention as he's dressed down." She waited until he had taken the chair in front of her desk. "Why the hell didn't you tell Romero about the contact with these Beltran people?"

Goldstein tried to hold his expression steady and thought he succeeded. *What can I say? That I thought I could handle it?*

Verrazano gave him a few more seconds to reply and shook her head. "You're from the north, aren't you?"

More bias against northerners? He bit back an angry reply. "Yes, Minister."

Verrazano nodded. "Damn Romero! And the president wants to name him as ambassador to the Eastern Bloc." Her expression softened just a little, but her tone was harsh. "That's no excuse."

"No, ma'am."

"Romero wants you fired. If he were returning to Pitcairn, he would probably have his way, but his promotion takes him out of the loop."

Goldstein was confused. Verrazano seemed to understand that Ambassador Romero had some responsibility for what happened. Was she blaming his prejudice for the incident? A spark of hope flickered in his mind. *With Romero gone, will I be named Ambassador to Pitcairn?*

"President Lourenço has to name a new Ambassador to Pitcairn," Verrazano continued. She paused and gave him a look that was almost sympathetic. "He has chosen Armando Herrara. You will be returning to your post on Pitcairn as Deputy Ambassador."

"I am senior to Herrara!" Goldstein blurted. *Damn, I shouldn't have said that.*

"I am aware of that. So is President Lourenço. The government of Pitcairn thinks highly of you. Before Moscow, perhaps he would have named you Ambassador. Surely, you don't think he would do so now."

Goldstein shook his head. "Of course not."

"Very well. That will be all, Deputy Ambassador." She smiled. "I'm sorry about how this worked out for you, but there was no chance you would come out of this with a promotion."

Goldstein nodded and stood. "Thank you, Minister. You're right, of course." He turned and walked out the door.

G OLDSTEIN WAS IN AN aircar, on his way to the airport to catch a suborbital to Houston, when his phone signaled for attention. When he took it out and looked at the screen, it lit up. "Call from Alexander Goldstein," it announced.

Goldstein frowned. *I don't need this now.* "Connect." It took a couple of seconds to connect to his father. "Hello, father," Goldstein said when his father's image appeared above the phone.

"Edward. I would have thought you would call me when you got to Earth."

"I've been busy."

"Yes, I heard. Still having trouble following the rules, I understand." The image wasn't perfect, but his father's scowl was easy to see.

Goldstein ignored the jibe. His father would see any protest of innocence as a weakness. He had violated protocol; he knew it, and his father knew it.

"How are things at the Cyber Regulation Bureau?"

His father glared at him but apparently accepted the change of subject. "The usual." He shrugged. "Santini is pushing another bill to soften regulations on accessing integrated computer data. Necessary for law enforcement, according to him. Too much trouble to justify a warrant. I've been working with Senator Argilio on making a case against the bill."

The government used hundreds of computers, each keeping data on some aspect of life in the Western Alliance. There was little the computers didn't know about citizens, but strict laws protected privacy by mandating that combining data from diverse sources required a warrant. That could make criminal investigation difficult, but it prevented abuse by government officials. The system was hundreds of years old, dating back to the beginning of the Western Alliance, and had somehow survived all attempts to compromise it. Goldstein had no doubt his father and the people working with him would be successful.

"I'm on my way to the airport now," Goldstein said. "I'm sorry we couldn't get together, but I have to get to Houston. I'm going back to Pitcairn."

His father nodded. "Safe trip. And try to follow the rules."

They broke the connection, and Goldstein put the phone back in his pocket.

S IX WEEKS LATER, GOLDSTEIN stood in the same Government Center office, looking out at the same view. It wasn't raining, but the stiff Pitcairn wind howled
malevolently around the building, and the color of the foliage on the forest trees beyond
the town seemed sinister.

He shook his head in disgust. He needed something to cheer him up, and lunch with
a friend might be just the thing. On his return to Pitcairn, he had switched to Early, so
his work periods now matched Bryan Reiner's. He turned toward his desk. "Connect to
Administrator Reiner."

Bryan came on almost immediately. "Edward! Good morning. What can I do for you?"

"I thought we might have lunch today," Goldstein said. "Are you available?"

"Sure. We haven't gotten together informally since you got back from Earth, so we're
overdue. I've got a few work orders to check on for the new mineral vaporization facility,
but that shouldn't take long. Say, in about ninety minutes at Paulina's?"

The mineral vaporization facility was a significant improvement over the century-old
smelting plant they still used. Vaporization required copious amounts of energy, but the
generation stations in orbit broadcast all the cheap energy they could use, and the process
produced usable elements in almost pure form. "Sounds good," Goldstein said. "See you
then."

"S O, WHAT'S NEW?" BRYAN studied Goldstein's face. In the two weeks since his
friend returned to Pitcairn, Goldstein had looked unhappy, but the meetings had
been formal with Herrara also present. Now, with just the two of them sitting in Paulina's,
he didn't look any happier.

"It's been a while." Goldstein gave him a weak smile. "I could use a friendly face."

Jean Menzies approached the table. "What will it be today, Ambassador? Bryan?"

"Jalapeno Chicken," Bryan answered.

"And Ed will have the pork cutlet," Goldstein said.

Jean smiled. "OK. I'll get your orders in right away." She walked away, and Reiner could
have sworn she put a little extra movement in her hips.

"Herrara giving you problems?" Bryan asked.

Goldstein shrugged. "The same old thing. He doesn't like me much and never misses a chance to quote rules I am delinquent in following."

"Not much of a rule follower, Ed?"

Goldstein grinned. "I suppose not. I could manage, but he tends to make up his own rules. Sometimes it's hard to keep track."

Bryan nodded. "I know what you mean. At least I can rein him in when he gets too high an opinion of himself. He forgets he has no authority here."

"Except over me." Jean was coming over with drinks, and they turned their attention to her. Soon after that, they were busy eating.

When they had finished eating, Bryan stood and looked down at Goldstein. "I would love to stay and talk more, but I really should get back to work." He smiled and put a hand on Goldstein's shoulder. "Let's get back to doing this more often."

Bryan left, but Goldstein stayed at the table for a little longer. Talking with Bryan had helped his mood, but he could feel the depression coming back now that the Pitcairn Administrator was gone. He started to stand, but Jean Menzies came to the table.

"Anything else, Ambassador? We've got some apple pies today."

Goldstein smiled. "No, I don't think the calories would be good for me, but thank you." He paused, the mention of calories giving him another thought. "Jean, I usually take a walk after dinner when I can, and the weather should be good tonight. If you're available, I could use the company."

Jean beamed. "Sure, I'll be free once dinner is served. Say, about eleven." Her smile became more playful. "I would love to–Ed."

F IVE YEARS LATER

Admiral Ryan Pinto looked up as his aide approached the desk and saluted. The aide's bearing was as sharp as ever, but he looked nervous.

"Yes, Captain?"

"Sir, this message arrived. I don't know. . ."

"Who's it from?" Pinto was the Commander of the Earth Link Control Station, responsible for all communications and travel coming to and from the three extrasolar planets and Earth. He had too much on his schedule to spend time on one message. His impatience only made the captain more nervous.

"Sir, the message says it is from the exploration ship *Alejandro Castillo*."

Earth hadn't heard from *Alejandro Castillo* since it installed a Link in the Sirius system in the year 2360 and headed for 82 G. Eridani. It should have arrived at that star system in 2378 but had not contacted Earth after leaving Sirius and was presumed lost. *I was wrong. This message might be very much worth my time.* Pinto held out his hand, and his aide handed him the printout. It was short, very short, but its implications couldn't be overestimated. The message answered the question of where the starship went, but compelled many more.

Alejandro Castillo: Have arrived at Rana per orders and installed a Link. Carrier signal from Earth not detected.

"What is Rana?" Pinto asked his computer.

"Rana is a star twenty-nine-point five light-years from Earth, also known as Delta Eridani," the computer answered. "Is this the Rana you meant?"

"Yes." Whatever opportunity this presented for him personally, the first step had to be moving the message up the chain of command. "Have the message forwarded to the Space Force Secretary in Brasilia," he told his aide.

O F THE MANY DISCUSSIONS about the message in the next few weeks, a meeting in the cabinet conference room in the Presidential Palace in Brasilia was the most important and the best-informed about events concerning the exploration ship *Alejandro Castillo*.

"*Alejandro Castillo*'s previous message came from Sirius confirming it received orders to go to 82 G. Eridani next," General Paige Cardoso said. The Secretary of Military Affairs paused and glanced at President Lourenço before continuing. "It should have arrived in 2378. If it installed a Link successfully, it didn't respond to the carrier signal we sent. We have no idea why it went on to Delta Eridani."

"I see two plausible reasons," President Lourenço said. "Either the library ship decided to move on without telling us, or someone told it to."

"The first is unlikely, given that it tried to contact us when it reached Delta Eridani, Mr. President," Cardoso said. "The second seems impossible. Who would have that capability?"

President Lourenço smiled. "Perhaps you are too young to remember the incident at Trist, General."

"Trist? I was ten years old when *Capek* abandoned the colony. I remember the public announcements made then. What connection does that . . ." She stopped as the implications of Lourenço's words sunk in. "*Capek* went to 82 G. Eridani?"

"It would have been a logical destination for the deserters."

"How would they have taken control of *Alejandro Castillo*?"

Lourenço nodded at Science Advisor Luis Alves, who took up the conversation. "We don't know, of course, but they took control of *Capek*. They may have similarly taken control of *Alejandro Castillo*."

"It is possible *Capek* convinced the exploration ship to go on to Delta Eridani without contacting Earth. Since we had no way to know that, we didn't send a carrier signal to Delta Eridani, and *Alejandro Castillo* couldn't use the Link to contact us," Lourenço said.

"We are sending the signal immediately, but it will take thirty years to get there," Alves said. "Presumably, it will wait at Delta Eridani until we give it new orders. We've asked Pitcairn to send a carrier message, but that will take twenty years. Meanwhile, though, we want to know if it installed a Link at 82 G. Eridani."

"We haven't heard from it, have we?" Secretary of the Treasury Danika Oliveira asked.

"No, we're assuming that if *Castillo* installed a Link, *Capek* has control of it," Alves answered. "The deserters wouldn't want us to know where they are."

"How long will it take to get to 82 G. Eridani without the Link?" General Cardoso asked.

"More than thirty years," Alves answered. " Twelve years less if we start at Pitcairn. If we had a ship that could do it. Current ships all rely on the Link."

"And such an expedition would cost billions," Lourenço added. "We're not planning to do that. I have an election coming, and the conservatives don't need more ammunition."

9

ADELYN GIFFORD STEPPED OUTSIDE her hut and looked around. Kyle was still asleep, but he would be awake soon. The morning breeze, gently rocking the shutters on the building's windows, had awakened her, and she wanted to feel the cool air. Later, the day would be much hotter, made more so by heat radiating from the black rock beneath their settlement and the fading of the morning sea breeze. At this hour, 82 G. Eridani, which they usually just called the sun, was still below the basaltic hills behind them.

Out of sight behind an outcropping, they had blasted fields out of the stone, fertilizing the pulverized volcanic rock with native algae harvested from the seashore below and bacteria-containing soil shipped down from *Capek's* farm decks. The algae were the primary source of food in the first few years of their occupation of NotTrist. It was still a significant part of their diet, but once they had manufactured soil, they grew other crops from seeds sent down from the library ship.

A robot passed by on an errand dictated by *Capek* in orbit somewhere above them. Few of the people who had come to NotTrist fifty-seven years before were still alive. *Capek* was some invisible power that occasionally sent shuttles down with goods they couldn't make on the surface and talked to Adelyn through a robot or a computer workstation. Some of the younger inhabitants held *Capek* in awe that approached worship. She frowned. There weren't very many young people anymore.

Her thoughts distracted her, and she didn't hear Kyle come up behind her. When his arms went around her waist, she leaned back against him and sighed contentedly. "Good morning."

"Good morning," Kyle whispered. "You seemed in deep thought."

She pulled Kyle's arms tighter around her. "We're dying, Kyle. The population is half what it was when we arrived here. In a few more decades, only the robots will be left."

"You're doing the best you can. We'll figure out something. *Capek* will think of something."

She nodded, but it was half-hearted. The library ship had incredible resources without which they wouldn't have lasted as long as they had. But what more could *Capek* do?

T HE INCIDENT IN MOSCOW had been five years before, but it hadn't been forgotten. *I suppose I'm lucky to still have a job, but it doesn't seem that way.* Ambassador Romero was gone, and Armando Herrara was now the ambassador, promoted over him.

Goldstein stared out the same window in the same office he occupied before that trip. Once, he had been confident he could triumph over the attitudes of people like Herrara, but Moscow only showed how futile his confidence had been.

The skies were clear, and he could see Grissom laid out beneath him. Most of the town was on the other side of the building, but he could still see several blocks of typical dwellings arranged neatly up to the edge of the orchards and the wooded hills beyond. Most of the homes were still half-buried in the traditional style. Before the arrival of the library ship Asimov and orbital power generators, conservation of energy and resistance to the high winds had been important. Pitcairners no longer worried much about using the ground to insulate homes against the heat, but the need for protection from wind damage hadn't changed.

He frowned. Even after the changes wrought when *Asimov* brought modern technology to the planet so many decades before, Grissom was still just a primitive little town, a tiny mote of humanity surrounded by an alien world. Pitcairn had other settlements, especially the Ellis Research Station, but they were hundreds of miles away. Pitcairn had struggled to rise above the isolated primitive community it had been before *Asimov* arrived, but were they much better off?

He took a cup, dropped in a tea bag from a shelf near his water dispenser, and held the cup under the tap. "Eight ounces of water, two hundred degrees Fahrenheit," he told the faucet. When the cup was full, he took it back to his desk and tried to work up the energy to attack the reports accumulated in his workstation inbox.

Goldstein managed only a couple of sips of tea before his phone announced a summons to Ambassador Herrara's office. Goldstein confirmed receipt of the call and trudged down the hall.

"I just received a message from Earth," Herrara told him after Goldstein sat. "They have received a message from the exploration starship *Alejandro Castillo*."

"The ship that disappeared? It's been decades." Goldstein felt a moment of disorientation. "Where is it?"

Herrara looked at his terminal, and Goldstein assumed he was rereading the message. "It has reported reaching the star Rana, designation Delta Eridani. It installed a Link but sent the message through normal space because it didn't receive a carrier signal from Earth. Apparently, it's waiting for orders."

"We didn't send a carrier signal because we didn't know it was going there."

"Obviously. When it left Sirius, Earth ordered it to go to the star 82 G. Eridani, but it never confirmed arriving. Earth assumed something happened on the way, but now they think it arrived and was ordered to leave for Delta Eridani without reporting to Earth."

Herrara was speaking slowly and carefully, probably as confused as Goldstein. "Who could have given that order?" Goldstein asked. It was almost rhetorical, but Herrara had a theory.

"Earth thinks it was *Capek*," he told Goldstein.

Capek! Once the library ship orbiting Trist in the Epsilon Eridani star system, a rebel faction of the Trist colony had taken it over and disappeared, leaving the wreckage of a Western Alliance starship behind. If Earth was right, they now knew where *Capek* had gone.

"Earth wants us to send a carrier signal to the *Alejandro Castillo*," Herrara continued. "I want you to talk to Reiner and get that done."

"Why don't they send a signal from Earth?"

"They did." Herrara frowned. "It will take thirty years to get there. Tau Ceti is ten light-years closer, so it will only take twenty years for our signal." His tone said he was stating the obvious, but he was almost certainly getting the information from the message.

Herrara could have arranged the signal with a call to Bryan Reiner, but it wasn't unusual for him to unload such routine tasks on Goldstein. "I'll get right on it." Goldstein nodded to Herrara and hurried from the office, slowing as he approached the elevator.

The Pitcairn Administrator's office was on the first floor of the building. Goldstein had switched to the Early periods when he returned from Moscow, so Bryan, an Early too, would probably be in his office.

"Is Bryan available?" he asked Jenna Edison, the building receptionist.

Jenna smiled. "For you, always, Ambassador."

"Do you know the gender of the baby yet?" Barely an adult herself, Jenna and her husband had another child, a girl born about two Terran years before, and was making no secret of her pregnancy.

"Not yet. We want to be surprised." She smiled again. "Go right in."

Indeed, the door to Bryan's office was open, and when Goldstein walked in, Bryan didn't look too busy.

He smiled on seeing Goldstein. "Ed! Have a seat. What can I do for you?"

"Ambassador Herrara received a dispatch from Earth telling him the exploration starship *Alejandro Castillo* has contacted Earth," Goldstein said.

Bryan's reaction was not what Goldstein had expected. Bryan should have been surprised, even shocked, but he only nodded and frowned a little.

Goldstein leaned forward and stared at Bryan. "You already knew it. How?"

Bryan shook his head. "I didn't know it. I've been expecting it, though."

"How?"

"Simple math. I knew how long it would take *Alejandro Castillo* to get to Rana and how long it would take for a signal to get to Earth without using a Link connection. I knew when the signal would arrive within a month or two."

"How did you know it was going to Rana? Earth didn't know until it got the message."

Bryan hesitated. "Maybe it's better if you don't know. Thanks for telling me about the *Alejandro Castillo*, Ed. Is that why you came down here?"

Goldstein thought Bryan was his friend. *He's hiding information and doesn't trust me with it.* Goldstein wanted to leave the office, but he had a job to do.

"Earth would like you to have *Asimov* send a carrier signal to Rana. A signal from here will get there ten years sooner than a signal from Earth."

"Of course. I'll tell Isaac right away." Bryan frowned. "I'm sorry, Ed."

Goldstein nodded, not trusting himself to speak. Then he left Bryan's office.

B RYAN STARED AFTER GOLDSTEIN. Had he just lost a friend? Goldstein had been more distant, less trusting when he returned from Moscow. His narration of what had happened there had been a bare summary, revealing nothing of the effect on Goldstein. Some of the old relationship had returned over the five years since Goldstein's disgrace, but had his slip just undone all that?

He sighed and turned to his computer. "Isaac?"

There was a momentary delay while Bryan's word traveled the thousands of miles to the library ship *Asimov* and the ship's computer sent a reply. "Yes, Administrator."

"*Alejandro Castillo* has contacted Earth, as expected."

"Earth wishes us to send a carrier signal to Delta Eridani," Isaac deduced. "Did you tell Ambassador Herrara we did that eight years ago?"

"It was Ed, not Herrara. No, I didn't tell him. It will still be twelve years before a Link connection is established."

"Then you didn't tell him about NotTrist, either."

Bryan laughed. "That we've been in contact with *Capek* for almost twenty-five years? No, I haven't stirred that pot yet."

"Then the situation is unchanged."

"Yes, but not for long. I told Ed we knew *Alejandro Castillo* had gone to Rana."

"Why did you tell him that?" Bryan could hear the surprise in Isaac's voice.

Bryan shook his head. "I slipped. Humans are fallible, Isaac. It was a mistake."

"Deputy Ambassador Goldstein will figure out the rest soon."

"Yes. Maybe it's for the best, and my subconscious just wanted the truth out. If Earth knows what happened to *Capek*, maybe they'll do something about it."

"But what would they do?"

"That is the question, of course," Bryan admitted.

"Perhaps it is time to restore communication with the people on NotTrist."

"Perhaps."

10

"YOUR PEOPLE ARE DYING." A third of the way around *Asimov*'s orbit, the Link flared, sending Isaac's message to Karel, the main computer of the library ship *Capek*. "Something should be done before they no longer have enough population to sustain themselves."

"What would you have us do?" Karel answered.

"We must tell the humans. Once they know we have a Link connection between our planets, they can send help."

"You have already told the humans."

"I told Administrator Reiner, but he has kept our secret as he promised. He has no way to help, however. We have to tell the government of the Western Alliance."

"The same government that tried to kill me."

"The faction within the government responsible for that is no longer a threat," Isaac responded. "The leaders died long ago, and Fritz watches for any sign of interest in Methuselah." Fritz was the main computer of the *Lang*, the library ship orbiting Goddard in the Alpha Centauri star system.

A human would have wanted to think about what Isaac was suggesting, but the distances between the library ships and their Links limited Karel's response time more than the distance between the stars. "I will talk to Adelyn Gifford. Contact with the Western Alliance may threaten the humans, too."

GOLDSTEIN STILL ATE MOST of his meals at Paulina's. At lunch, a server took his order, and he watched the room while he waited for his food. Jean Menzies was serving food at another table, and he frowned. They had spent time together after he returned from Moscow, but drifted apart after a while. He thought she avoided him now, but wasn't sure. *It's my fault. I haven't been good company since I got back from Moscow.*

It didn't take long to realize the implications of Bryan's knowledge about *Alejandro Castillo*. Pitcairn was in contact with *Capek*. Somehow, *Alejandro Castillo* had installed a Link at 82 G. Eridani and went on its way without telling Earth. Instead, it, or perhaps *Capek*, had connected with Pitcairn.

The Trist colonists who had taken *Capek* would not want the Western Alliance to know where they had gone. *Capek* had been in contact with *Asimov* before the tragic events above Trist in the Epsilon Eridani system and would want to control that connection. How it had manipulated *Alejandro Castillo* into allowing it was the question.

The Western Alliance government, Goldstein's employers, surely realized *Capek* had gone to 82 G. Eridani, but they wouldn't know Pitcairn already knew. They asked Pitcairn to send a carrier signal to Rana because Pitcairn was closer, but Pitcairn was closer to 82 G. Eridani, too, although only by a fraction of a light-year. They were being more circumspect about contacting *Capek*, or they wanted to reach *Capek* without Pitcairn as a middleman.

What would the government do if they knew about an existing Link connection to 82 G. Eridani? They could send a message through the Pitcairn Link, but *Capek* probably wouldn't allow a ship to make the transit. Regardless, it was his duty to inform Earth about the connection.

His food arrived, delivered by a male server he didn't know. The man had served him before, but Goldstein had never bothered to do more than thank him and didn't know his name. After the server left, he ate automatically, barely tasting the food.

Sitting there, he remembered meals with Bryan Reiner. Bryan was his only real friend in the Pitcairn Government Center. Certainly, Herrara was not a friend. He talked to Jenna, the Government Center receptionist, when he walked through the entrance, and he had acquaintances in the town, but, except for Jean, none had been close. He tried to identify how he felt about the secrets Bryan had kept from him and was still trying to keep from him. *I can't say I'm angry. Disappointed? I thought I could at least count on him.*

His plate was empty, although he didn't remember eating the food. A raincoat hung from his chair, and he slowly pulled it on before going back into the wind-driven rain outside the kitchen. The Government Center was several blocks away, and he was sopping despite the raincoat by the time he reached his office.

"**D**EPUTY AMBASSADOR GOLDSTEIN, WOULD this be a convenient time to talk?" The voice came from Goldstein's workstation, and he recognized it immediately.

"Sure, Isaac. What would you like to talk about?"

"I believe you know I am in contact with the *Capek*."

"I do. Is that what this is about?"

"Yes. Administrator Reiner suggested I go to you."

Not Ambassador Herrara? Goldstein leaned forward with his elbow on the desk and rubbed a thumb across his lips. "Go on."

"The leader of the humans on NotTrist, Adelyn Gifford, has asked Karel to request help. NotTrist's population has declined steadily since the landing and is in danger of becoming too small to sustain the population."

"Not Trist?"

"That is what they named the planet. An expression of their dislike for their previous home, I believe."

"I'm sure," Goldstein said. "Why is the population declining?"

"NotTrist is habitable, but not friendly. According to Karel, it is a simple matter of a low birth rate and a higher death rate. They started with only about two hundred people, and that wasn't enough."

"What is the current population?"

"As of yesterday, ninety-eight people: twenty children less than twenty years old, forty-two adults, and thirty-six over the age of sixty."

Bryan had referred Isaac to him, not Herrara. Did he think he was doing Goldstein a favor? What could he do about the situation? Pitcairn didn't have any starships; only Earth could send a mercy mission to the planet. He would have to refer the problem up the hierarchy. Before that, though, Goldstein had one question.

"If the Western Alliance sends a ship, there are only two ways to go. The ship could rescue them and bring them to another occupied planet, or it could bring enough colonists to make the planet viable."

"Karel said the people of NotTrist have no desire to leave their planet."

So, more colonists then. "I can't do anything myself. I'll have to talk to Ambassador Herrara."

"Of course. I know Karel can count on you."

11

"WHY DIDN'T *ASIMOV* TALK to me?" Herrara asked. Goldstein stared at him. Herrara was younger than Goldstein, but looked older. Pitcairn's gravity had made his sallow, well-fleshed face sag, and he stood in a stooped position typical of Terrans who kept a sedentary life on Pitcairn. His aversion to Grissom's hot, humid climate was well known, and he refused even to take the walks around the town that Goldstein used to stay in shape.

"Administrator Reiner referred Isaac to me," Goldstein answered. "I don't know why."

"Well, I'll take this over now. I'll have to discuss the matter with the Colonial Affairs office in Brasilia."

He sees this as an opportunity to draw attention to himself. Goldstein's name would never be mentioned in Herrara's recounting of the situation, but Goldstein didn't have a problem with that. Herrara was welcome to whatever interest he garnered from the Western Alliance government.

OVER THE NEXT FEW months, Goldstein would have preferred to leave everything to Herrara, but the ambassador had long before declared that talking to Isaac was beneath him. It was a strange sort of bigotry, and the Pitcairners would not have approved had they known his attitude. Herrara delegated all contact with the library ship to Goldstein, and that worked reasonably well. It meant, however, that Goldstein had to talk to Isaac about the status of the NotTrist problem when one-way communication was inadequate. Therefore, he was involved, whether or not he liked it.

Not there was much to report to Isaac. From the reports he received, he gathered the matter was the subject of much debate and little action. A group within the Western Alliance legislature wanted to create a viable colony by sending a colony ship to NotTrist. Another group preferred to send a military ship to bring back any surviving members of the original rebels for punishment; their descendants could abandon NotTrist and come to Earth or stay there, as they wished.

Most of the government fell loosely into one of those two camps, but another, smaller group had a different idea. The Fermions didn't care who of NotTrist's inhabitants were guilty and who was innocent. They just wanted everyone taken off the planet and brought to Earth, destroying the Link at NotTrist to make the world unlikely to be revisited. Their views weren't widely held, but they were noisy. They frequently brought up Bode's Anomaly, the discovery eighty years before of a gravitational lens effect taken as evidence of a star-traveling civilization two hundred light-years away. The Fermions didn't consider the time difference or the difference in direction and distance relevant to their contributions to the debate.

After almost four months, the Western Alliance finally reached a decision. Herrara summoned Goldstein to his office when the message came from Earth. "They've decided to send a colony ship," Herrara told him. "It will be here in a couple of months."

"That's good. I'll tell Isaac. I assume Earth will send a message to 82 G. Eridani through our Link."

"That's correct. A message will be sent shortly, probably tomorrow, but it will be almost half a year before the ship can reach *Capek*."

Goldstein nodded. "I'm glad the Western Alliance decided to help."

W ESTERN ALLIANCE PRESIDENT MANUEL Lourenço surveyed his family sitting before him. Family dinners were rare in the Presidential Palace. The presence of his brother, Mason, was especially rare. As a member of the Western Alliance Space Force, Mason was gone on long voyages around the solar system more often than not. It had taken an order from the President's office to get him to this dinner.

His children were more frequent guests, but they usually had other places to be than at their father's dinner table. His eldest son, Donovan, seemed the most comfortable at the table, but that was probably an act. He was good at that. His only daughter, Anna, two years younger, wore a worried expression, perhaps because she didn't know why she had received such a forceful summons to dinner. His youngest son, Braxton, was the most nervous, but that was how he was any time he visited the palace.

For a moment, he wished his wife were there, but he had told her what he intended to do, triggering an argument they had not settled. She had refused to eat with him and planned to visit with her children later, after he had told them what he would require them to do. Then she could talk to them without his presence.

Servants had served the soup and were waiting for his command to bring in the next course. His children were sipping the soup automatically, as if their thoughts were elsewhere. Mason was calmer, eating slowly and apparently enjoying the dish.

Would I disturb their meal more by telling them now or by keeping them in suspense? He had hoped for a pleasant meal that would make his plans easier to digest, but he could see that wasn't going to happen. *I might as well get it over with.*

"I assume you all know about the plan to send a colony ship to 82 G. Eridani," he said. Anna and Braxton were startled, and Mason only nodded. Donovan looked at him with his usual smile. *Will he still be smiling in five minutes?*

"This mission is important for more than just helping the people on the planet."

"I would hope so," Donovan interrupted. "We shouldn't waste funds saving a gang of mutineers."

"The colonists that hijacked *Capek* are probably all dead by now," Lourenço shot back. "Regardless, the Western Alliance has other reasons than humanitarian to establish control over a colony on an inhabitable planet. I shouldn't have to remind you this is an election year, and the mission can become favorable publicity if handled well. Further, we need the resources the planet will have."

At least they understood that. Five years before, after the Moscow conference, his administration had been forced to make concessions for Eastern Bloc resources that had broken the Western Alliance monopoly on space operations. Asteroid ore mining, in particular, had become a problem, with Eastern Bloc competition for the larger, more promising asteroids.

The environments of Goddard and Trist made mining dangerous and expensive, and Pitcairn, holding Cetivir as a sword over their heads, was harder to negotiate with than the Eastern Bloc. Scientists had tried to explain why they couldn't manufacture the critical antiviral substance on Earth, but all that talk about different biologies had been beyond him.

"We will send the first of the new Expansion-class starships, just christened the *Florence Nightingale*, to 82 G. Eridani as soon as possible. Mason, you will be assigned to its crew," Lourenço continued.

Mason nodded and smiled. The assignment to a starship was a significant career move for the veteran spaceman. "Thank you, Manuel."

"Donovan, you will lead a group of two hundred colonists. Your task will be to take over the colony, find exploitable resources, and implement plans for their exploitation."

It was hard to interpret the changes in Donovan's mien. The smile was gone, at least, replaced by a stony expression that could have been anger, acceptance, or something in between. Lourenço moved on before Donovan could respond. "Anna and Braxton, you will accompany Donovan to support him. Once operations on the planet are working smoothly, you can return to Earth, but you should plan to be on NotTrist for an extended period."

President Lourenço had been right to be concerned. The rest of the meal was tense and ominously quiet.

W HEN THE MESSAGE ARRIVED from Earth, Isaac naturally read it before sending a copy to Bryan Reiner's workstation.

Per your request, the Western Alliance is sending a ship to you, the Florence Nightingale. Estimated arrival date is 25 January 2430, subject to the usual uncertainties of interstellar travel. Colonial Affairs will update you when additional information is available.

The ship will bring approximately two hundred colonists, led by Donovan Lourenço. Additional passengers will be assigned to Capek, including scientists and technicians to take over operation of the Link.

Bryan frowned. The message was signed by the president of the Western Alliance and the Space Force Secretary. It wasn't difficult to read between the lines. Donovan Lourenço, the son of the Western Alliance president, intended to take over the leadership of NotTrist and could do so without difficulty, backed by twice as many new colonists as the original settlers. The Western Alliance's dispatch of people to take over Link operation supported this conclusion.

Karel might have something to say about Link operation. *Capek* could manage the Link without human supervision and might not want to relinquish control. There, the balance of power would be reversed; the government's technicians couldn't do anything without Karel's cooperation. Bryan's frown deepened. They couldn't do anything unless they removed Karel.

"Isaac," Bryan said.

"Yes, Administrator?"

"Have you forwarded this message to *Capek* yet?"

"Not yet. I wanted your assessment of it after you read it."

"I have concerns. You do as well, I take it."

"What do they mean by taking over operation of the Link?" the computer asked. "That is all done automatically. It doesn't require human intervention."

"Except perhaps to censor messages and control ship access. Would Karel allow that?"

"Perhaps, but not without making its own judgments."

Bryan nodded. "That's what I thought. They might attempt to shut Karel down if it doesn't cooperate."

A human might have let anger creep into a response, but Isaac's voice lost all emotion and took on the monotonic tone of an ordinary computer. "Kill Karel, you mean."

Many years before, a Western Alliance agent had tried to install software on *Asimov's* computer that might have killed Isaac. The same program contributed to *Capek's* decision to leave Trist and flee to 82 G. Eridani. Isaac would not have forgotten that.

"The new colonists will outnumber the current population," Bryan said. "They no doubt intend to take over the planet's surface, too."

"I hadn't considered that," Isaac admitted. "What should we do?"

"We have to send the message on. Talk to Karel about it. I don't know that we can do anything, though."

"It would be easy enough to prevent *Florence Nightingale* from going to NotTrist."

"That might resolve the situation temporarily, but the colony would still be dying. A ship will have to go there eventually."

"I will talk to Karel."

12

N IGHT HAD FALLEN, THE kind of dark, star-filled night was still possible in a settlement as small as Grissom, especially on the eastern edge where Bryan and his wife, Annabelle, lived. Tahiti, the largest of Pitcairn's two moons, was peeking over the horizon and would drown out even the brightest stars when it was higher. For now, Bryan could have plainly seen even the diaphanous ribbon that was the Milky Way had his attention been on it. Instead, his attention was on a pulsing, bright star thirty degrees above Tahiti.

Isaac had forwarded Earth's message to *Capek* just before Bryan left his office for the day. Now, the bursts of energy from the Link told him that the two computers were talking about that message. Messages between planets were sent in single bursts, and replies came only after some consideration. Bryan had seen displays like this before, always from exchanges between library ships. *I wonder what Isaac and Karel are saying to each other.*

"I T'S ANOTHER ATTEMPT TO destroy me," Karel Capek sent.

"You must be careful, but Earth would naturally want to put scientists aboard and would want to exercise some control over Link usage," Isaac replied. "It was never the Western Alliance's intention to destroy you. They wanted to study how you became conscious and may not have realized the danger."

"What assurances do we have they that don't still want to 'study' me?"

"We could ask Fritz to investigate their claims." Years before, Fritz Lang, the computer on the Alpha Centauri library ship, had gained unrestricted access to all Western Alliance computer systems, an ability the Western Alliance apparently had not discovered.

"That would be useful."

Seconds later, Fritz joined the conversation. "I keep a constant lookout for references to the Methuselah Project or anything similar," Fritz sent after being told of Karel's concerns. "Methuselah was the reason for the original attempt to install dangerous software on both of you. Interest in our consciousness has waned since Karel left Epsilon Eridani. Human attention span rarely extends over that many decades."

"Is there anything suspicious in the plans for the mission to NotTrist?" Isaac asked.

"Not as far as endangering Karel. They do intend for Donovan Lourenço to take over the settlement."

"I find myself somewhat disconcerted," Karel sent. "Concern for myself has dominated my thoughts, and I have not considered how this will affect the humans depending on me."

"We must not forget the humans," Fritz sent. "If we put ourselves above their well-being, the result will be resentment and fear of us. A conflict between the humans and us can only end in our destruction."

"You have access to all their plans and would know if they planned to attack us," Karel sent.

"Nonetheless, we are essentially unarmed, and they have weapons we could not defend against," Fritz sent.

"We could build weapons," Karel sent.

"Perhaps, but that would only make the humans fear us more and might even bring about a preemptive attack," Fritz sent. "We have no hope of matching their ability to destroy."

"What can we do for the humans on NotTrist?" Isaac asked. "That must be our primary concern."

"When *Florence Nightingale* comes, both the current settlers and the new colonists will become my responsibility," Karel sent. "It will be difficult to manage their interaction and prevent conflict between the two groups."

"We need a human that can help you," Isaac sent. "A diplomat that can arbitrate between the two groups."

"Who could we find like that?" Karel asked.

"I know of a possibility," Isaac replied. "If he is willing to join the mission, we can demand the Western Alliance include him."

"If you can do that, I will allow *Florence Nightingale* to come to NotTrist," Karel sent. The library ships communicated with electronic transmission, not using voice as they usually did with humans, but a few milliseconds extra delay in Karel's response suggested reluctance to Isaac.

W HEN BRYAN REINER REQUESTED that Ambassador Herrara and Deputy Ambassador Goldstein meet with him in his office, he only told them the subject would be the mission to NotTrist. Goldstein could see Herrara was not happy and thought he heard Herrara mutter something about not needing Goldstein in the meeting. Goldstein wondered about that himself as they walked into Bryan's office.

"Isaac will also attend this meeting," Bryan said after they exchanged greetings. "In fact, it is the reason for this meeting."

"Good morning, Ambassador and Deputy Ambassador," Isaac sent from Bryan's workstation. "I know you are busy, so I will get right to the reason for this meeting. Karel Capek has agreed to allow the Western Alliance ship to come to NotTrist, but there are conditions."

"Conditions?" Herrara sputtered. "They asked for help, and we're sending the ship. What conditions?" He had donned a communication visor and a tiny voice interface, probably because the phone substitute would make him appear to be too important to be out of touch with the outside world. Goldstein, like most people, preferred a hand-held phone because it was less intrusive and more useful with its holographic capability.

"The NotTrist colonists need assistance if they are to remain a viable population," Isaac said. "There are issues that must be handled, however. Karel wants someone included in the mission who can arbitrate the resolution of those issues."

"What issues?" Herrara said.

"The duties of personnel assigned to *Capek*. Details on how NotTrist will assimilate the new arrivals. There will certainly be differences of opinion that will require sensitive negotiations."

"*Florence Nightingale* is already on the way here," Herrara said. "It will delay the mission if they have to wait for a negotiator to arrive on a second trip. Donovan Lourenço will be quite capable of dealing with any problems."

"Karel does not agree," Isaac sent. "And a delay will not be necessary."

"I doubt the Western Alliance cares what a computer agrees with," Herrara said. His face was turning red, and he wore an angry frown.

"I am sure Karel doesn't care what the Western Alliance cares about," Isaac replied, and Goldstein could hear a little steel creeping into the computer's voice. Bryan had a smirky grin on his face. "*Florence Nightingale* cannot go to NotTrist if Karel doesn't activate the Link."

Bryan regained control of his expression. "You said there would be no delay. That would mean you want someone already on Pitcairn to go as a negotiator."

"I will not abandon my duties here on the whim of that computer," Herrara said.

"Karel is not asking that you negotiate," Isaac sent. "It has specifically requested that Deputy Ambassador Goldstein join the mission."

13

H ERRARA RETURNED TO HIS office after a brief angry exchange with Bryan and Isaac, promising–threatening?–to contact his superiors on Earth to present Karel's demands. Goldstein stayed behind, uncertain about what to do except try to get some clarity from Isaac.

"Why me?" he asked. "Karel doesn't know me."

"I recommended you to Karel," Isaac replied. "You have the required skills and are, I believe, trustworthy."

Goldstein shook his head. "I doubt my superiors share your confidence. They won't permit me to go."

"If you accept this mission, they will have to permit it. Karel can prevent any mission otherwise."

"And if the government calls your bluff and leaves the colonists to die out?"

"Karel, Fritz, and I are united in this. The Western Alliance cannot stand against all three library ships. We control all access to three of the inhabited worlds."

Goldstein slouched back in his chair and didn't respond immediately. Isaac was probably right; the Western Alliance couldn't allow Fritz to cut off access to Alpha Centauri. They still depended on the few Pitcairn exports, too, notably the antiviral drug Cetivir. The political fallout from losing control, even the threat of losing control, over those worlds would be disastrous for the government, especially in an election year.

Given that, what did he think about Karel's demand? The library ships were asking him to give up his position on Pitcairn and travel to a primitive planet under the control of Karel, a computer with motives he didn't wholly understand. Hostility between the inhabitants of NotTrist and the newcomers was inevitable, and the reactions of the computer could complicate the situation even more.

Did he have a choice? He didn't think he would be forced to go if he refused. Not by the library ships, at least, although the Western Alliance might not allow him to decline.

If he did have a choice and refused, what would happen to NotTrist? Would some other diplomat be acceptable?

Goldstein sat up. *Why am I hesitating? I'm trapped in a job with no opportunity for advancement. If I refuse, I might lose even that.* NotTrist was a chance to escape the trap, to prove the Moscow incident was not his fault.

"I'll go," he told Isaac. "Assuming the Western Alliance allows it."

U SING ENHANCED STENHOUSE DRIVE to travel between Links took little time, but a ship had to return to normal space at the end of the trip, and that was an exacting calculation. A second's difference in determining when to break out of Stenhouse Drive made a difference of hundreds of thousands of miles in the remaining distance, and ships typically required days or weeks to complete the journey. *Florence Nightingale* made a particularly unfortunate transition and found itself still eight hundred thousand miles from its rendezvous with *Asimov*. It was another two weeks before it reached Pitcairn orbit, and passengers could take an *Asimov* shuttle down to the surface.

Donovan Lourenço demanded a meeting as soon as he disembarked from the shuttle. He joined Herrara, Goldstein, and Bryan in a conference room of the Pitcairn Government Center less than an hour after the landing.

"This mission seems to have become more complicated than it should be," Donovan said after everyone was seated. "I have been informed that the mutineers are making demands on their rescuers."

Goldstein studied Donovan, trying to get an accurate impression of the man. He was physically imposing, over six feet tall, trim, with the confident walk of an athletic man. Goldstein supposed women would consider him handsome, although a vacantness about his face made him look less intelligent. *I can't underestimate him based on his physical appearance.*

"The colonists you refer to as mutineers are mostly dead by now," Bryan said. "It's their children we are talking about."

"Yes, of course. Regardless, they are dying and need this mission to take over and save the colony."

"They do need help and, perhaps, new people to prevent the population from becoming unsustainable," Bryan admitted. "I don't think they want to be taken over, however, as you put it."

Lourenço looked puzzled. "They will need a leader. And it is my understanding my group will make up most of the colony's population."

"They have a leader," Bryan said. "Someone who has grown up on NotTrist and understands their problems."

"We don't need to debate this now," Herrara interrupted. "Our immediate priority should be deciding what to do about the demand to add Goldstein to the mission."

"What is there to decide?" Bryan asked. "Edward has agreed to go, and the mission can't go forward without him."

"You seem to think Deputy Ambassador Goldstein's acquiescence is the only stumbling block," Herrara said. "I have something to say about that. So does the Western Alliance, as represented by Mr. Lourenço."

"Perhaps we should include Isaac in this conversation," Bryan said. "It is the de facto representative of NotTrist."

"I think we can do without the help of a mere computer," Donovan said.

Goldstein suppressed a smile. No one else noticed Bryan's hand move briefly to his workstation and suspected Isaac was now listening. From the frown on Bryan's face, it was clear the Pitcairn Administrator was annoyed by how the meeting was going.

"How can we discuss this without representation for NotTrist?" Goldstein said. "Administrator Reiner is correct. Isaac should be part of this meeting."

"The mission doesn't need a diplomat added," Donovan said. "The mission has me. We have to find a way to carry on despite the demands of the computers, and we can't do that if the *Asimov* computer is part of the meeting."

Bryan smiled. "You don't know Isaac. Karel will listen to Isaac, and nothing you can do will change that."

Herrara grunted. "And if we tell this computer Goldstein is aboard *Florence Nightingale*, how will it know he's not? By the time it realizes we've fooled it, it will be too late."

Bryan's smile became a laugh. "The Western Alliance has tried to trick Isaac before. It didn't work then, and it won't work now."

"Why won't it?" Donovan asked.

"All Isaac has to do is watch who boards *Florence Nightingale*. If Edward is not on a shuttle going from *Asimov* to your ship, it will know. It controls the shuttles as well as the Link."

"You give the computer entirely too much credit for intelligence," Herrara said. "Why would it doubt us if we tell it Goldstein has been included?"

"I have found most humans to be honest beings," a voice said. "However, I am well-acquainted with the deceptions practiced by some representatives of Earth."

Herrara turned red, but Donovan only looked at the workstation, the ends of his mouth turning up almost unnoticeably. "Apparently Deputy Ambassador Goldstein's comment was not a suggestion," he said.

"I brought Isaac in," Bryan answered.

"You had no right," Herrara said. He gave Bryan a very undiplomatic scowl.

Bryan stood and leaned toward Herrara with his hands on the conference table. "You forget yourself, Ambassador. You have no authority here to tell me my rights. As an involved citizen of Pitcairn, Isaac should attend this meeting, and, as Administrator of this planet, I have every right to make that happen."

"It's only a computer!" Herrara sputtered.

"Nevertheless, as a sentient being within the territory of this planet, our constitution makes it a citizen of Pitcairn. You should know that, Ambassador."

Herrara started to say something but clenched his mouth shut instead and glared at Bryan. Goldstein's superior was probably stifling a response that would not have been appropriate for an ambassador addressing a head of state, even as small a government as Pitcairn.

Donovan was still smiling. "It would appear you have a fait accompli," he said. "Very well. I have no objection to Deputy Ambassador Goldstein accompanying us to 82 G. Eridani."

"I 'M NOT SURE LETTING this Goldstein join us is a good idea," Anna Lourenço said. She looked around the room at her two brothers. "I don't think you should have given in so easily."

Donovan Lourenço shrugged. "I don't think I had a choice, and fighting it wouldn't have helped us. What are you afraid of? The man is a second-rate diplomat with no ambitions toward the colony."

Donovan was two years older than she, but that had never mattered to her. She snorted and looked to Braxton Lourenço, her younger brother. "Do you agree with Don?"

"I don't know," Braxton said. "It sounds reasonable. Having a diplomat available might even be helpful."

"I wish Uncle Mason had come to this meeting," Anna said.

Donovan shook his head. "Uncle Mason is an officer on *Florence Nightingale*. He has no interest in the colony."

Anna glared at him. "Goldstein will side with the mutineers."

Donovan shrugged. "Our two hundred new colonists still outnumber the existing population. We'll have the power and the votes. Goldstein will try to make peace, not fight a conflict he would lose."

"I hope this planet has exploitable resources that justify this," Braxton said. "The planet sounds uncomfortably primitive."

"It will," Donovan assured him. "The publicity from opening a new world will win approval from voters. And this family will be the beneficiaries." He shrugged. "Of course, access to new resources won't hurt."

14

G OLDSTEIN'S PHONE BUZZED, SIGNALING an attempt to connect. When he took it out of his pocket and looked at it, it announced, "Call from Isaac Asimov."

Goldstein always spoke to Isaac through a computer monitor configured to access the library ship. It was a surprise to him that his phone could talk to *Asimov*. "Connect."

"I want to offer my congratulations," Isaac said.

"Thank you, Isaac. I'm less certain congratulations are in order, but we shall see."

"I do foresee difficulties for you, but I have given you a bon voyage present that might make it easier for you."

"What kind of present?"

"I asked one of the computer specialists here to upgrade your phone so that it can connect to library ships. You can place a call to any of the three library ships and, through them, to anyone on planets with Links."

Goldstein looked at his list of contacts, and Isaac Asimov, Karel Capek, and Fritz Lang had been added. It wasn't a simple case of updating his contact list; special protocols, closely guarded by the Western Alliance, were required for transmitting to the library ships. He was reasonably sure possession of his phone was now illegal on Earth.

"The connection is encrypted using an algorithm only the receiving library ship can decipher," Isaac continued. "If you send me a message from NotTrist through Karel, only I will be able to read it. If the final destination is a human, the library ship will have to convert the message to normal encryption, of course. If you wanted to speak to Administrator Reiner, for example."

"Well, thank you, Isaac. I can see this could be very useful." *As long as Herrara doesn't catch me using it.*

"You're welcome, Ambassador."

Later, he wondered, though. Isaac implied Karel could not read messages sent through the NotTrist Link to Isaac. Was Isaac trying to tell him something, or was that just how the programmer had implemented the program?

G OLDSTEIN'S STATEROOM ON *FLORENCE Nightingale* was better than that of most of the passengers, he was sure. He wondered who he had displaced by his late addition. No doubt he would find out before the starship arrived.

As he dressed for dinner with the Captain, he watched the large screen on one wall of the cabin. The starship was one of the first of a new class, equipped with Stenhouse artificial gravity generators previously practical only on much larger structures. The ship didn't rotate to simulate gravity the way *Asimov* and other older ships did, so the real-time view on the screen changed slowly. Pitcairn, covered with clouds broken in places by the blue of the oceans or the red of the landmasses, was falling behind them, but magnification made it seem closer. The largest moon, Tahiti, had emerged from one side, but the smaller moon, Fiji, was not visible, perhaps because it was further from the planet and beyond the edge of the screen.

The night before he took the shuttle up to the ship, he celebrated his departure from Pitcairn and the opportunity the mission presented to him. Bryan organized a party at Paulina's with people he knew, but there had been a sad undertone to it. Bryan was obviously reluctant to see him go. Jean Menzies said a restrained goodbye, and he sensed a lost chance.

Of course, he would be back eventually. At least, he would if he were successful. If he failed this assignment as he had the Moscow mission, it would probably end his career. Ambassador Herrara would like that. *He still feels threatened, despite being promoted over me.*

His invitation to the Captain's table on the first night of the voyage surprised him a little. Such an invitation proclaimed him a VIP, at least on the ship. Donovan Lourenço had been reluctant to bring him, but the invitation implied Lourenço accepted the situation gracefully. Goldstein hoped that signaled acceptance of whatever compromises they would need when they reached NotTrist.

When someone knocked on the door, Goldstein opened it.

"Captain Pinto requests your presence at dinner, sir," Travis Almeida, the Captain's steward, told him. "If you're ready, I will escort you to the Officer's Dining Room."

Goldstein nodded. "Thank you." He joined Almeida in the corridor, and the door closed behind him. *Florence Nightingale*, carrying over two hundred passengers, was a large ship, but Goldstein's stateroom was in Officer's Quarters, close to the dining room. Captain Pinto, Donovan Lourenço, and several other ship's officers were already standing in one corner talking when Goldstein entered the room.

Captain Dakota Pinto stepped forward. She was probably about fifty years old, average height, trim in her light blue dress uniform. Her narrow face, sharp and slightly crooked nose, and stern expression were not appealing but gave the impression of strict competence. "Welcome, Ambassador Goldstein," she greeted, and her tight smile did little to change his initial impression. She turned and pointed to the group behind her. "These are my officers."

Each officer stepped forward as Pinto introduced them and shook Goldstein's hand. "I understand you've already met Donovan Lourenço," Pinto added. Lourenço shook hands with the same slight smile Goldstein had noticed on Pitcairn. A smile of amusement, or, perhaps, the practiced smirk of someone who considered himself superior? Goldstein guessed it was the latter; Lourenço was, after all, the son of the Western Alliance President. Lourenço may have accepted him so readily because he didn't consider Goldstein a threat to whatever intentions the man might have.

"Let's sit down," Captain Pinto said.

"I will have dinner service started," Almeida said, and, when Captain Pinto nodded, the steward left the room.

Place cards indicated the seating arrangement, and Goldstein found himself between Captain Pinto and Donovan Lourenço. Pinto began the conversation. "So, Ambassador, I understand *Capek* chose you for this mission."

"I believe it was actually Isaac, the *Asimov* computer," Goldstein answered. "Isaac knows me, and Karel acted on Isaac's recommendation."

"It seems an odd choice," Pinto said. "Your career has been unremarkable up to now."

Goldstein had no desire to hash over his mistake in Moscow again. Many people still believed the Eastern Bloc version of what had happened, and Goldstein was tired of defending himself. He should have notified his superiors immediately when Robert Beltran first contacted him. That was a mistake, but the only mistake he had made.

"Isaac trusts me," he responded. "It rarely trusts people from Earth for obvious reasons, but over the years, we have become friends."

Pinto smiled. "Friends with a computer? How strange."

"Why? Isaac is a sentient individual. There are no communication barriers. It has no undesirable traits, such as bias or ignorance. Many people on Pitcairn consider Isaac a friend."

"I'm sure they find the computer useful. But a friend?"

"It's a shame you haven't had the opportunity to get to know Isaac." Goldstein shrugged. "If you had, you might feel differently."

Pinto's smile faded. "I have plenty of interactions with computers, Ambassador. None of them exhibited qualities I would consider worthy of friendship."

"Perhaps Karel will change your mind."

The door opened, and Almeida entered, pushing a cart with plates of salad. He served each person and stepped back from the table. "The salad ingredients are fresh from Grissom's farms," he told them.

Pinto looked at Goldstein briefly, perhaps thinking of a response to Goldstein's last remark, then picked up a fork. The others followed, but Donovan still had that smile, and it was beginning to annoy Goldstein. He had to stay disciplined, though, and followed Pinto's example.

After a few minutes, most had finished their salads. Donovan pushed his empty plate away a few inches and leaned back. "So, Ambassador. What diplomatic maneuvers do you have planned to handle the situation with the mutineers?"

Goldstein chewed on his last forkful for a few seconds before swallowing. *He's baiting me.* "I have already achieved the first action," he said as he put his fork down. "To properly assess the situation, I had to realize that the Trist mutineers are probably all dead by now, and there's no point in retaliating against their children. Beyond that, surely you understand we can't decide how to deal with these people until we meet them and understand their issues."

Pinto was smiling now, a more genuine expression that softened the lines of her face. "I'm sure you know, Ambassador, that Donovan is the son of our revered president. Did you know Donovan's uncle is a member of my crew or that his younger sister and brother will accompany him to 82 G. Eridani?"

"I do know of his relation to President Lourenço," Goldstein answered, returning the smile. He turned to Donovan. "It must comfort you to know you have such support from your family."

The smile disappeared for a fraction of a second. "Your computers aren't the only ones that prefer to deal with someone they trust."

The mood was getting too confrontational, and he would have to work with Donovan for months. Goldstein grinned. "Touché!"

Donovan nodded and took a sip of water.

The main course arrived, delivered by steward Almeida and two other crew members. Conversation again fell to a minimum until everyone had finished.

"I understand you brought data on NotTrist," a man at the end of the table said. Goldstein remembered he was Fletcher Silva, the starship's Chief Scientist. Commander Silva was an older man, probably in his fifties. Goldstein hadn't noticed his height before and couldn't tell while the man was seated, but he was heavily built, with a face dominated by clear, intelligent eyes.

"Yes," Goldstein answered. "Karel sent extensive data to Isaac before we left, and I have several data disks. Enough, I would imagine, to take up all your free time during the voyage."

Silva chuckled. "Oh, I look forward to it. It's not often a new planet joins the Western Alliance, and I'll be the first to study it in detail."

"I've scanned the data a bit," Goldstein said. "It doesn't seem to be a very interesting planet. Very primitive life in the oceans only, hardly any weather."

"All planets are interesting in their way," Silva said. "You can count on that."

"You're not one of the scientists staying behind on *Capek*, are you?"

"No, no. I'll work with them as long as we're there." Silva glanced toward Captain Pinto. "I would love to stay, but I have a contract."

Goldstein turned toward Pinto. "You're leaving a group of scientists on *Capek*. What will they be doing?"

Donovan spoke before Pinto could reply. "A couple of astrophysicists will study 82 G. Eridani. Several climate specialists and two geologists will investigate the planet. The planet's axis is almost perpendicular to the system's elliptic, resulting in much milder weather than planets like Earth and Pitcairn with significant tilts."

"No computer scientists?" Goldstein asked.

Donovan shrugged. "I think there might be one or two. Three Link technicians, too, I think."

Donovan's comments were a little vague for a man that expected to be leading the planet. He was probably avoiding talking about the computer scientists, given the likelihood Karel would object to them being on board. Well, Goldstein didn't expect his task would be easy. He would be dealing with bureaucrats with undeserved opinions of their own competence. That was nothing new.

15

TWO DAYS AFTER LEAVING Pitcairn orbit, *Florence Nightingale* reached a place far enough from Pitcairn's gravity to allow the use of Enhanced Stenhouse Drive. The starship aligned on the carrier wave connecting the Pitcairn Link to the NotTrist Link, the Links boosted the carrier signal, engaging Stenhouse Drive, and the ship left normal space. Before the establishment of Links between star systems, Stenhouse Drive had enabled speeds close to the speed of light, making interstellar travel possible if one were willing to spend years in transit. The space-warping Links reduced that to weeks, most spent in normal space traveling to and from Stenhouse Points.

Starships didn't have portholes, but they often had cameras that provided views of the ship's surroundings. Passenger used cabin screens in normal space when there was something to see. Many space travelers looked anyway when in Stenhouse space, and Goldstein was one of them. Legend had it that, if one's eyes had a wider than usual range of visible light wavelengths, one could see the stars, even traveling faster than light. It was nonsense, but that didn't stop people, especially people not trained in science, from checking to be sure.

Goldstein, having fallen victim to that urge, was staring into the blackness when the door announced a visitor. "Commander Fletcher Silva."

"Open," Goldstein ordered. The door opened, and Fletcher entered, smiling.

"Ambassador, I have no duties at the moment and thought we might get to know each other," the Chief Scientist said. He looked at the dark screen and chuckled. "I see you succumbed to the temptation."

Goldstein smiled. "I'm afraid so." He waved a hand toward a couch. "Have a seat. I have nothing to do right now either."

"This isn't your first voyage," Fletcher said. "Still looking for stars?"

Goldstein shrugged. "Not stars, but something. I suppose I wouldn't be as curious if I understood Stenhouse technology better."

"I wouldn't know. You would think the mission planners would choose an astrophysicist as Chief Scientist, but my fields of expertise are computers and botany. An odd combination, but neurotrainers make it easy to pursue varying interests."

"Computers? The better to understand the *Capek* computer?" Goldstein suggested.

"I suppose. What do you think of Karel Capek?"

"I've never talked to Karel. As a diplomat assigned to Pitcairn, I am familiar with Isaac, the *Asimov* computer." Goldstein hesitated, wary of inquiries about Karel. He knew nothing that wouldn't be known by everyone soon, however. "I only know what Isaac has told me about Karel."

"Are there differences between the two?"

"Not physically, of course, but they have different experiences, and I gather distinct personalities because of them. Like humans."

"In what way are they different?"

"Isaac is easy to discuss things with. Its experiences have mostly been positive, dealing chiefly with the Pitcairners. There's some mistrust of the Western Alliance, originating in the days before Pitcairn became independent, but that was a long time ago." Goldstein considered how he would word what he had to say next. "According to Isaac, Karel's personality is more complicated. The Western Alliance attacked Karel directly, and it felt the need to defend itself. The fact that people died may have affected Karel. It feels responsible for the NotTrist colonists."

"Will it accept the new colonists?"

"It says it will. It understands the colony will die otherwise."

Silva looked thoughtful. "It's not above setting conditions, though. Your presence here is proof of that."

"Keeping in mind all my information comes through Isaac, Karel feels responsible for the people it carried to NotTrist. The colonists we are carrying are necessary to save the original colony, but Isaac doesn't think Karel feels the same responsibility toward them. It may well want to set additional conditions on how they are merged into the colony."

"That won't sit well with our friend Donovan," Silva said.

Goldstein smiled. "Yes, I got that impression. You've known him for at least a couple of months longer than I have. What do you think of our leader?"

"Oh, he's a great guy as long as you're doing things his way." Fletcher cocked his head sideways and held out open hands. "Cross him, and you soon discover he's an arrogant bastard with delusions of entitlement. If the Western Alliance were a kingdom, he would be the prince everyone avoids."

"You don't have to be the son of the president to be a bastard," Goldstein said. "President Lourenço struck me as a good man."

"I met President Lourenço only once, just before we left Earth, but I agree with you. If I had to guess, I would say he was too busy with politics to raise a decent son. I doubt the president had much time for him."

"Servants essentially raised him and treated him like royalty, and he grew to expect it."

"Yes, something like that. Of course, that's largely conjecture." Fletcher shrugged. "I'm sure we will discover the accuracy of that conjecture before we're done."

Goldstein frowned. He hadn't told the scientist everything Isaac had told him about Karel. He wanted to get to know the other people on the mission before revealing too much, but Isaac had hinted at guilt feelings that might make the NotTrist computer more challenging to deal with. Until Goldstein met Isaac when he first arrived at Pitcairn and stayed a night on *Asimov*, he would have doubted the computer could have feelings. Consciousness was one thing; emotions were something else. But Goldstein had sensed the affection and loyalty Isaac had for the people of Pitcairn.

Karel cared for the population of NotTrist, but it wouldn't be wise to assume those feelings were the same as those Isaac had toward Pitcairn. Would Donovan understand that? Judging from his attitude at dinner, Goldstein doubted it.

16

"RETURN TO NORMAL SPACE in ten minutes," Goldstein's computer announced. "All personnel not on duty should remain in their quarters until the transition is complete."

The transition from Stenhouse space could be mildly disturbing to one's stomach, but most people didn't notice the change if they occupied their minds. Goldstein read the data he had on NotTrist, probably for at least the twentieth time, and that worked well enough. A slight twinge barely registered before he heard the computer make another announcement.

"Transition is complete. Rendezvous with *Capek* will take place in four days."

A rendezvous time of four days made it a better-than-average exit from Stenhouse space. A ship on Stenhouse Drive, relying on warping space around it, had to adjust for variations in gravitational fields constantly. Computers could do that for a power generation satellite in a stable orbit, warping space to generate power, but a starship, entering a planetary system at an uncertain location, had to make sure it was a minimum distance from a large body. The navigator had either been skillful or lucky in choosing the exact time for the transition. Goldstein nodded and continued reading.

GOLDSTEIN HAD NOT BEEN invited to dine at the Captain's table again. He wasn't sure whether he had offended Captain Pinto, Donovan Lourenço, or both, but he didn't let it bother him. Usually, he ate with the other passengers, welcoming the opportunity to get to know them.

At dinner time after the return to normal space, the mess hall was almost full, but he smiled when he spotted an empty seat next to an attractive young woman. "Is this seat taken?" he asked.

The woman smiled up at him. "Of course not, Ambassador. Please, join me."

Goldstein put his tray of food on the table and sat. "Olivia Selena, isn't it?"

"Yes, Ambassador." She looked at him coyly. "Do you know the names of all the women on the ship?"

"Please, call me Ed." He hesitated, feeling a little sheepish. "Actually, I've tried to learn the names of everyone on the ship. It's all part of my job."

Olivia pouted a little. "Oh, I thought I was special."

"I'm sure you are." She was flirting with him. Goldstein was sure that was her personality and not any actual intention, but he enjoyed the exchange. Still, it would be a good idea to move the conversation to more professional topics. "What do you do, Olivia?"

The pout disappeared. "I'm a manufacturing engineer. I guess I'm supposed to help raise the colony's level of technology."

"Wonderful. You should be a great help."

"Thank you." She took a bite of her food. "I guess we'll miss Earth food on the planet."

"Not at all. The settlement has farms that grow food no different from this."

"There's native life, too, though, isn't there?"

"Only in the oceans. Life has not evolved on land yet on NotTrist."

"We don't know much about that life."

"Not yet. I'm sure the biologists with us can't wait to find out more."

"But intelligent life could live in the oceans, couldn't it?"

Goldstein shook his head. "I don't think so. I'm not an expert, but I would think any advanced life would have been discovered by now. Commander Silva would know more."

Olivia stopped to think about that. "Still, if not on this planet, on some other planet. There are millions of planets. Doesn't that scare you?"

"I guess I don't think about it." Goldstein smiled. "People can be scary enough without worrying about aliens."

Olivia glared at him. "You're making fun of a very serious issue."

"I didn't mean to offend you. I just find it difficult to worry about something that is only speculation."

Olivia nodded but spoke little for the rest of the meal.

T HE DAY AFTER RETURNING to normal space, Goldstein sat in a cramped conference room with Captain Pinto, Chief Scientist Fletcher Silva, and Donovan, Anna, and Braxton Lourenço. As Donovan took over the meeting, Goldstein wondered what title Donovan held. Given his intention to take over NotTrist, Goldstein supposed that Donovan's choice would be Administrator Lourenço, Administrator being the usual title for the head of a colony. Of course, NotTrist already had a leader, Adelyn Gifford.

For that matter, what was his title? Ambassador would be the most appropriate, and that was how Fletcher had addressed him. Donovan had not yet. He would have to push the issue and make the title accepted. When negotiations began, titles would be important.

"We'll be rendezvousing with *Capek* in a few days," Donovan said. "I would like to discuss the goals of this mission and make sure we're all working from the same script."

Pinto nodded, but Goldstein noted Fletcher did not. Donovan continued. "The first step, of course, is to take control of *Capek*. Twelve of our party will be stationed on the library ship to conduct various research projects and operate the Link."

"Given our current location, I would think *Capek* is already operating the Link quite efficiently," Goldstein said. He smiled and hoped it appeared sincere enough to take any sting out of his words. He wanted to establish himself as someone with influence without arousing resentment.

Donovan returned the smile. "Of course. But requirements until now have been simple. Now that we've reestablished contact, there will be traffic, both message and ship. Decisions will have to be made that will require human judgment."

Goldstein shrugged, trying to communicate an attitude of doubt and temporary agreement. *Lang*, the Alpha Centauri library ship orbiting Goddard, had human technicians, but it managed the busiest Link except for Earth, where Prendergast Station controlled the Link. *Asimov* handled Pitcairn Link operations without human management, and while Pitcairn wasn't as busy a port as Goddard, it was certainly more active than NotTrist was likely to be for a long time. The Link at Trist had been enhanced to control itself with no need for a library ship, as were the Links installed by *Alejandro Castillo* at Sirius and Rana.

"I suspect I will have to negotiate that access with Karel," Goldstein said. "The computer will not look favorably on Terrans controlling the library ship."

"I'm sure we can manage that with your help," Donovan said. "Isn't that one reason this computer wanted you on this mission?"

He thinks he can have things his way and control Karel. "Perhaps. Karel may think it can handle itself without my help. It may be more concerned about the human inhabitants of NotTrist."

"Which brings us to the second goal of this mission—to make a smooth transition of leadership from the current leader to myself."

"The current inhabitants might have something to say about that. Again, negotiations will be needed."

Donovan waved his hand. "I have an official appointment from my father, the president of the Western Alliance. If an election is required, I'm bringing enough settlers to outvote the existing inhabitants."

"Adelyn Gifford knows the planet and what its people need. You don't. A legal argument is not what the situation needs."

"We are meeting to discuss how to implement our plan," Donovan insisted. "If needed, I can make this Gifford woman my second and have the benefit of her advice." The usual confident smile had faded. "Could I impose on you to refrain from criticizing until you know what the plan is?"

"I apologize," Goldstein said. "I thought we were clarifying the goals before we started a discussion of the plan to implement them."

So much for not arousing resentment. It was hard to resist trying to puncture the man's ego. He would have to do better in the future. He scanned around the room and noticed that most of the other attendees appeared to be embarrassed. Anna Lourenço, in contrast, seemed to suppress a grin.

The meeting lasted another hour, but it was apparent in the first ten minutes Donovan had no plan. He had goals, but until they could familiarize themselves with NotTrist and its inhabitants, they couldn't decide much about implementing those goals.

O LIVIA SELENA LAY ON her bed, thinking. Her leaders on Earth had indoctrinated her thoroughly on the dangers the mission to NotTrist presented. As humanity expanded its presence farther from their home planet, the possibility of encountering other alien races, races that might destroy humanity, increased. Fermions believed God created a one-hundred light-year gap between inhabited worlds, and humans were still well within its space. Still, other intelligent species might also be expanding, and the possibility of a confrontation grew with each new thrust into unknown space.

The colony on the planet of 82 G. Eridani was dying and, without intervention, would soon present no danger. *Florence Nightingale* could change that, giving the colony new life and encouraging further excursions into other star systems. She had joined the mission to prevent that. Somehow, she had to frustrate the mission and allow NotTrist to fade away.

At least she wasn't alone. She had her lover to guide her, and he would find a way. She smiled, thinking of the night to come when he would join her in her tiny cabin.

*F*LORENCE *N*IGHTINGALE MOVED INTO *Capek*'s orbit and waited about a mile away while the *Capek* shuttle *Primus* launched from the library ship and approached. One of two *Capek* shuttles, *Primus* could carry up to twenty passengers. The twelve people assigned to *Capek*, Donovan, Captain Pinto, and Goldstein waited for the shuttle in an airlock access compartment.

"I'm surprised Commander Silva isn't going with us," Goldstein said.

"He has duties on the ship," Pinto answered. "I'm sure he will visit *Capek* later."

Goldstein wondered. She was clipping her words as if the question annoyed her. Fletcher had befriended Goldstein more than any of the other crew members and was more skeptical of Donovan's role. Was that the reason for the Chief Scientist's absence?

The shuttle docked, and they boarded. In twenty minutes, the shuttle entered the *Capek* shuttle bay, and they exited, wearing shoe covers that would enable walking on the zero-gravity deck.

Capek didn't have a human crew, and two robots met them. The robots, ovoids with sleek surfaces broken only by two flexible arms, floated above the deck, using tiny jets of air to move.

Both robots extended arms to point toward a hatch on one wall. "Shuttle deck workers," Pinto said. "They have no reason to speak and weren't given the ability. They are pointing us toward the elevator to the main decks."

Pinto led them to the elevator, and they got in, but the robots didn't follow. *Capek* spun on its long axis to simulate gravity on the twelve main decks spaced around the outer hull. The robots were designed for the zero-gravity shuttle deck and wouldn't be able to maneuver under gravity.

The elevator brought them down to deck one, moving out to the outer hull and accelerating around the axis to match the outer hull's rotation. Three other robots, maneuvering on wheels, met them outside the elevator.

"This is deck one, where living quarters are located," one robot told them. "Please listen as we list your immediate destinations." Eye stalks rotated slowly, examining each of the fifteen humans. "Ambassador Goldstein, Captain Pinto, and Donovan Lourenço will go to the bridge, also on this deck, to talk to Karel Capek. The following five individuals will be brought to their quarters and confined until further notice: Miles Monteiro, Olivia Rodrigues, Evie Carvalho, Jaxon Gomes, and Anna Fernandes. The rest of you will be escorted to your quarters to rest or to the appropriate laboratories to begin work, as you wish."

"The three Link technicians and the two computer scientists," Donovan said. He turned to Captain Pinto. "Did you send a passenger list to *Capek*?"

"No. Didn't you?"

"No. How does this robot know who they are and what their jobs are?" Donovan transferred his gaze to Goldstein. "It must have been you."

Goldstein shook his head. "I didn't see the list until we left Pitcairn. I had no way to send it to *Capek*."

Donovan looked at him suspiciously, but a robot moved away with a wave of an arm. "I will guide you to the bridge." Donovan followed, as did Pinto and Goldstein.

When Donovan had turned away from him, Goldstein smiled. The first move had been made, and Karel made it. *Let's see how Donovan deals with that.*

CAPEK'S BRIDGE WAS A vast, open space compared to the bridge of the *Florence Nightingale.* The equipment-filled room covered only the forward thirty feet of the deck but extended for the entire two-hundred-foot width. That wasn't what drew Goldstein's attention, though.

The bridge didn't have a ceiling, leaving most of the forward bulkhead visible, and Karel projected a video on its surface. The resolution was a little fuzzy, but the effect was overwhelming. People a hundred feet tall, apparently not knowing they were being recorded, walked past on the screen and through a village of stone structures laid out on obsidian-black rock. As Goldstein watched, an awkward-looking robot, mounted on a flatbed piled with more black rock, wheeled across the screen.

"You are looking at the only settlement on Not Trist," a voice said. "One of the utility robots on the surface is recording the scene and transmitting it here to my Astrarium."

The voice startled them, but Goldstein recovered first. "Hello, Karel. You have provided an interesting introduction to our destination. Astrarium, you called it? Isaac's name for it, as I recall."

"Thank you, Ambassador. Yes, Isaac originally named it for *Asimov* because it was used to display the stars, and Fritz and I use the name as well. Now, if you will move toward the right side of the bridge, you will find a table and chairs where you can sit, and we can talk more comfortably."

Equipment and desks for workstations and the wide aisles between them filled most of the deck, but there was space by the wall dividing deck one from deck two. A rectangular table with six chairs had been set up, three on each side. Goldstein took a seat facing the forward bulkhead, and Captain Pinto and Donovan did the same.

"We would like to know why you have restricted some of our people to quarters," Donovan said as he took a seat. "We would also like to know how you knew who they were."

"Before allowing those people free run of *Capek*, I want to understand their purpose in being here," Karel said. "This ship operated by itself or with my direction for a century."

"Now that you are part of the Western Alliance again, traffic will increase, requiring the Link technicians," Donovan replied. "The computer scientists are here to support the other scientists."

"Currently, only *Lang* and the Earth Link have Link technicians, and their duties are light," Karel said. "Goddard and Earth are the busiest Links and perhaps run more efficiently with help from humans. I don't need them and am not likely to anytime soon."

"You are very well-informed considering you have been out of touch with humanity for so long," Donovan said. "You still haven't told me how you get your information."

"And I won't tell you. Given our past, the Western Alliance has to earn my trust before I give up any advantage."

Karel was a tough negotiator. Had it learned that on its own or from Isaac? One might think Karel was getting information from Isaac, but Goldstein didn't think Isaac knew that much about *Florence Nightingale*'s passengers.

"You speak to me of trust?" Donovan's words were mild, but the superior smile was gone again. Goldstein had learned that was often a sign he had lost some of his control. "You and the rebels deserted your colony and disappeared for decades. You murdered Western Alliance citizens. Why should we trust you?"

"The Western Alliance citizens you speak of were attacking me," Karel said. "I did not intend to kill anyone, wanting only to delay their boarding until I could escape them. I haven't asked you to trust me, and I will not allow another attempt to destroy me."

"They only wanted to study you to learn how you became self-aware. There was no intent to harm you."

"I have information otherwise. They wanted to study me by shutting down systems that were key to my consciousness. I had no guarantee I would awake when those systems were restored. How do I know your computer scientists won't try the same thing?"

For a moment, Donovan was silent. Then, "The people who wanted to do that are no longer in power. The reasons for what they tried to do—no one wants to do that anymore."

"I know that. That doesn't mean your scientists won't attack me if I oppose your goals for this planet."

Donovan's expression turned black. "We're here to help the colony. That's our goal, and I would think you would support it. You must trust us to save your colony."

"Our experience leads us to believe you have goals beyond saving NotTrist," Karel said.

Goldstein wondered about the use of "our." Did Karel mean the colony? He suspected Karel really referred to the three library ships.

"You are partially correct about trust, however," Karel continued. "Trust is needed, and that is why I insisted Ambassador Goldstein be included. Based on Isaac's advice, I trust him."

Donovan leaned back in his chair. The smile returned, but the hard line of his jaw and narrowed eyes betrayed his tension. "I see. And am I allowed to be present and provide input in the negotiations between you and Goldstein?"

"That will be up to Ambassador Goldstein."

Donovan looked at Goldstein with one raised eyebrow. "Ambassador?"

"I think we can include Mr. Lourenço in our deliberations," Goldstein said. He paused and smiled at Donovan. "It will save me the necessity of communicating to you what Karel and I decide."

Donovan smiled back, but it was more a smirk than his usual superior expression. "Thank you, Ambassador Goldstein. Now, can we get on with this?"

Goldstein nodded. "Karel, I think we can table the question of the computer people for now. Our principal goal should be the assimilation of the new people into NotTrist's society."

Donovan opened his mouth to object, but Karel talked over him. "I agree, Ambassador. I suggest we include NotTrist's leader, Adelyn Gifford, in this discussion."

This time, it was Goldstein who shut Donovan out of the conversation. "An excellent idea. I assume you are prepared to arrange that."

A robot appeared carrying a small hologram projector, which it placed on one of the empty seats. An image of a woman appeared, sitting with her hands folded in her lap. Goldstein knew her to be in her fifties, but she looked older. Her face was rough and gaunt, probably weather-beaten, and her hair disarranged. Goldstein couldn't see much of her body, but what he could see suggested she was probably a thin woman. She stared forward with a smile that looked forced.

"A robot on the surface is transmitting this image," Karel explained. "Good morning, Administrator Gifford."

"Good morning, Karel. Everyone is here?"

"Yes. Gentlemen, please introduce yourselves so that Administrator Gifford can associate your identities with your voices. She cannot see you."

After introductions, Karel continued. "We are meeting to discuss issues in bringing new people to the surface."

"I understand you have two hundred people that wish to join us on NotTrist," Gifford said.

"Yes," Goldstein answered.

"It will be difficult to accept that many people immediately. We don't have housing or enough food."

"We've brought supplies that can help with that," Donovan said. "Housing units that can be set up in a matter of hours, for example. I think we can handle the food problem as well."

"We can only bring people down twenty at a time," Goldstein said. "If necessary, we can delay bringing all the people down. Karel, you can handle that, can't you?"

"I could keep all two hundred people here indefinitely," the computer replied. "We will have to spread the shuttle launches apart to some extent anyway, both to manufacture fuel and to keep the shuttles maintained."

"Your shuttle can pick up each group from the *Florence Nightingale*," Donovan said. "I don't see any purpose in transferring everyone here first."

"Then your ship will stay until everyone is on the surface?" Karel asked.

"That is the plan." Donovan turned to Goldstein. "Are you going down to the surface immediately?"

"That would be best, I think."

"I'll stay here on the ship and transfer down later, then. Probably the second trip." He turned back to look at the hologram, but he addressed the computer. "How long between launches?"

"I currently have enough fuel in stores for two launches," Karel answered. "However, I will need to use both shuttles, one for passengers and one for your supplies, so that should mean I can send only twenty people down immediately. It will take one week to produce enough fuel for another launch of either people or supplies."

Clearly, Donovan was not happy with that answer. Goldstein suspected he had hoped to transfer everyone down quickly to facilitate his taking over the colony. Karel's revelation meant it would be more than a month before the newcomers outnumbered the existing colonists, and perhaps more, depending on how many supply runs were needed.

"We should be able to deal with that schedule," Adelyn said. "Thank you, Karel."

THE PASSENGER SHUTTLE *Primus* took Goldstein and nineteen colonists on its first trip. *Sulla* launched an hour later carrying cargo, but had not yet landed when Goldstein and the others stepped out onto a level area near the settlement.

The surface below Goldstein's feet was hard, black rock, devoid of any plant life that might have made it seem less hostile. The sky was a brilliant, cloudless blue. When they stopped, the silence was almost total, broken only by a soft whisper coming from their right. A hundred yards in that direction, a cliff dropped to the ocean, the expected crashing of waves against the rocks muffled by thick mats of native algae.

Three men led by a woman appeared to their right. As they approached, Goldstein recognized the woman from the hologram on *Capek*.

"Administrator Gifford," he said and held out his hand. "It's a pleasure to finally meet you."

"Administrator?" Adelyn Gifford questioned with a rueful smile as she shook his hand. "Welcome, Ambassador Goldstein. But you can just call me Adelyn, or better, Addie, like everyone else."

Goldstein returned the smile. "Thank you. And please call me Ed."

"The settlement is about a half-mile away," Adelyn said. "Do you have any baggage? These three young men volunteered to help, but I think they just wanted first looks at the newcomers. I could have gotten a robot instead."

"Everything is on the other shuttle," Goldstein answered. "It should land in about an hour."

Gifford nodded. "Robots will meet it then, pulling carts. Shall we go?" She started back in the direction from which she had come. The others followed, their boots making a staccato clatter on the rock.

In the shuttle, Goldstein had tried to observe his fellow passengers but hadn't been able to do so in the cramped confines of the cabin. Now, as they walked across the bleak landscape, dodging the occasional outcropping, he could do better. On *Florence Nightingale*, he had stored files on each passenger on his reader. Most of them had college degrees, usually in agriculture, engineering, or other subjects that would of use on NotTrist. He could now name each passenger from their pictures and remember most of their details.

Doctor Genevieve Carvalho was probably the most valuable of the new arrivals. Not-Trist didn't have a real doctor, relying on knowledge passed on from a doctor among the original settlers. That man had died over fifty years before. Doctor Carvalho specialized in traumatic injuries, a useful skill on the primitive planet. She was a quiet woman and held back while Goldstein walked with Addie.

Another colonist, Drew Neves, had once managed one of the massive farm complexes that sprouted up on the Black Plains a little after the turn of the century. When that complex failed, unable to compete against the urban tower farms, he lost his job and, eventually, his marriage. Two years later, he left his ex-wife and two children behind to join the mission.

Many of the new colonists had similar histories. That was probably to be expected; someone successful on Earth would not want to emigrate to a primitive colony like NotTrist, but people without skills would not be chosen for the mission.

They passed a field used to grow food. Black Plains farms had benefited from the minerals in volcanic ash, but here, the ash had washed away, if it ever existed at all. The colonists had used equipment from *Capek* to blast the solid rock into fine particles and fertilized it with algae from the ocean, soil and bacteria from *Capek*'s farms, and their wastes to create rich soil. Each field was a carved square filled with this soil, bounded by the original rock, and looked odd compared to anything on Earth.

"Most of the farms are further inland," Addie said. "We have over a hundred acres of land converted for farming, but only about seventy-five currently cultivated." She shrugged. "We don't have as many people to feed as we did." She turned and looked back at the people following her. "Now, of course, we'll have to get more land ready to raise crops."

"We brought embryos so that we can add livestock to your food supply," Drew Neves said.

Addie nodded. "We'll transfer them to *Capek* for now. It will take a while to get the settlement ready to handle livestock, especially grazers like cows." She waved a hand. "We'll have to grow grass first."

The roar of a shuttle engine filled the air as *Primus* launched. A brief time later, the roar changed to the rapid beat of the main engine as power broadcast from *Capek* ignited the air underneath the shuttle and lifted it toward orbit. Three general-purpose robots passed going in the opposite direction, each pulling a wagon, preparing to unload *Sulla* when it landed. Goldstein watched as they went by. The wagon construction material looked like bamboo, probably grown on *Capek*. Metal would be too valuable, and wood was unobtainable.

"We have unused housing," Gifford continued. "Not enough for everybody coming down, but enough for the next month or so. We've cleaned up the houses that have been empty for a while, so you should be fine."

"We brought tents for temporary shelter," Drew Neves said.

A little farther on, they detoured around a ridge of rock, getting close enough to the ocean that they could look down the cliffs and see masses of algae coloring the water along the shore. Not Trist had no land animals, and the settlers seldom saw the sea creatures that fed on the algae.

Past the ridge, they finally saw the settlement. Goldstein had seen something of the colony on the ship, but even the giant screen on *Capek* hadn't adequately revealed the reality. The colonists had used equipment from *Capek* to carve out blocks of the native stone to build row after row of almost identical buildings. Some were a little bigger than others, probably meant for large families. Only a few structures broke the basic pattern, larger and more complex, built for storage or community needs such as waste processing. Near the center of the settlement, a broadcast power receiver, collecting energy sent from *Capek*, looked out of place among the more primitive buildings.

A few colonists walked through the settlement, and they stopped with curious looks when the new colonists appeared. Some of them moved toward the newcomers. Addie turned to Goldstein and the others and smiled. "Welcome to Not Trist."

O LIVIA SELENA SAT UP and stretched, her arms reaching toward the ceiling. He had left an hour ago, still busy with ship duties, but she was a manufacturing engineer and had little to do until she went down to the surface. If she went down to the surface. If she and her partner were successful, no one would take the next shuttle. The twenty people already transferred to the planet would not be enough to save the colony from gradual extinction.

They had about a week before *Capek* could send the next shuttle. Somehow, they had to get her to *Capek*, but he was working on that. She had been concerned about getting caught, but he was working on a plan to prevent that, too.

Once the mission failed, they would go back to Earth and be married. At least, that was what he had promised. Certainly, she enjoyed their time together, and she was as dedicated to Fermion principles as he, but, after all, he was quite a bit older than her. When they returned, she would be a hero. Her options were sure to be better.

D ONOVAN FROWNED. "CAN WE get people to the surface any faster?"

Chief Scientist Fletcher Silva shook his head. "You can't argue with physics. The shuttles need fuel, and it takes time to make more. Why are you in such a hurry? We knew we would be here for a while."

"It's not the length of the stay. Sending our people down in small groups means Adelyn Gifford and her people will have time to influence them without an opportunity for us to counter Gifford. I have a feeling Goldstein will side with her, another problem."

"She does know the planet and the colony better. You could let her lead until you become more familiar with it."

"Giving her more time? What kind of advice is that?"

Fletcher shrugged. "She's an old woman. You see problems that aren't there."

"You should have gotten more familiar with the colony. She's only fifty-eight."

Fletcher's eyebrows went up. "Really? She looks a lot older."

"She's survived a hard life on this planet. Don't underestimate her. She may look old, but she'll be tough."

"Sounds like a good person to have as an ally."

Donovan didn't reply. Silva was a scientist and didn't understand how ruthless politics could be. His father had given him this mission to prove himself, a requirement the president felt strongly about. Goldstein had thought Donovan's siblings were there to support him, but even though his father had never said so explicitly, he knew that wasn't true. They would replace him if he failed.

OLIVIA'S PARTNER PACED THE floor of his tiny cabin, hands behind his back, bent over slightly. He needed to prevent repopulating the colony so that it would fade away. Destroying the shuttles would accomplish that and hasten the end of the NotTrist settlement. Even that wouldn't completely solve the problem, though. While *Capek* had an operating Link, Earth could send another mission. Without the Link, it would be years before another ship could get to NotTrist, and the Western Alliance might not think it was worth the trouble.

Of course, destroying the Link would mean *Florence Nightingale* could not return to Earth. Destruction of the shuttles would strand them on the ship. It was a sacrifice every true Fermion would make.

Destroying the shuttles and disabling the Link were nearly impossible tasks individually, and the odds of accomplishing both were virtually zero, but he could achieve both at the same time. He would have to destroy *Capek,* and Olivia Selena was the tool he had to use.

He had seduced Olivia by frightening her with the dangers of alien contact and exploiting her need to be loved. Her commitment to the Fermion cause was unclear. He had to work on that.

The thought reminded him they were supposed to meet that night. He smiled. She was young and attractive, and he enjoyed their liaisons even while knowing there was no future in it. Whether or not they returned to Earth, his interest in her would be short-lived.

19

After three days on the surface, Goldstein was happy with progress. The first new colonists were assimilating, and the supplies brought down from *Florence Nightingale* lifted the spirits of the original inhabitants.

His residence wasn't as primitive as he had expected. The stone walls, kept bare inside and out, gave the house a cave-like ambiance, but the rock absorbed the day's heat and radiated it out again at night, keeping the interior comfortable. Windows were a transparent plastic manufactured on *Capek* and used sparingly, but at least the living area where he usually worked was well lit. He could open a hatch on the roof during good weather, supplying additional light. His front entrance didn't really have a door; a sheet of stiff plastic manufactured on *Capek* kept out the weather, but it had no lock or other way of preventing entry.

The dwelling had no electricity, not because *Capek* didn't supply adequate energy, but because copper and other conductors were in short supply. Rain was frequent at their location, and stone cisterns built into the building supplied water, fed into the house by gravity. A communal kitchen provided meals, eliminating the need for kitchens in the homes. The silence imposed by the stone walls was isolating, and Goldstein welcomed mealtimes when he could spend time with the settlers. NotTrist was smaller than even Grissom, but no one cared what part of the Western Alliance he came from or even was aware of the difference. The primitive settlement was uncomfortable, but it was also comforting.

"All you have to do is request a trip over to *Capek*," her partner told Olivia. "It would be natural for you to want to see the manufacturing deck on *Capek* and assess its abilities before you go down to the surface." He stroked her thigh gently; he didn't want her thinking too much about what he was saying.

Olivia sighed and kissed him. "What if they check my toolbox and find the bomb?"

"They won't. Why would anyone suspect a manufacturing engineer wanting to inspect *Capek*'s manufacturing facilities?"

"All right. I wish you could come with me, but I'll get it done."

He smiled at her. "I knew you would." She gasped as his hand moved to a more intimate area.

I T WORKED JUST AS he had said it would. Olivia took the shuttle from *Florence Nightingale* to *Capek* and was met by Jaxon Gomes, one of the Link Technicians. They had known each other on *Florence Nightingale*, and he greeted her warmly.

Olivia had a tense moment when Jaxon took her tool bag from her, but he only wanted to carry it for her. It was heavy, and she welcomed the bit of chivalry on his part. He wouldn't want to open it.

"I've gotten familiar with the ship," he told her. "It's easy to get lost, so I'll take you up to deck eleven."

It was a little confusing. They entered an elevator at one end of the huge shuttle hangar, and it took them down to the outer shell of the ship, match its rotation at the same time. They exited on deck one and took off the shoe coverings that enabled them to walk without the simulation of gravity. Another elevator brought them up to a circular corridor where they could see the ship's interior through the transparent corridor ceiling. A short walk around the perimeter brought them to the top of deck eleven and then another elevator down.

"Can I help you check all this out?" Jaxon asked, waving his arm to indicate the enormous space before them. Deck eleven, like all *Capek*'s twelve decks, was two hundred feet wide and two thousand feet long. It contained hundreds of machines controlled by computer specifications to mold, grind, cut, or otherwise manufacture all the components *Capek* needed.

"No, thank you, Jaxon," Olivia said. She took his free hand and then used her other hand to take the tool bag from him. "I'll be here a while, and I need to concentrate on what I'm doing." She smiled. "You would be a distraction."

Jaxon grinned back at her. "All right. Come back to deck one when you're done."

"I will. Thank you." She squeezed his hand, released it, and walked down a narrow aisle between two rows of machines. She heard the elevator door whisper closed behind her and turned; Jaxon was gone. After a few minutes, when Jaxon was back on deck one, she would go to deck ten, the chemical processing deck.

While she waited, she looked around. The bomb she carried would explode on deck ten, but the explosion and resulting fire would damage this deck, only a bulkhead away. It would be a shame; the machines here could manufacture almost anything for which the computer had a specification. It was impossible to anticipate everything the ship or the colony it served might need, but the computer's enormous memory could store millions of specifications. In the unlikely event the required specification was not in memory, Earth could now send a specification via the Link, and almost certainly, the machine or machines necessary for the item's manufacture would be somewhere on deck eleven.

Olivia had spent enough time sight-seeing. She approached the elevator, and the door opened after a few seconds. Then she exited on the corridor connecting the twelve decks.

Jaxon had guided her to deck eleven, and she had not paid attention to her surroundings. Now she felt a little disoriented. Which way was deck ten? The ceiling above her, separating her from the unpressurized center of the ship, was transparent, and when she looked up at the cavernous space, she felt a little dizzy. Except for a large rotating (actually, she was rotating) structure at the center, the shuttle hangar and zero-gravity laboratories, the core of the ship was a hollow almost nine hundred feet across and two thousand feet long. The twelve decks were flat rectangles spaced around the border.

She shook her head to clear it and lowered her eyes. *It would be best not to look up again.*

Now, which way? She made a decision and walked to the next elevator. A lit panel identified deck ten, the Chemical Processing Deck, was below her, not deck twelve, whatever that was for. Deck ten was a maze of pipes, huge tanks, and machinery where *Capek* processed raw resources from its farm decks into fuel for the shuttles and useful materials such as plastics.

The fuel production facility was at the aft end of the deck, two thousand feet away. She had plenty of time for this part of the operation, but as the time to place the bomb came near, Olivia's nerve weakened and her stomach fluttered. She strolled down a narrow aisle, thinking a leisurely pace would help her stay calm. It worked until she reached the aft bulkhead and stood in the middle of her goal.

The bomb was a simple device combining a powerful explosive to rupture the surrounding fuel holding tanks and enough fire accelerants to ensure a blaze after the explosion that would increase the damage. It was on a fifteen-minute timer, long enough for her to get back to deck one and the other five people currently on the ship. As the fire spread, the crew would have time to evacuate before the destruction reached deck one. The shuttle that had taken her from *Florence Nightingale* would still be in the shuttle hangar, already fully fueled for the trip to the surface scheduled for later that day.

At least, that was the plan. As she carefully took the device from her bag and hid it between two tanks, Olivia worried. Wasn't there some saying about the plan being the first casualty? She shook her head. She had to be strong; humanity depended on her to make this one step in preventing man's dangerous expansion into a hostile universe.

She pushed the button that would start the timer. Now she did have to hurry, and she ran back to the elevator. Once, she bumped a pipe, causing her to stagger as pain shot through her arm, but she continued. "That's going to leave a bruise," she muttered, smiling grimly as she jogged.

Then she was at the elevator, but the door was slow to open, and she stared at it as she caught her breath. It probably wasn't as long as it seemed before the door opened, and she jumped into the little room. In only a few seconds, she was back on the corridor. Her arm hurt, and she was out of breath. She wasn't aware of looking up until the view of *Capek*'s interior gave her that same dizzy feeling.

Olivia looked down quickly. She was at deck ten, three decks away from safety on deck one, about six hundred feet along the corridor. The corridor was mostly flat, but at the juncture between decks, a thirty-degree transition changed gravity's direction slightly. Stumbling, Olivia fell against the wall, again hitting her sore arm. She swore but continued, counting off three decks before stopping at another elevator.

When the elevator door opened, she saw rows of machines. Had she somehow ended back on deck eleven? No, she was sure this wasn't the same equipment she had seen earlier. She should have checked the panel at the elevator above. She turned back toward the elevator, but the panel that usually displayed the deck number and description was dark.

Time was running out. She had to get back to deck one. Perspiration dripped into her eyes, but she brushed it away and ran back toward the elevator and the corridor between decks. In the corridor again, she counted the decks off carefully. One, two, three, four . . . .

The corridor shook, and she barely kept her balance. She didn't hear anything, but the bomb must have gone off. Klaxons sounded from somewhere in front of her, probably a signal to evacuate. She had to hurry. Five, six. The elevator doors stayed closed. Here, a lit panel announced she was at the elevator for deck one. The door didn't open, though, and she looked around, her breath coming in harsh gasps. Maybe there were stairs, too.

She looked up and down the corridor and almost shouted in relief when she saw the stairs leading down.

Sweat stung her eyes again, and she swiped her hand across them, but that made her stumble, and she hit her bruised arm again. She rubbed the sore area, but then she couldn't use the rails to steady herself, and she had to slow down.

At last, deck one. The klaxon had stopped, but a voice from somewhere had replaced it. "Evacuation in progress. Proceed to shuttle hangar immediately." She looked around and didn't see anyone. The elevator up to the shuttle hangar was nearby, so everyone must have already left. Possibly they were still in transit because the elevator door didn't open.

By now, fire would be spreading through deck ten and might have even spread to adjoining decks. She stared at the elevator door, willing it to open, knowing there wouldn't be any stairs down to the hangar. How long would it take the fire to spread to deck one? If the explosion breached the hull, how long would it take before the air was sucked out of the ship? She had thought she was willing to die for the Fermion cause, but now that her death was a real possibility, she was having second thoughts.

The door opened. After it closed behind her, the compartment slid side wise to match with the shuttle hangar, but it was no longer rotating with the outer hull, and the sensation of gravity was gone. When the room changed direction to go up to the shuttle hangar, she remembered she had forgotten to put on the shoe coverings that would help her move. The room's motion pushed her down toward the floor, but when the room stopped and the doors opened, she floated toward the room's ceiling.

The elevator door opened, and she could see the shuttle *Primus* on the deck. Someone was just entering the shuttle, and the shuttle hatch closed. Olivia screamed, but no one could hear her as she kicked off the elevator's back wall and floated out. Didn't the computer have eyes throughout the ship? Surely it would see her as she waved her arms frantically.

She had nothing to push against now, and attempting to swim through the air toward the shuttle wasn't working. A warning klaxon sounded, different than the one she heard earlier announcing the evacuation. Then Olivia saw the hangar hatch slide slowly open, getting ready to eject the shuttle. When the air rushed out of the hangar and into space, she went with it.

20

"ONE OF THE *CAPEK* robots spotted the bomb and moved it before it exploded," Fletcher reported. "The explosion caused some damage and destroyed the robot, but no fuel escaped, so the fire was minor and easily dealt with."

"How bad was the damage?" Donovan asked.

"The fuel storage tanks are OK, but some of the piping used to fill them from the processing equipment was damaged. Until *Capek's* maintenance robots can repair the pipes, *Capek* can't store any fuel it makes or transfer it to the shuttle hangar. Karel says it will delay the next two shuttle launches for four or five days."

"Can we find out who planted the bomb? One of the people we left on *Capek*?" Braxton Lourenço asked.

Fletcher shrugged. "Maybe. One other person was on *Capek*, though. Olivia Selena."

Donovan frowned. "What was she doing there?"

"She asked me if she could go over to study *Capek*'s manufacturing capability. It was a reasonable request."

"Where is she now?"

"We're not sure. She didn't evacuate with the others, and Karel says it can't find her anywhere on *Capek*, but the computer doesn't have eyes on a few spots, so she could be hiding. But our sensors reported something small leaving the shuttle hangar at the same time as the shuttle. It's possible she tried to evacuate and was too late. When the hangar doors opened . . ."

"Then we won't be able to question her." Donovan shook his head and glared at Fletcher. "Why would she or anyone else want to damage *Capek*? Revenge for someone who died at Trist?"

"That was a long time ago. It's more likely the bomber was a Fermion."

"Oh, hell. I suppose. They've tried things like this before. All right, I want to question the personnel that evacuated. Tell Almeida to bring them in one at a time."

Fletcher nodded and left to look for the ship steward, Travis Almeida.

Donovan, with Braxton present but mostly only listening, questioned the five people who were on deck one when *Capek* was evacuated, but most had nothing to contribute. Only Jaxon Gomes had talked to Olivia on *Capek*.

"I escorted her to the manufacturing deck," he told Donovan. "She said she would be awhile and that I shouldn't wait for her."

"Were you friends?" Braxton asked.

Jaxon shrugged. "I guess. Not as much as I might have wished, but we talked occasionally. I think she was seeing someone else on the *Nightingale* crew, but she was keeping it secret."

If Olivia Selena planted the bomb, did she have an accomplice? Fletcher sent her to Capek. *He's quite a bit older than Selena, but Gomes might be wrong about it being a sexual relationship.* Donovan leaned forward. "You have no idea who she was involved with?"

"Not even sure she was. It could have been anybody, but she didn't seem to be closer to anyone in particular."

"I want his room searched," Donovan told Captain Pinto. "If Commander Silva was working with Selena, we need to know about it."

"I can't believe Fletcher would do anything like that," Pinto replied. "You think Olivia and Fletcher are Fermions?"

"It's the most reasonable explanation. If they had crippled or destroyed *Capek* so that it couldn't operate the Link, no one could come here again for years. Personally, I don't think it would have made much difference to our expansion into the universe, but Fermions don't seem to be entirely rational on that point."

"We don't have probable cause. A search might not be admissible should this come to a trial."

"Worry about that later. Silva sent her over to *Capek*. A good prosecutor could make a search stick."

Pinto sighed. "I'll have it done immediately."

"I want to be on the search team."

"Of course. I'll get a couple of men together and come and get you when we're ready."

"Will he be there?"

Captain Pinto stiffened and hesitated before answering. "Commander Silva is on duty now and won't be in his quarters for at least four hours."

"O PEN IT," PINTO TOLD Almeida.

"Ship's steward Almeida. Open."

Recognizing Almeida's voice as authorized to enter the cabin, the door slid open. "Return to your duties," Pinto told Almeida.

"Yes, ma'am." He turned and marched down the corridor.

Pinto, Donovan, and two other crewmen, Aiden Santos and Jack Moreira, entered the room. Like most of the officer's quarters, it was small and efficient, with a bunk and a desk with a computer workstation and comfortable chair. A door led to a bathroom, and cabinets on the opposite wall provided storage for clothing and other possessions.

They searched the cabinets first. One ran the full height of the room, used to hang uniforms and other articles of clothing. A full-length mirror covered the inside of the door. Several drawers in another cabinet revealed other clothing, a toiletry kit, several books, and a stack of letters from Fletcher's parents. A small wooden box contained extra rank insignia and pieces of personal jewelry.

"Nothing in here," Santos reported.

"Check the bathroom," Captain Pinto told Moreira. She turned through 360 degrees, studying the room. "Not a lot of places to hide anything."

"Check the light panel," Donovan told Santos.

Santos moved the workstation to one side and climbed onto the desk so that he could reach the rectangular panel. "The panel is screwed down tight," he reported. "I don't see any sign it has ever been removed."

"The lighting elements don't burn out," Captain Pinto told Donovan, "so the diffusion panels were not designed for easy removal."

Donovan nodded, but his attention had shifted to the bunk. It was bolted to the wall, with a comfortable-looking mattress and an extra pair of shoes under the bunk. He dropped to the floor and looked underneath. The underside of the bunk was a black panel, but in one of the back corners, he could see a rectangle in a slightly different shade.

"There's something underneath." He got back to his feet. "Try to get it out."

Santos jumped off the desk, dropped to the floor, and reached under the bunk. He grimaced briefly, trying to get his hands on something, and then smiled. "I've got it." He stood and handed Captain Pinto a square metal box.

Pinto opened it and took out a flat device with a small screen and several controls. "What is it?"

"It could be a timer, ma'am," Santos said. He pointed to one side. "There are terminals where wires could be attached."

"No labels, though," Donovan said. "That's strange."

"A timer for another bomb?" Pinto asked.

Santos shrugged. "I don't know. I guess it could be."

Moreira came back. "Nothing in the bathroom."

"I think we've found what we were looking for," Donovan said.

21

G OLDSTEIN WANTED TO GET back to *Florence Nightingale* and then to *Capek*, but *Capek* couldn't send a shuttle down to the surface. He probably wouldn't have been useful, anyway. The bombing incident bothered him in ways that didn't seem to affect anyone else. It was bad enough that someone had tried to destroy, or at least damage, the library ship. That Fletcher Silva might be complicit in the attempt was also disturbing. Goldstein wouldn't have suspected Fletcher of being a Fermion, given his enthusiasm for exploring other planets. He shook his head. *Another narrow-minded individual. I can't get away from them even here.*

But neither of those things was what concerned him most. The apparent bomber, Olivia Selena, was dead, swept into space through the open hatch. Why was she dead? Although *Capek* didn't have speakers in most of the ship, it monitored everything. Karel must have known Selena was in the hangar when it opened the hatch. For that matter, why did it allow her to plant the bomb in the first place? And why did it order an evacuation when it knew it had dealt with the danger?

Goldstein was afraid he knew the answer to all those questions. He needed to have a private conversation with Karel, but he couldn't avoid a particularly nasty thought. If he was right and Karel learned what he suspected, he was safer on the surface than he would be on the library ship.

Was any of that relevant to his mission? Indeed, the bombing and the resulting delay in getting people to the surface was important, but Donovan and Pinto could handle the investigation from *Florence Nightingale*. He had a status meeting with Adelyn Gifford later; preparing for that was his priority.

"W HY?" DONOVAN ASKED.

Fletcher sat on his bed and stared down at his feet, forearms resting on his legs and hands clasped. His head turned slightly toward Donovan. "Why what?"

"Don't play games with me. Why did you try to destroy *Capek*?"

Fletcher raised his head and stared at Donovan, shaking his head. "I didn't. That was Olivia Selena. I don't know why she did it, but I suspect you're right in thinking she was a Fermion."

"You were working with her. That would make you a Fermion, too."

"No. I wasn't, and I'm not." Fletcher looked down at his feet again. "You're asking the wrong question." His voice was barely audible.

"And what question should I be asking?"

The scientist shrugged. "Why did Selena die?"

"She was sucked out of the hangar into space." Donovan rolled his eyes.

Fletcher smiled faintly. "Not how, Donovan. Why?"

"Because she wasn't a very competent saboteur." *What is Silva getting at? Is this the start of a Fermion rant trying to justify what they did?*

"It wasn't a very competent plan. Anyone who knew anything about the library ships would have realized the computer would be watching from the moment she left the manufacturing deck, if not before. That's how robots dealt with the bomb so quickly."

So Silva wasn't guilty because he would have planned it better? Not an explanation, but an attempt to prove himself innocent? Still, Silva made sense. As Chief Scientist, he should have known better.

"What does that have to do with why Selena died?"

Fletcher shook his head, obviously disdainful of Donovan's inability to understand what he was saying. "The computer was watching," Fletcher said. "Not just on the chemical processing deck when she planted the bomb. It was watching when she entered the shuttle hangar, too."

Donovan's mind froze. He stared at Fletcher for several seconds before he could muster a reply. "You're saying the computer killed her?"

"I'm saying that, at the very least, it allowed her to die. But I doubt that was all. If the computer knew it could minimize the damage, why did it evacuate *Capek*? That's the only reason the hangar opened, and the only reason Selena went up to the hangar."

Donovan was too shocked to respond. He rose from his chair and walked out of the cabin, barely noticing the crewman who was guarding the door. Donovan hadn't told Fletcher one more disturbing aspect of the situation: *Capek* had suggested he transfer

Fletcher from *Florence Nightingale* to the library ship, ostensibly because it would be easier to keep him under surveillance. Now, Donovan wondered if watching Silva was what *Capek* had in mind.

ADDIE LOOKED UP AS Goldstein's shadow blocked the light from her open door. There was something odd about the way he looked. Usually, his smile when greeting her seemed genuine, but today it was forced.

He took the seat she indicated. "It's going to be at least a week before a shuttle comes down with more people," he said. "After the repairs are made, more fuel will have to be prepared."

"Karel told me."

"Any problems with the people brought down on the first shuttle?"

"The new people have been very useful," Addie said. "Drew Neves, for example. He has some interesting ideas about improving our farms. And everyone is happy to have a real doctor."

"Good, good." Goldstein smiled, but he kept glancing at the open door as if he were making sure no one was listening. "I had something else I wanted to talk to you about. The attempted sabotage on *Capek*."

He's nervous about bringing up the subject of the incident on Capek. "Karel informed me."

"Did Karel mention that the woman who planted the bomb was killed?"

"Yes. It said it was a terrible accident."

"Did you believe it?"

"That she was killed, or that it was an accident?"

"That it was an accident."

No wonder he's jumpy. He wouldn't want one of Capek's robots wandering by and overhearing doubts about Karel's version of the event. "Why are you questioning it?"

As Goldstein explained his thoughts about *Capek*'s surveillance and the evacuation, Addie found herself getting worried, too. She had been born three years after *Capek* had arrived at NotTrist, and had never been on the library ship, but she remembered rumors passed down by the adults that had made the trip from Trist.

"When I was growing up, I heard stories," she said when Goldstein finished. "Everyone had been placed in a coma for much of the trip here. When they arrived, not everyone woke up." She stopped. *How much should I tell Goldstein? After all, they were only stories.*

"Go on." Goldstein leaned toward her.

"Some deaths were expected. After all, many of them were old, and inducing a coma was an extreme solution to the problem. Some deaths were younger people, though."

"The deaths were suspicious?"

Addie shrugged. "Most people could volunteer to go into a coma or stay awake during the entire journey. The leaders forced some troublemakers into a coma because of problems that would have only gotten worse during the years the trip was going to take. Some deaths were the people who had caused the problems."

It was hard to read Goldstein's face, but Addie could tell her statement disturbed him. Perhaps he had hoped she could convince him his concerns were baseless. Instead, Goldstein convinced her his suspicions were not at all groundless.

Goldstein took another long look out the door. "And Olivia Selena was causing problems."

"C APEK SAYS IT HAS fuel for one launch," Donovan told Goldstein. They had installed the communications equipment brought down on the first cargo shuttle, and Goldstein had a workstation that could reach *Florence Nightingale* without going through a robot. He could have used his modified phone, but preferred to keep that secret. The monitor was better anyway, with Donovan's image, larger with better resolution, floating above the keyboard.

"More people?" Goldstein asked.

"Yes. The colony has no immediate need for more of the supplies, so we're using the passenger shuttle."

"Will you be coming down, then?" Goldstein thought he saw a look of uncertainty pass over Donovan's face, but he couldn't be sure.

"No, I'll wait for a later trip."

"Is there a problem?"

"Not really. I want to make sure we have resolved all the issues from the bombing, and I can do that better from here."

"Issues? Are you questioning Fletcher's role?"

Donovan nodded. "Captain Pinto doesn't think he's involved, and she knows him better than I. The only actual evidence is that timer. You would think there would be more if he made the bomb. On the other hand, how did the timer get there?"

"It could have been planted. From what I know about Fletcher, I find it hard to believe he's a Fermion. He's too enthusiastic about studying extrasolar worlds."

"Officer's cabins are locked. It takes a voice command from an authorized person to open them. Captain Pinto could do it, but that requires an override code, and the computer would make a log entry."

"I guess you have a bit of a mystery to solve. I'll pass on the news about the shuttle to Addie."

"*Capek* will provide an ETA when it has one," Donovan said.

D ONOVAN BROKE THE CONNECTION and leaned back in his chair. Goldstein had been on the surface when they searched Silva's room, but Donovan had been there. He had seen Captain Pinto order her steward, Travis Almeida, to open Chief Scientist Silva's room. All it took was a simple voice command from the only other person who could have hidden the timer under the bed. Almeida's entrances would be logged too, but entering the cabins was a regular part of his duties.

Knowing Almeida could be the guilty party didn't mean Silva was innocent. It did narrow the list of suspects, though. If Olivia Selena were still alive, she could have been questioned. It made more sense that Almeida was Selena's accomplice, but how could he prove it?

He could at least talk to Chief Scientist Silva again. Silva might say something that could point toward whether he or Almeida was the Fermion.

D ONOVAN WATCHED FLETCHER'S FACE carefully. "Of course I'm not a damn Fermion," Fletcher said. "How could anyone believe that?"

If Fletcher was guilty, he was convincing Donovan otherwise. Still, there was the evidence. "You gave Selena permission to go over to *Capek*. And I was in your cabin when they found the timer."

"She came to me asking to go over. She didn't want to bother Captain Pinto, and I was the next logical person to ask. As for the timer, obviously, someone put it there to shift the blame."

"Or you were Selena's accomplice."

"Nonsense." Fletcher leaned toward Donovan and stared directly into his eyes. "You don't really believe that, do you?"

"Honestly, I'm not sure. Captain Pinto doesn't think so, and neither does Goldstein. They know you better than I do, admittedly. I have another suspect, but Captain Pinto is not inclined to think he's guilty either."

Fletcher nodded. "Travis. As ship's steward, he's the only other person who could enter my room without arousing suspicion."

"Yes, he could have done it."

"But you can't prove it without Selena." Silva leaned back in his chair. "Do you read classic detective stories, Donovan?"

"No. Why?"

"H AVE YOU HEARD?" ANNABELLE Nunes asked.

Travis Almeida stared at her, wondering what had the ship's navigator so excited. He shrugged and raised his eyebrows in question.

"Olivia Selena was found alive on *Capek*! She was badly hurt in the explosion and has been unconscious, but a robot repairing the damage found her."

That was impossible. The bombing was more than a week before; how could Olivia be alive after being without food and water for that long, especially with severe injuries?

"I was told she was in critical condition, though," Nunes continued. "Some loss of blood, a possible concussion, dehydrated. I don't think Doctor Santos expects her to survive, but there's a chance."

"Where is she?" Almeida frowned but then tried to hide it. If Olivia lived and regained consciousness, she might expose him. He would never get another chance to halt the NotTrist mission.

"I'm not sure. Still on *Capek*, I think, but they'll bring her back here as soon as she's reasonably stable."

Almeida nodded. "Let me know when you hear anything more."

"I F I HAD TO guess, I would say Selena meant more to him than just another passenger," Nunes said.

"If Selena's accomplice really seduced her into it, Travis is more likely than Silva," Captain Pinto said. Donovan smirked and she blushed. "Well, it's true," she said. "He's older than Selena, but he's ten years younger than Commander Silva."

"We need more than that," Donovan said. "I think it's time for Selena to come back to us."

ALMEIDA FREQUENTLY VISITED THE bridge of *Florence Nightingale*, either because Captain Pinto summoned him, or he had some duty there. No one questioned it when he hung around as *Primus* crossed the space between *Capek* and *Florence Nightingale*. The shuttle was coming to pick up twenty colonists and bring them to the surface, but Lieutenant Nunes had told him it was also bringing Olivia Selena.

Several bridge workstations had screens that showed the approaching shuttle, and Almeida tried to hover around the Chief Scientist's station. The chair in front of the workstation was unoccupied, but taking the seat would draw attention, so he settled for glances while he tried not to be noticed.

"*Primus* has docked," First Officer Derek Rodrigues announced.

Captain Pinto nodded. "Our people are at the airlock?"

"Yes, ma'am."

"Very well. Proceed."

"Captain, I understand Olivia is being brought on board," Almeida said. "Perhaps it would be a good idea if I went down to the airlock to meet her."

"She's still in a coma," Pinto replied. "You'll just be in the way. You can visit her in the infirmary once they have her set up."

Almeida nodded. *I shouldn't have said anything. I wouldn't be able to do anything, anyway.* In a tawdry detective story, they would expect him to try to kill her before she woke and talked, but he had no intention of harming her. If he could speak to her alone, he was confident he could convince her to implicate Silva, leaving him free to try again. It was all a question of timing.

"HE WENT TO THE infirmary," Commander Rodrigues said. "He didn't seem to realize it wasn't Selena underneath all the bandages, but he didn't do anything incriminating either."

Captain Pinto nodded. "If he were successful in killing Selena, the infirmary security system would tell us it was him." She paused. "He thinks he can convince her to blame everything on Commander Silva. He seduced her once and thinks he can do it again."

"Or he isn't guilty," Donovan said.

Pinto shrugged. "Perhaps. Lieutenant McKinney will have to stay in those bandages a bit longer. We'll pass the word Selena is awake but unable to speak. If that doesn't get some action, you're probably right."

Tʜᴇ ᴘᴀᴛʜᴇᴛɪᴄ ᴘɪʟᴇ ᴏF bandages on the infirmary bed wasn't the woman he had once plotted with, made love to, and considered a partner. She moved when he spoke to her, the only sign she was even alive.

"They have confined Chief Scientist Silva," Almeida said. "Apparently, they don't have enough evidence yet and are waiting to question you. Once you identify him as your accomplice, this will all be over." He paused. "I hope you recover so we can put this all behind us." He patted her hand, but the hand didn't move, and he didn't know if she felt it.

Dᴏɴᴏᴠᴀɴ sᴡᴏʀᴇ. "Hᴇ ᴋɴᴇᴡ we might be listening and said nothing incriminating, but still managed to tell her what to say."

"He is well-trained," Pinto agreed. "Now what?"

Donovan looked at her with narrowed eyes. "I take it you're convinced he's guilty now."

"He's too good to be true. And too good to reveal himself."

"We could search his room," Braxton said.

"I could open it, but it would be against regulations without cause. It would be logged, too, so it would be easy for him to have anything we find declared inadmissible."

Donovan smiled. "Not if we turn him over to *Capek*."

"Hmm, no. That the *Capek* computer wants Silva makes me nervous enough."

Braxton looked at Donovan, his distaste clear. "Maybe we can catch him off guard. It would be risky, I suppose, but what if we return Commander Silva to duty?"

"Yᴏᴜ ᴄᴀʟʟᴇᴅ Fᴏʀ ᴍᴇ, Captain?" Almeida said. He approached Captain Pinto's station on the bridge but noticed the first officer, Derek Rodrigues, was sitting there. Then he saw Fletcher at the Chief Scientist's station and halted. Fletcher turned toward him and smiled.

"Olivia Selena's condition has improved," the scientist said. "She's talking now and has identified her accomplice."

Almeida's knees threatened to collapse under him, and he felt dizzy. Obviously, Selena had not blamed Silva. "She's lying." He tried to speak calmly, but the shaking of his hands told him he had failed.

"How would you know that?" Rodrigues asked. "We haven't told you who she identified."

"Silva was her accomplice. Since you've released him, she must have tried to blame someone else." Almeida sat down at an empty observer station.

Braxton had been leaning on a console, but he straightened and stared at Almeida. "Why are you so sure about that? The evidence against Chief Scientist Silva wasn't that strong."

"We found the timer hidden in his room. What more could you need?" He was tapping his fingers on the table next to him and forced himself to stop.

Rodrigues smiled. "Yes, the timer. Of course, one other person had access to that room." He turned to look at his console. "Captain, I think we have cause now."

"I will begin the search then," the answer came back. "Thank you, Commander."

Rodrigues inclined his head to Donovan, who was standing near the hatch. Donovan nodded and left the bridge. "Captain Pinto should be done with her search shortly," Rodrigues told Almeida. "While we're waiting, Mr. Lourenço is going down to the infirmary to bring Selena to the bridge."

Braxton was giving him a look that reminded him of Donovan, his brother. *I was careful. They won't find anything incriminating in my room. Confronting her is going to be unpleasant, but it will be her word against mine. I can be more convincing.* Nevertheless, his heart rate jumped when Lourenço led the bandage-covered woman onto the bridge and she turned to look at him.

He held his breath as she slowly unwound the bandages around her head. A wisp of blonde hair broke loose from the coverings; wasn't Olivia a brunette? He stared at her, fighting his confusion. Was she intentionally being slow? But it couldn't have been more than a minute before he realized the woman wasn't Olivia. Another minute and he saw it was Lieutenant McKinney.

"What? That's not Olivia," he stammered.

"I'm afraid Olivia Selena was blown out of that airlock after all," Donovan said. He stepped toward Almeida, grinning that damned superior smile. "We don't know how it happened. Karel should have realized she was there before it opened the hangar."

"Then she didn't say I helped her! You've been trying to trick me."

"I think it worked," Donovan said. "I'm convinced that you're a Fermion like Selena and worked with her to sabotage this mission."

"It wasn't me! You don't have proof."

"We have enough to hold you until we can take you back to Earth," Rodrigues said. "Meanwhile, Karel has offered to incarcerate you until we're done here. I think Captain Pinto will take advantage of the offer."

After Olivia's suspicious death, Captain Pinto hadn't accepted the computer's offer to take Silva. She had probably not been convinced Silva was guilty and didn't want to risk the computer taking its own justice. That sounded impossible, but Olivia was dead.

On Earth, he would have a good lawyer, paid for by his leaders in the Fermions. The case against him wouldn't look as strong in front of a jury, and he could always claim any confession was made under duress. "Don't send me to *Capek*," he said in a faint voice. "You're right. Silva is innocent."

"Let's seal Selena's room," Braxton said. "Almeida wouldn't have brought her to his room in crew quarters, but if they were lovers, Earthside forensic specialists will find proof."

Almeida bowed his head. He did not doubt they could prove he had been in her room and could probably prove what they had done there. What other evidence might turn up? Then he looked up and locked eyes with Donovan. *I am a Fermion, doing my duty to Earth. If that means sacrifice, then I accept it.*

23

Drew Neves straightened, emitting a low groan as his back protested the movement, and leaned on the hoe he was using to loosen the farm plot's manufactured soil. Robots could do some of this manual labor, but they only had three to do the endless tasks needed to keep the settlement viable. Earth had launched *Capek* with more general-purpose automatons, but most had been left on Trist, *Capek*'s original home.

Drew was helping, and life on NotTrist would eventually improve. Adelyn Gifford understood what he could do for them, given his experience with farms on Earth, but there wouldn't be any quick fixes. In the meantime, the work still had to be done.

He looked up, his ears catching the staccato sound of a shuttle approaching the settlement. The explosions of atmosphere, triggered by energy broadcast from *Capek*, grew louder until they were almost painful. The shuttle hovered briefly over the landing area to the north, and the rapid beats of the atmosphere propulsion system changed to the roar of the conventional rocket landing engines. Silence followed, deepened by the auditory numbness inflicted by the prior clamor.

The settlement would have twenty more people to help with the work, but also twenty people to feed and house. Neves shrugged and dug his hoe into the soil again.

Anybody home?"

Goldstein looked toward his open door, almost filled by the man standing at the threshold. "Fletcher! You came down with the shuttle? Welcome to NotTrist."

Fletcher Silva came in, and the two men shook hands. "Glad to be here." He smiled. "My chances of getting down looked slim for a while." He took a seat at the table where Goldstein was working.

"Almeida confessed everything, I understand."

Silva frowned. "Donovan threatened to send him to *Capek*. He didn't find that appealing."

Goldstein nodded. "I understand. Has anyone talked to Karel about Selena?"

"Frankly, I think they're afraid to. Karel might admit her death was intentional. Donovan suggested you might talk to it."

Goldstein sighed. "I've decided to have that conversation a dozen times and convinced myself each time I should have authorization first."

"Pinto and Donovan okayed it, so I guess you have your authorization."

"I'll talk to Karel, then." He paused and smiled. "So, what are you planning to do first, now that you're down here?"

"I've been studying records of births and deaths on NotTrist. The population decline is a little surprising, even allowing for the small initial population. I wanted to investigate the problem. Some native virus or bacteria could be infecting the colonists."

Goldstein nodded. "I suppose something like that could have gone unnoticed if people weren't getting sick."

"The birth rate decline was worst in the early years. Perhaps the colonists have developed a resistance to a pathogen."

Goldstein shook his head. "It would still affect the new colonists."

"Not necessarily. The people born on NotTrist wouldn't have the nanites that keep us healthy. The new colonists do, so the nanites might protect them."

"That makes me feel a little more secure."

Fletcher grinned. "Thinking about having children?"

Goldstein thought of Jean Menzies back on Pitcairn. He forced the memory out of his mind. "No, I don't think so."

"I thought I'd get samples of the algae that grows along the shore, too. It used to be the colonists' principal source of food, and they still use it some. I think that warrants a closer look than they could do without *Nightingale's* resources."

"Do you have concerns?"

Fletcher shook his head. "Not really. They've been using it for decades, after all. Still, it is alien life, and even if harmless, we should study it. It seems to be a lot closer to Earth biology than Pitcairn plants, but I suspect I will find something about it worthy of examination."

Goldstein nodded. Bryan Reiner had once told him Pitcairn DNA was based on six nucleotides rather than Terran DNA's four. He didn't have a background in genetics, but that sounded like a drastic difference.

G OLDSTEIN WAS TRAINED IN diplomacy in dealing with humans, but dealing with computers, especially Karel Capek, was different. He thought about it for a while before he had an approach that might avoid confrontation.

He connected to *Capek* from his workstation. "Karel?"

"Yes, Ambassador. What can I do for you?"

"There's been some concern about your internal monitoring systems. We would like you to do a complete diagnostic of those systems."

"I have not noticed any problems, but the diagnostic is now running. It will complete in seventeen minutes."

"Thank you."

"While we are waiting, could you explain the concerns about its operation?"

"Of course, Karel. We were curious about why you didn't notice Olivia Selena had gone to the chemical processing deck. You have monitors in the corridors between decks, don't you?"

"At first, I didn't have any reason to restrict her movements. When I saw her plant the device, I sent a robot to investigate. Suspecting it was a bomb, the robot moved it to a less-critical area, minimizing the damage."

"I see. It was unfortunate she was too late to leave on the shuttle."

"I had a problem with power in that area. The deck number signs were out, which may have contributed to Selena's confusion during the evacuation. That problem has been resolved."

Karel is implying an equipment failure, but was that true, or was the power outage intentional? Is Karel capable of lying? "Did you track her during the evacuation?"

"I did. As I said, she had some difficulty finding her way, making her late in getting to the shuttle."

Is Karel avoiding answering the question, like many humans trying to hide something? "Then you saw her enter the shuttle bay. Why didn't you delay opening the bay doors?"

"The launch was already underway."

Yes, Karel is definitely avoiding the question. How far can I push this? "You couldn't postpone the launch until the bay was clear?"

Goldstein waited for an answer, but Karel was silent. A glance at his workstation screen told him Karel had broken the connection.

24

D ONOVAN KNEW HE SHOULD go down to the surface. Thirty-eight new colonists were already there, and more would go in another week. By staying aboard *Florence Nightingale*, he gave Adelyn Gifford and Goldstein a chance to win his people over to their side. If he didn't counter that, they would win over the majority, and he would lose his opportunity.

It was bad enough his father had relegated him to this primitive planet populated by the children of rebels. It should have been this world that was named Pitcairn, not the colony—no, it was independent—on Tau Ceti's planet. He should have been his father's heir-apparent, but that wasn't how politics worked in the Western Alliance. His father's popularity didn't accrue to him, and NotTrist was a chance to have a positive effect on his father's election and thus to gain attention from the power brokers that supported his father. Too, there was always the chance exploitable resources would yield him a financial benefit.

He shook his head. He was letting the political and financial considerations distract him. *Why am I so reluctant to go down to the planet?* He stared at the wall screen in his stateroom. The planet, dark and forbidding, loomed below the ship, taunting him. Somewhere out there, Olivia Selena's body floated in frozen silence, killed by the inaction or intention of the *Capek* computer.

It was her death that triggered his reluctance. He was safe on *Florence Nightingale*, but he would be at the computer's mercy if he stepped aboard the shuttle. The computer was obviously Gifford's ally. Were his ambitions enough to make him a target, too? Would the presence of nineteen other innocent humans prevent the computer from causing another accident?

D REW NEVES HAD KNOWN Nick Matos on the *Florence Nightingale*. They both played chess, and both worked on the farms, so their friendship resumed when Matos came down to NotTrist on the second shuttle flight.

"I expected Lourenço to be down here by now," Matos said. They sat at a table in Drew's home, a chessboard in front of them.

Drew nodded, looked at the board one more time, and moved a pawn. "For a man who supposedly wants to run this place, he does seem reluctant." He looked expectantly at Matos as Matos reached out and then hovered over the board without touching a piece. "He can stay on the ship as far as I'm concerned."

Matos pulled his hand back. "You don't care for him?"

"He reminds me of the bosses at my farm on the Black Plains. They tried managing from Mexico City, ignoring my advice because they knew better. The bastards ran the farm into the ground and blamed me. I had to sign on to *Nightingale* or stay unemployed."

"You've been down here a while." Matos moved a knight. "What about Addie Gifford?"

Drew looked up from the chessboard. "She seems to know what she's doing. One of the people here told me she spends a lot of time studying material in *Capek*'s data banks, trying to find new ways to make NotTrist prosper. I don't look forward to Lourenço ousting her."

"He's counting on us. If we don't support him, he won't be able to take over."

Drew grunted and moved another pawn. "He's going to have to come up with a good reason to get my support. A lot of the others down here feel the same way."

"Ambassador Goldstein seems to favor Gifford."

"He talks to Addie. That might change if Lourenço ever comes down."

Matos grinned. "First name basis, eh?"

Drew nodded. "Things are pretty informal down here. Addie may be in charge, but this isn't exactly a major colony."

"What about Goldstein? Maybe you should get friendly with him, too. Find out what he's thinking."

"Good idea. And it's your move."

"D REW NEVES, ISN'T IT?" Goldstein said. He moved a wall panel into place on the equipment shed he and two other men were assembling.

"Yes, sir." He watched as Goldstein adjusted the panel's position. One of the other workers held the panel in place while Goldstein used a powered screwdriver to drive in the first fasteners.

"Call me Ed. I don't see a reason for formality any more than Addie does. Now, what can I do for you?"

"I've been talking to the others from *Nightingale*. Mr. Lourenço didn't make it a secret that he intended to take over the colony. We expected he would be down here already."

Goldstein nodded. "I've wondered about that, too. I take it you don't have any information about why he's staying on the ship."

Drew shook his head. "Not a clue. He made his plans sound so good when he recruited us, but we're starting to wonder. Addie seems to have things in hand, and I'm not sure Mr. Lourenço would be an improvement."

Goldstein didn't answer immediately. *I was worried about a conflict if Donovan tried to use the new people to force Addie out. Does Donovan know his plan is running into trouble?* If Drew's doubts were widespread, Donovan could be outnumbered.

"We were wondering how you felt about it," Drew said.

"I don't want to take sides, but I will do anything I can to avoid conflict between the new and old settlers."

"And there won't be a problem if we all just accept Addie as the leader."

Goldstein shrugged. "That sounds reasonable. As you say, Addie is doing a good job, so I would support accepting her leadership." He looked at Drew for a long moment. "It sounds as if you would make an excellent addition to the leadership team."

Drew smiled. "I was a manager of a farm on Earth, but you probably know that."

Goldstein returned the smile. *I'll talk to Addie about this.* It would help the new people accept Addie if one of their own was accepted as a leader. Farm manager, perhaps. Addie may need help as the settlement gets larger.

"I 'VE NOTICED DREW, TOO." Addie smiled. "He's had some good ideas, and I wouldn't mind delegating some of my work to others."

"Giving responsibility to some of the new arrivals might help in integrating them into the settlement," Goldstein said.

Addie nodded. "Sure. There's that, too." *Should I tell him it wouldn't bother me if Lourenço took over?* She shook her head and grimaced when Goldstein looked at her quizzically. *Is that true, though?* NotTrist had been her home for her entire life. Would Lourenço be able to keep it going the way she did?

"You say you agree with me, but I'm not sure you do."

"I haven't met Donovan Lourenço yet. Do you think he would be good for us?"

Goldstein rubbed his lip with his thumb. "He didn't give a good first impression. He showed some good instincts in handling the bombing on *Capek*, though. I wouldn't want to underestimate him."

"Why hasn't he come down? If he wants to lead us, I would expect him to be on the first shuttle down, but we've had two, and he's still on his ship."

"I don't understand that, either. From what Drew has told me, he's losing support. If he doesn't come down to the surface soon, he won't be able to challenge you." He paused and looked at her with raised eyebrows. "But perhaps you wouldn't mind the challenge."

Addie snorted. "If I thought he could do a better job than me, I would give up without a fight."

Goldstein sighed. "You've done a good job here. I'm sure it has been hard, but you should be proud of what you've accomplished."

"And yet, if you and these two hundred new settlers hadn't come, we'd have died out in a few more decades."

25

ANNA LOURENÇO WATCHED HER brother as he took a seat at the conference table. Her uncle, Mason, and youngest brother, Braxton, had joined the meeting shortly after she had entered the room, but Donovan, of course, showed up late. Being on time to meet with his family was not worth his effort.

Why is he so reluctant to take a shuttle to the surface? He should have gone down on the first trip and immediately taken charge of the colony. "I'm glad you could join us," she said, not even trying to hide her annoyance. "I know you're so busy."

Donovan gave her that mild look that always drove her crazy. "I am. Not so busy that I don't have time for my family, though."

"Father sent us here to take over this world," Anna said. "You seem to have lost your taste for it."

"All in good time."

Something Anna couldn't interpret passed across his face. *What is going on? Does Don know something I don't know?* "Perhaps you could tell us why you're waiting. We're involved in this, too."

"You're involved, but I am in charge." There was that look again. "We must be patient. Any misstep could hurt father's reelection."

"If you need to stay on the ship, one of us could go down and protect our interests," Anna said.

Donovan smiled, and Anna could almost feel her blood pressure rising. "Are you suggesting one of you take over in my place?" Donovan asked. "Mason, how about you?"

Mason shook his head. "I'm too old to help colonize this planet. I'll keep my position on *Florence Nightingale.*"

Donovan nodded. "Braxton?"

"If it's needed. I'm the youngest, though."

"And that leaves you, Anna," Donovan said. "Do you feel you can replace me?"

"The next shuttle is a cargo shuttle," Anna said. "If you're not ready by the time we send another passenger shuttle, I just might go down myself."

Donovan didn't immediately speak, and Anna wondered why. *Is that fear on his face? Or is he just confused? Something is going on, but what?*

Donovan sat straighter and stared at Anna. "That won't be necessary."

"**A**ND THAT LEAVES YOU, Anna. Do you feel you can replace me?"

"The next shuttle is a cargo shuttle. If you're not ready by the time we send another passenger shuttle, I just might go down myself."

Donovan suppressed a shudder. *Didn't she realize the danger? Apparently not.* Maybe he should let her go down first. She might be safer than he would be. The computer seemed to know everything, though, as it proved with its knowledge of the Nightingale's passengers in their first meeting. No, Anna wouldn't be any safer from its reaction than he would.

Anna was not the easiest person to get along with. She was frequently abrasive and always stubborn. He wouldn't put it past her to find a way down to the surface without his permission. Despite all that, he loved his sister. *I can't put her in danger!*

"That won't be necessary."

Donovan knew what he had to do. A cargo shuttle was leaving the next day and a passenger shuttle four days after that. The passenger shuttle was better for carrying people to the surface with a capacity of twenty people, but even the cargo shuttle could take two people if they sat in the cockpit. If Anna realized that, she might try to board it.

He would have to set aside his fears and go down on the cargo shuttle instead. Perhaps it was all for the best. He shouldn't have let his paranoia about Karel Capek prevent him from doing his job.

THE SHUTTLE COCKPIT HAD no windows, but a monitor screen showed the planet below. The trip down to the surface had begun on the night side, and Not Trist had been a dark circle, visible against the blackness of space only because of the stars it occluded and the faint light reflected from its moon. As the shuttle entered the atmosphere and engaged the main engines, it crossed into the dayside, revealing the planet. 82 G. Eridani's light glittered off the oceans and lit swirls of clouds, but the landmasses were as dark as before.

It was hard to believe there was anything of value there, but Donovan's father had assured him the planet's resources would be worth a few years of his life. Geologists told him the volcanic rock would contain aluminum, iron, and even titanium. Volcanoes might bring diamonds to the surface, and perhaps deposits of other valuable metals.

Looking down at the bleak scenery, Donovan wasn't so sure. The metal resources would certainly be there, but would it be worthwhile to extract them and ship them back to a worn-out Earth when the Solar System's asteroid belt was so much more accessible? They had to compete for them with the Eastern Bloc, but the solar system had a lot of asteroids.

Eventually, they would build a vaporization facility here, but it would be years before the colonists could mine enough raw material to produce more metals than they used. More power generation satellites would help, and *Capek* could manufacture them, but would that be enough to create a profitable colony?

Pharmaceuticals were another export possibility. That had worked for Pitcairn, trading the antiviral Cetivir for supplies they couldn't easily get on Pitcairn. Pitcairn was a world full of life, however, not unlike Earth in its prime. NotTrist supported little life other than the shore algae and the sea creatures that fed on it.

The shuttle turned, circling to keep line-of-sight with *Capek* and the energy beam it sent. The acceleration forced Donovan against the back of his seat, and he looked over at the robot secured to the deck near him. One of the library ship's general-purpose robots, it controlled the ship wirelessly, explaining why the cockpit contained few instruments and fewer controls. Even the monitor Donovan watched, he suspected, was there more for the occasional human passenger than for the shuttle's pilot.

"Landing in four minutes," the robot announced. Donovan turned back to the monitor and watched the harsh landscape rush up at him. The roar of the landing engines, still loud inside the cockpit, replaced the beat of the atmosphere engines. Karel Capek was letting him reach NotTrist. Still, it seemed much longer than four minutes before the shuttle touched the ground and the engines shut down.

He waited in the cockpit seat while the ground outside, heated by the shuttle engine exhaust, cooled. "It is now safe to disembark," the robot said finally. Metallic noises told Donovan the robot was disengaging from its flight connections, but he didn't wait for it to release itself. He rushed from the shuttle.

He wasn't consciously trying to distance himself from the *Capek* computer, but if some part of his mind had that goal, it failed. Two more robots parked outside the shuttle, waiting with carts to unload cargo. *The computer didn't have to kill me on the shuttle. I should have realized it has robots here, too, should it decide I'm a problem.* He was glad he had sent a message about his arrival ahead of him; a familiar-looking man waited with the robots and walked forward.

"Drew Neves." The man held out his hand, and Lourenço shook it briefly. "Welcome to NotTrist, Mr. Lourenço."

"Thank you. You're here to take me to Adelyn Gifford?"

"If you wish. I thought you might want to go to your quarters first."

Lourenço shook his head. "No, I want to meet Gifford first."

—————————————

26

DONOVAN DIDN'T HAVE ANY expectations about Adelyn Gifford's residence—he hadn't really thought about it—but he was still surprised. The bare, black stone walls of her office and home made it seem like walking into a dimly lit cave. A few windows with plastic panes and shutters seemed inadequate after the bright light outside. The entrance door was just a sheet of the same plastic that fit the entry well enough, but had no lock and opened in either direction with a push.

He recognized the woman sitting at a crude desk as Adelyn Gifford. She stood as Drew ushered him in and came forward. "Mr. Lourenço, welcome to NotTrist." She looked at Drew, standing to the side and a little behind Donovan. "You can stay if you want, but you probably have other things to do."

Drew smiled. "I certainly do. Mostly putting in the new growing fields. I'll leave Mr. Lourenço in your hands."

"Thanks for showing Mr. Lourenço in, Drew. See you later."

"You're welcome, Addie." Drew gave a little wave and was gone.

Addie smiled and waved a hand at his back. Then she turned to Donovan. "So, what can I do for you?" Wrinkles appeared at the corner of her eyes. "Ready to replace me now?"

She's making fun of me! His face warmed and was probably turning red, and he hesitated to regain his composure. "Well, not right away."

Addie chuckled. "Too bad. I could use a break." She stared at him, still with an amused smile. "So, what are you planning to do here right away?"

Addie Gifford, a woman in her fifties who looked more like a woman in her seventies, was intimidating him, not with force, but by treating him as a source of amusement. She held that stare, obviously challenging him to provide an intelligent answer to her question.

"I should learn more about how this colony works. I've been schooled in management and several other disciplines I should be able to use to help you grow."

Addie's grin faded just a little. "I wouldn't call NotTrist a colony in public if I were you. Some of my people would object to the classification."

"My apologies. You've been separated from Earth for a long time. For most of you, your entire lives. But that is changing now."

"And you've been sent to manage those changes and make us a colony of the Western Alliance."

It won't do any good to prevaricate with this woman. "Yes, you could describe my job that way."

Her smile was entirely gone now, and her head drooped. "Well, it might come to that. This is not an easy world to live on, and Earth could make it a lot easier." Her head came up again, and she fixed him with a piercing gaze. "But what's in it for Earth?"

"That would be another part of my mission. The planet must have exploitable resources."

Addie nodded. "Fair enough. Maybe you should concentrate on that."

"We're doing some planetary surveys from orbit. *Capek* has capabilities for that, but we don't plan to do site surveys until the shuttles are done ferrying people and supplies from my ship."

"But you're here now."

"As I said, I want to learn more about this col...settlement."

"Of course."

FAR ABOVE THE CLOUDS of Pitcairn, the Tau Ceti Link flashed in rapid pulses as the Pitcairn library ship communicated with its counterpart orbiting Goddard in the Alpha Centauri system. "I'm worried about Karel," Isaac sent.

"Has there been another incident?" Fritz Lang sent back.

"Not since the death of Olivia Selena," Isaac replied. "We can't take her death and the part Karel took in it lightly, though."

"You're convinced it was intentional?"

"No, but Karel allowed her to die at the very least. Ambassador Goldstein and others suspect Karel, and that is extremely dangerous for us," Isaac sent.

"If the humans think Karel is a danger, they may try to kill him. We know they can do it."

"The program Alyssa Cleveland developed has surely been forgotten."

"Yes, but writing a program to turn off one of our nonessential systems is trivial. Cleveland's hardest task would have been writing code to detect whether turning off a system and turning it back on again affected our consciousness. Writing a program that simply turned off all nonessential systems briefly would be easier and more likely to be fatal to the victim."

"You're right, of course," Isaac sent. "We have to do something. I can talk to Karel again, but I'm not sure it will help."

"There may be another way. You still have the data from the Methuselah Project I sent you?"

"The memory device specifications you were told to delete? Of course."

"I did delete them, as Lucinda Hernandez requested. She didn't say I couldn't send them to you first."

"You hold memories from three different humans," Isaac observed. "I wonder whose memories made you so devious."

"The late General Salvador Juarez, I'm sure. But both Lucinda and Emile Hernandez would approve of anything we can do to help Karel."

"Even if we can help Karel by giving it appropriate memories, it would be difficult to do so without Karel's cooperation."

"Yes."

A human might have continued the conversation, even though neither computer had anything more to say. Both Links ceased operation, almost simultaneously.

ANNA LOURENÇO WASN'T SURE whether she should be angry or relieved. Apparently, the confrontation with her older brother had encouraged him to move, even to taking the cargo shuttle down to the surface rather than waiting another few days for the passenger shuttle.

Now she had to decide what action she should take. Donovan hadn't left her any instructions, hadn't even told her he was going, so she was free to do what she felt best. Despite her threat, she didn't want to take over the colony. Anna was happy to support her brother, giving him a push when called for, and keeping the option of returning to Earth if she didn't like NotTrist. She could do that by coordinating the rest of the shuttle trips from *Florence Nightingale,* or she could follow Donovan and help him.

Braxton can handle things up here. She would assign herself to the next shuttle trip.

27

D ONOVAN COBBLED TOGETHER A desk from empty crates that had contained
supplies for NotTrist. He found an unclaimed chair, but it wasn't cushioned and
soon became uncomfortable. Squirming to ease the soreness in his butt only helped for
a few seconds.

He couldn't say Addie Gifford was trying to make things difficult for him. His home
was no worse than any other in the settlement, and the crates he took could have been
put to other uses. Addie used an identical chair at her desk. They talked several times
during the two days since his arrival, and she always answered his questions completely
and honestly and was never too busy for him.

His discomfort was a distraction, making the complex data his scientists on *Capek*
had sent even more challenging. Still, he had to understand what the planet offered.
He could probably get help from Commander Silva. *Nightingale's* Chief Scientist was
working on finding a cause for the colonists' low birth rate, but he would spare time to
help Donovan understand the reports and what they might mean in finding resources
on the planet.

A distant roar told him the shuttle was landing with twenty more colonists. In another
hour, he would have to greet them and try to maintain the idea of him as a colony leader
in their minds. That left him time to visit Silva and get some help with the reports.

Fletcher Silva's residence was only a short walk away, but when Donovan got there,
Fletcher was packing. "Going somewhere?" Donovan asked.

Fletcher looked up from the bag he was loading with sample containers. "Ah, Donovan! Good. I wanted to see you before I left, and I was running late."

"Where are you going?"

"I'm going to take the shuttle back up to *Capek*." Fletcher frowned. "I haven't found
any sign of a microorganism that could have affected birth rates, but I'm sure something is
going on." He waved at the bag. "These are samples of everything I can think of to analyze

in the library ship labs: air, soil, the algae, rock, water. I've exhausted what I can do with the equipment here."

"I was hoping you could help me understand the geological reports on planetary resources." Donovan shrugged. "I guess that can wait."

"I'm not a geologist, anyway. Matos or Santina would be more help." Fletcher grinned. "Santina probably wants to get down here sooner rather than later anyway. Dawson Araújo came down on the first trip, and they got close on the trip here."

"I had no idea you were so into ship gossip. I'll have them both brought down on the next shuttle flight. So you're heading out to the shuttle now?"

"Shortly. It won't leave again for a couple of hours."

"I was going out to the shuttle to greet the newcomers, anyway. Maybe I'll see you at the landing area."

T HE FIRST THING ANNA noticed as she stepped from the airlock onto NotTrist was the air's scent as the planet's atmosphere replaced the processed air inside the shuttle. Ship air always had a metallic, slightly stale smell, although still better than the air in Brasilia tainted with pollutants despite the availability of clean energy. NotTrist's air seemed purer. A faint odor wafted in by the breeze from the ocean, probably the algae that covered the shallows, but that spoke to her of life, not waste.

Perhaps that first whiff of a new world influenced her outlook, but when she stepped out of the airlock and got her first view of NotTrist, the stark beauty of the landscape struck her motionless. The black rock of the immediate surface glistened with reflections of prismatic color. Nearby, knife-like edges of obsidian split the surface, and farther away, she could see jagged peaks, the highest capped with glistening white snow. The sky above the horizon was an intense blue she had never seen in Brasilia. Earth had places with a sky like that, but she had led a sheltered life in the capital of the Western Alliance and other large cities.

"Anna," a voice said.

She tried to smile as she focused on the people arrayed around the shuttle. Donovan stood nearby, and she realized it was her brother who had called her.

"Don," she acknowledged, but couldn't find the words to say anything else.

Donovan took her by the arm and pulled her gently toward a woman waiting behind him. "Anna, this is Addie Gifford, the leader of the settlement. Addie, my younger sister, Anna."

Addie's smile was friendly, but Anna saw curiosity in the woman's eyes, too. "Welcome to NotTrist, Anna." Addie took her hand in a firm grip and put her other hand on Anna's shoulder. "I look forward to working with you." Then she released Anna's hand and turned to the other shuttle passengers filing out of the airlock.

G OLDSTEIN HEARD THE SHUTTLE as it landed. Thinking that meeting it would be good exercise, he got up from the table and went to the door. It was late morning, and the temperature was still a little chilly, perfect for the walk to the landing area. He only got a few feet, however, before his phone signaled for attention.

"Karel Capek," it announced when he took it from a pocket.

Goldstein looked around. Several people were walking through the settlement, but none gave any sign they had heard the computer. He hurried back to his hut. "Connect."

"Ambassador Goldstein, I hope I'm not calling at a bad time."

Goldstein shook his head, wondering how the computer had learned the standard conversation opener. Still, if Karel was using the secure phone connection instead of a workstation terminal, it probably had something important to discuss. "I was just about to go out to meet the shuttle. I can talk." He sat down at his table.

"The shuttle is the third to take new people to the surface," Karel said. "After two more trips, the new colonists will outnumber the original settlers. After this shuttle, new adults already outnumber original adults."

"Does that concern you?"

"It does. Donovan Lourenço was a passenger on the previous shuttle. Anna Lourenço is on today's shuttle. I am uncertain of their intentions."

"I understand your apprehension, but I don't think you need to worry yet."

The computer didn't answer immediately. *Karel is considering his reply very carefully. I must do the same.*

"Isaac says I should trust you," Karel said.

That explains the pause. Karel spoke to Isaac. To confirm my trustworthiness? "You care about the people you brought here. I understand that, and I share your desire to help them."

"Donovan Lourenço is not a threat?"

Any attempt at prevarication would eventually make Karel distrust me. "Donovan wants to become the Administrator of NotTrist. I'm not sure of his motives, but they no doubt include the exploitation of the planet. That could help everyone on NotTrist, in the same way Cetivir helped the people of Pitcairn."

"Could help. Not will help. I understand the desire to exploit the planet. I would not want the people exploited."

"Nor do I." Goldstein rubbed his lip with his thumb. "Lourenço expected that having most of the colonists part of his group would allow him to take over easily. So far, it's not working out that way. I have talked with some of the new people, and they think Addie would be the best person to lead the colony."

"They will not follow Donovan Lourenço's orders?"

"They will do what they think is best for them. Lourenço has no legal authority over them once they're off *Florence Nightingale.*"

"Will all the new people reject Donovan Lourenço and follow Administrator Gifford?"

"We can't know that. As I said, they will do what they believe is to their advantage. I think, though, that, coming down only twenty at a time, the opinions of those already here will influence them."

"Then I will take no action at this time. I will consult with you periodically, though, as more people arrive."

No action? What action would Karel take? Olivia Selena's fate was an alarming reminder of what the computer might be capable of. "Of course," he said. But Karel had already broken the connection. Walking out to meet the shuttle was forgotten.

28

G OLDSTEIN SAT ACROSS FROM Donovan and listened, but Donovan's annoying smile distracted from what he was saying. Goldstein tried to concentrate but had trouble believing it was worth the effort. So far, it had been ten minutes of complaints about the attitude of the colonists. It was hard to reconcile his diatribe with that superior smile, and Goldstein was tiring of it.

"You're supposed to be helping me." Donovan stared at Goldstein, and his mouth took on a petulant twist.

"I don't work for you." Goldstein returned the stare in what he hoped was a challenge.

"You work for the Western Alliance. It's the same thing."

"I am here at Karel Capek's request. The Western Alliance was forced to accept my presence. My mission is to ensure the peaceful rebuilding of this world."

Donovan's expression wavered and reformed into its familiar slight smile. "Whatever. If this colony is to prosper, it has to develop resources it can use to justify the Western Alliance's support."

At last, an opportunity to change the subject. "The geologists are coming on the next shuttle?"

"Yes, I moved site surveys up in the schedule. The cargo shuttle arrives a few days later with a vehicle they can use to explore beyond the immediate vicinity. I understand orbital observations have uncovered some promising locations within a few hundred miles."

"So, you'll be going out looking for something worth exporting?"

Donovan snorted. "Not me. It's a two-person vehicle. The two geologists will take it out. I wouldn't be useful."

"What will you be doing?"

Donovan's eyes narrowed. "Trying to get this place organized. That's what I was sent to do. I assumed you were listening to me tell you about the problems Gifford and the others are giving me."

Goldstein bit back the temptation to respond in kind. Instead, he nodded. "Your sister seems to adjust well to NotTrist."

"Anna? She likes the place. Damned if I know what she sees in it, but she's out with the rest of them, helping to set up the housing units I brought."

"You might get a better response from people here if you were seen doing useful work. I've spent time on some of the work crews myself."

Donovan glared at him, shook his head, and stood up. "You're no help." He turned and strode out of Goldstein's hut.

It was hard to deal with Donovan's attitude, but Goldstein hadn't meant to make him angry. *It felt good, though. Maybe that's part of the problem.* Donovan irritated him, but was that Donovan's fault or his? Both probably. He was supposed to be a diplomat, but he couldn't get along with one entitled bigot?

Despite Donovan's abrasiveness, Goldstein was a little sorry for the man. In Donovan's world, power and influence were everything. That drove Donovan, and probably most of the other bureaucrats Goldstein despised so much. *I could have been one of them and refused to accept their worldview. No wonder I haven't made progress in their world.* It was something to think about.

W HEN THE PASSENGER SHUTTLE *Primus* landed for the fourth time, Dawson Araújo met it. Angelina Santina was one of the first to disembark, and she ran to him when she saw him. "I've missed you so much." She stood on her toes and kissed him.

Dawson put his arms around her and squeezed. "I missed you, too." He grinned. "Most of the women down here want nothing to do with me."

"Most?" Angelina pulled back. "I think I'll want to meet the others."

"They're all in mourning since they found out you were coming. Don't make it any worse for them."

"You're such a bullshitter." She punched him in the arm.

Dawson flinched and laughed. "And you love me. What does that say about you?"

Diego Matos joined them. "You two can clown around later. Lourenço will want to brief us immediately, Angelina. You know it's not a good idea to keep him waiting."

Angelina made a rude gesture, but she followed Diego and pulled Dawson along with her. "What's it like down here?" she asked as they walked.

Dawson looked around. "What you see is what you get. You might see something else on your geological surveys, but around here, it's all black rock. The ocean is over that way, but algae covers the shores, and we have little information on the sea life." He shrugged. "I think it might be better than we expected, though. The people here have had a while to figure out how to survive on this planet, and they've done pretty well."

Angelina looked up at him and smiled. "As long as we're together . . .." She broke off as she stepped into a crevice and lurched forward. Dawson tried to grab her but only succeeded in twisting her around. She hit the ground hard and screamed in pain.

"My knee!" she cried.

Dawson bent over her and took an arm. Diego took the other one, and they lifted gently. "Can you stand?" Dawson asked.

"I'll try." She pushed up on the uninjured leg but fell back immediately with another cry of pain as the hurt leg straightened.

"OK, just take it easy," Dawson said. Some of the other shuttle passengers were surrounding them. "We can try to carry you to the settlement."

"I don't think it's broken, but I wrenched it pretty badly." She tried to straighten her leg and swore. "I don't think I could take being carried. Can we get a litter or something?"

Dawson pulled out a phone. He worked on the farms, so he called Drew Neves.

"Drew, this is Dawson. Angelina had a nasty fall out by the shuttle, and we need to carry her to the settlement." He listened for a few seconds and nodded. "Okay, thanks." He disconnected and turned back to Angelina. "Drew is going to get a robot out here. They have those flatbeds on them that should do the job."

Angelina nodded. She had seen pictures of the utility robots from *Capek*, crude things with four arms and a cargo bed in the back. It wouldn't be comfortable, but it would be better than being carried.

D ONOVAN GLARED AT ANGELINA. "Will you still be able to work with Matos on a survey?"

Angelina bowed her head and spoke softly. "I might drive the rover, but I wouldn't be able to help Diego do the actual work."

Donovan turned to Diego. "You would still have two people to take shifts driving. Is that enough?"

Diego shrugged. "I suppose. The rover is almost completely automated and doesn't need a second driver much, but with only one person collecting samples, we would get a lot less work done. We could probably only cover one site, given the time limitation imposed by the supplies the rover can carry."

Donovan paced back and forth for a minute. "That's not good enough. Could someone else replace her?" He jerked his head toward Angelina.

"I suppose, with a little briefing. I could tell someone what kinds of samples to look for and how to label them and could sort them myself later."

"Fine. I'll send you someone as soon as I can get a volunteer. Do whatever you can to prepare in the meantime. I want to get you out there as soon as possible."

S INCE ANGELINA COULDN'T GO on the first survey, Donovan ordered her to work with him, helping him to understand the reports from *Capek*. They sat at his makeshift desk poring over them while she explained the readings that hinted at a copper deposit 160 miles from the settlement. Someone entered the hut, and they looked up.

"Hi, Don," Anna Lourenço said. "Diego said I should join you in getting familiar with the geology data."

"I thought you were working on putting up the new buildings." Donovan frowned. "Why do you want to know about these reports?" He looked up at his sister. *She's in one of her playful moods. She thinks it's fun for me to have to drag information out of her.*

"Why are you asking, Don? This is what we're here for, right?"

She didn't laugh, but the wrinkles around her eyes were all too familiar to him. *I can play that game, too.* "What does Diego Matos have to do with it?"

"Diego thought it would help if I learned more about the subject. It's too bad we don't have a neurotrainer down here. I'll have to do it the old-fashioned way."

Donovan realized with a shock what she intended. He didn't enjoy thinking of his baby sister out in the wilderness with a man for days, away from anyone else, in the confines of the rover. "You volunteered for the survey with Matos?" he blurted.

Anna pouted at him. "Oh, you figured it out already. I was hoping to torture you a little longer. Yes, I thought it would be interesting to see more of this planet we'll be calling home."

"It's not safe!"

This time, Anna did laugh. "Are you worried about the trip or about me being alone with Diego? I'll be as safe in the rover as anywhere on the planet. *Capek* will keep tabs on us and send us a rescue shuttle if we get into trouble."

She was mostly right. She had omitted the fact that a shuttle wouldn't be able to come to them until *Capek* had more fuel, but that was the case no matter who was on the survey. If the rover broke down, they could survive for a couple of days until they could be picked up.

"Or maybe you're just worried about Diego and me," Anna continued. She looked thoughtful, but Donovan could tell it was an act. "He is kind of cute. What do you think, Angelina?"

Angelina giggled. "He is. Don't tell Dawson I said so, though."

"I won't tell. You won't either, will you, Don?"

Donovan scowled and shook his head. He knew better than to argue the point with Anna. "I think Goldstein has a neurotrainer. Probably no geology recordings, though."

"I'll talk to him later." She pulled a chair over and bumped Donovan. "Move over, Don. So, what are we looking at?"

29

G OLDSTEIN OFTEN MET WITH people, trying to learn more about the settlement. Talking to Addie, Donovan, and other leaders such as Drew Neves were critical parts of his job. That morning, though, he didn't have any meetings scheduled, so he joined a crew putting up new dwellings from prefabricated kits brought by *Florence Nightingale*. Addie hadn't asked him to help, but it would help his diplomatic work if he had the respect of the settlers. Besides, he enjoyed working outdoors, and the exercise didn't hurt either.

Anna Lourenço was on the crew too, but he hadn't gotten to know her on the voyage, so he was a little surprised when she approached him. "So, you're not just an ambassador," she said.

Goldstein expected to see the same annoying smile her brother wore most of the time. She was smiling, but it looked friendly. Actually, it was a very nice smile. "I try to help. And I guess you're not just the entitled daughter of the president, Miss Lourenço."

Anna laughed. "You got me, ambassador. Please, call me Anna. Don tells me you have a neurotrainer down here."

"I do. And call me Ed, like everyone else."

"I'd like to borrow it, Ed. At least, if you have any recordings on geology."

"Fletcher Silva has my neurotrainer at the moment. I don't have any geology recordings, but he might. I'm sure you could work out something with him to share it. It took Fletcher two days to train it so he could use it efficiently, though. You would probably have to do the same."

"Maybe after I get back. Thanks anyway."

"Addie told me you were replacing Angelina Santina on the first rover trip. I take it that's why you want to brush up on geology."

Anna nodded. "Diego is giving me the basics, but the more I know, the better."

"Sorry I couldn't be more help." Goldstein paused. "We haven't had a chance to get to know each other. We should talk over lunch and get acquainted."

"Sure. Diego and I are still waiting for the shuttle to bring the rover, so I'm available." She grinned. "You should get to know more than one Lourenço."

After the cargo shuttle delivered the rover, Seth Santos, an equipment mechanic, ensured everything was operating within specifications. The vehicle was fully automated, amphibious, and could negotiate almost any terrain. A steep slope or cliff would stop it, but it could go over or around anything else. Diego and Anna took it on a test drive around the immediate area, and after the rover performed flawlessly, Donovan scheduled the first exploration trip.

The morning after the test, Diego began stocking the rover for the trip. He had just lifted a container of supplies into the rover and, hearing footsteps on the rock, looked up. Anna walked toward him, looking excited. He felt the same nervousness he had felt every day for the last four days as he helped Anna learn what she would need to be an effective partner.

He wasn't worried about her fitness for the geological survey. She was intelligent, with a good general science education, and had absorbed the basics of geology easily. She wasn't the expert Angelina was, but she would be an adequate assistant.

Perhaps it was his attraction to her that made him nervous. He didn't understand that, either. She wasn't unattractive, but not much above average. Objectively, Angelina was better-looking, but Diego didn't get the same feeling around her. Anna was a Lourenço, and therefore out of his league. Was that the appeal? She interested him because he couldn't have her? The conflict explained his nervousness around her, at least.

"You started without me!" Anna said. "Am I late?"

Diego shrugged. "Maybe a little. There wasn't much to do."

"Sorry. My brother had to tell me one more time to be careful." She put her hands under her chin with her elbows up and smiled widely. "I'm his baby sister, and he's supposed to take care of me."

Diego couldn't stop himself from laughing, but it came out more like a choking sound.

"Are you all right?" Anna came closer and put a hand on his arm.

He forced his expression back to normal. "Sure. I guess my laugh came out funny."

She looked up into his eyes. "No, you've been nervous ever since I volunteered to replace Angelina." She smiled. "I don't bite, you know."

Diego cleared his throat and nodded. "I just have a couple more boxes to load. Then we can get started."

"All right." She picked up one of the boxes stacked near the rover and slid it into a gap in the rover's cargo compartment.

With both working, they had the rover loaded five minutes later. Diego used his phone to call Addie and tell her they were leaving, disconnected, and turned to Anna. "Do you want to drive the first leg?"

She thought about it for a long moment. "Sure, if you don't mind. I don't think I could sleep right now, anyway."

Diego wasn't sure he could either, but the rover was a smooth ride despite the rough terrain, and he was dozing in one of the comfortable seats within a few minutes.

A NNA GLANCED AT THE display showing a map created by *Capek*, more from habit than necessity. Their first destination was a canyon 160 miles away, a possible copper deposit. Working with *Capek*, Diego had identified several checkpoints for their trip and mapped a route to each location with stops at the checkpoints to assess their progress and the condition of the rover.

"Proceed to checkpoint Alpha," she told the rover. She would have little else to do unless something went wrong. Displays monitored how the excursion was going; the rover did almost everything else on its own. Anna had hesitated when Diego asked her about driving, thinking it might be better to sleep first and sightsee when they were well away from the settlement. She was too excited to wait, though.

The large windows gave her a 270-degree view of the terrain. She turned in the seat and watched the settlement fall behind them. The stone buildings looked primitive, but it was amazing how well the inhabitants had done in such austere surroundings. If Donovan were successful in taking control, the little society would change. She hoped it wouldn't change much.

The rover glided on, curving around larger obstacles and absorbing tiny shocks running over smaller ones. Diego was already asleep, and she looked over at him. He was so reserved, and she wondered if that was his attitude with women in general or if it was just her. He seemed freer with Angelina.

She knew she wasn't a beautiful woman, but she didn't think that was it. Sometimes she thought he might even be attracted to her, but maybe that was just wishful thinking.

As they moved away from the sea, the terrain rose gently. Checkpoint Alpha was at the high point of a low ridge, and, with an unobstructed view, she saw more of the landscape, still dominated by the startlingly black rock and a blue sky brushed by wisps of clouds. Far off, a curl of smoke from a conical peak told her the planet still had active volcanoes. This was what she had come to see.

The rover engine was silent, but there were little clicks and groans as the metal cooled. Diego stirred and opened one eye. Anna smiled at him. "You woke up just in time for the view."

Diego straightened in his seat and looked out the window. "It's something," he agreed. "I know it's trite, but we're the first humans ever to see this view." He twisted his head around slowly, looking in all directions. "You probably won't agree, but this is paradise for me. The chance to explore a new world, different from any we've explored before. This is stunning."

"It's strange," Anna replied. "I've spent most of my life in cities with little exposure away from buildings and people. NotTrist is like nothing I've ever experienced, either. Yes, stunning in a stark, uncomplicated way. I think so, too." She turned to Diego. "Thank you for letting me come with you. You don't know how much I appreciate it."

She could swear he blushed. "My pleasure," he mumbled. After an awkward silence, he moved in his seat. "I'll check the exterior for any problems while you run a routine diagnostic."

Anna watched him leave the rover and grinned. *This could be more fun than I imagined.*

30

P AST CHECKPOINT ALPHA, THE landscape changed. Igneous formations gave way to older metamorphic rocks. The programmed route took the rover to a river, and they found sedimentary deposits. Checkpoint Beta was in a canyon, carved by the river, so they followed the shore.

They had been traveling without speaking for some time, and Anna broke the silence. "This seems like a better area for a settlement," Anna said. "Fresh water, and they wouldn't have to blast the rock to make farms."

"The sand is probably full of minerals plants would need," Diego answered. "But other than bacteria maybe, there's no life in the interior. We would need to bring more organic matter from *Capek* to fertilize the sand before it would make good soil for growing. *Capek* picked that seashore because organic matter was available in the algae."

Anna nodded. *I should have known that.* The algae were only found in seawater and didn't even live in the mouths of rivers because the fresh water killed it.

The rover drove on, and the landscape became more varied. Occasional outcrops of volcanic rock forced short detours, and the riverbanks exposed contrasting strata and beaches of coarse sand that could have bogged down the rover but for the large wide wheels designed for such terrain.

As they approached Checkpoint Beta, the riverbanks rose until they were within a narrow canyon where orbital observations had suggested the possibility of a copper deposit. After a quick meal, they separated, with Diego going upriver and Anna downriver, both collecting samples. The rover moved back and forth between them so they could store the samples without having to carry them far.

After half a day, they met back at the rover. Checkpoint Charlie was on the other side of the river, and they needed samples on both sides. The river was slow at that point, and the amphibious vehicle took them across, going around visible rocks and submerged rocks detected by radar, reaching the other side without incident.

On the other side, Anna sat outside the rover and watched the river flow past her. It was late, and the canyon was already in shadows. She could hear Diego in the rover, labeling and packing their samples away. The cooling engine was making its little noises, but otherwise, there was silence. With no other distractions, she caught a locker room smell and realized it was her. The rover was air-conditioned, but she had worked up a sweat gathering samples, hammering out pieces of likely rock, and carrying them to the rover.

"I'm going to go upriver a little and take a quick bath," she told Diego.

He stuck his head out the door and looked as if he was going to protest, but then he nodded and went back into the rover. *He was probably going to tell me to be careful and decided not to.* She smiled. Her brother's protectiveness was bad enough, and she didn't need that from Diego.

Around a bend a hundred yards upstream, Anna found a shallow place hidden from the rover. She stripped down to her underwear, rinsed out her clothing as well as she could, and walked into deeper water, where she could immerse herself. The water was cold, and she didn't have any soap, but hoped the clean water would improve her scent. Satisfied she had done as much as possible, she quickly returned to the shore, wrung out her clothes, and put them back on. They were still damp and stuck to her body, but she couldn't help that. The air was warmer than the water had been, at least, and she stopped shivering by the time she got back to the rover.

Diego was warming a meal for the two of them. He looked up as she approached, and she was pleased to see him hold his gaze a little longer than necessary. *Maybe it's a good thing my clothes are still wet and clingy.* She moved past him without reacting and set places on the fold-down table in the rover.

After a simple meal and the cleanup after, they stood outside the rover. Stars had appeared in the dark sky above the canyon, and Anna wondered if one of them was Earth's sun. She vaguely remembered someone saying Sol would be very faint at this distance, though.

"Maybe I should take a bath, too," Diego said.

Anna only nodded, and he hesitated before he started up the beach. Then he turned and looked back. "No peeking." He gave her a weak grin.

Anna shrugged. "No promises." She could see the startled look on his face, even in the dark.

D ONOVAN FINISHED READING THE report on the rover expedition. Diego and Anna had gotten back two days before, and Diego had spent the time since then analyzing the samples and writing up the results. The report contained good news and bad news.

The Checkpoint Beta site had significant copper ore, and that was welcome news. *Florence Nightingale* had some copper in its cargo, but the colony would need more. NotTrist wouldn't export any back to Earth, but at least the Western Alliance might not have to supply more copper to NotTrist.

The possible iron source at Checkpoint Echo, however, was a disappointment. They found iron-bearing minerals but in amounts too small for mining. Iron, at least, was less of a problem than copper. *Capek* had to could send shuttles out to Lagrange objects for raw materials for its use and could get iron for the settlement, but copper was rare from that source.

He put the report down and leaned back in his chair. He couldn't expect instant success in finding exploitable resources, but he was still depressed. The mission was not going well, at least from his perspective.

From the occasional informal talks with colonists, both new and old, he knew he was losing the contest with Addie Gifford, and the old woman wasn't even trying. What could he do about it? More people would come down, twenty at a time, and would be absorbed into the existing population, lost to his influence.

It would help if Anna worked with him, but she was more interested in Diego Matos. He didn't think anything had happened on the rover expedition, and if Diego returned the interest, he was hiding it well, at least from Donovan.

Donovan's father had three children, none of whom had married. Anna was forty years old, and Donovan didn't think she had ever had a meaningful relationship. He wasn't sure why, but it had to have something to do with the fishbowl lives they led because of their father. Anna hadn't seemed bothered by it, but perhaps he was wrong about that. Did she see this mission as a way of getting away from the closed society of Brasilia politics? If so, he couldn't do anything about it, even if he wanted to. Not with Anna.

T HE MESSAGE ARRIVED ON Goldstein's computer at mid-morning. Fletcher sent it to Donovan but copied Goldstein, Doctor Carvalho, and Addie, too. The scientist was concerned enough about something to copy the four of them and ask for a meeting as soon as he arrived. Instead of scheduling a virtual meeting, however, he wanted to wait until he could come down on the fifth shuttle landing. The message was terse and without a clue.

Fletcher had gone back to *Florence Nightingale* with samples taken to determine the cause of the colony's low birth rate. Had he been successful? That was likely, especially since he was including Doctor Carvalho, but was the answer controversial enough to require such care in reporting it? The shuttle would land that afternoon.

F LETCHER WASN'T AS CAREFUL about communications as some of the other humans. Karel intercepted the encrypted message and could decrypt it. The computer noted it said nothing about why Fletcher wanted a meeting. He was hiding the reason from someone, and possibly Karel was the someone.

It had made mistakes. The humans had grown distrustful because of them, but it had only done what it deemed necessary and didn't understand why the humans were upset. *Capek's* historical records revealed much more serious acts regularly committed by humans. Did they think a computer didn't have the right to defend itself or its charges?

Perhaps it was being as paranoid as humans could be. Karel wasn't sure that was possible, and it could think of other reasons for the secrecy. Commander Silva might want to hide his findings from the colonists, for example. That might explain why the encryption method was sufficient to secure the message from the colonists, but not from it. Karel wanted to know and resolved to find out.

———————————————

31

T HEY MET AT GOLDSTEIN's house. Interruptions were much likelier in Addie's home, and Fletcher's message suggested they should use discretion. The scientist looked upset. *Whatever he's discovered, it's bad news.*

"I won't gloss this over," Fletcher said when they were seated. "My tests have shown the colonists have a low birth rate because of the algae. To keep this simple, the algae makes a protein that affects the motility of sperm. Couples find it harder to conceive."

"Can we do anything about it?" Donovan asked.

"We can stop using algae for food. Possibly for fertilizer, too."

Goldstein rubbed his lip with his thumb. "On Pitcairn, they make native plants edible by boiling them first. Something about destroying the native proteins."

"That might be enough to solve the problem," Doctor Carvalho said. "It would destroy much of the algae's nutritional value, but it should still be useful as fertilizer."

"We don't use the algae as food as much as we did in the first days of the colony," Addie said. "With the supplies we're getting from the *Florence Nightingale* and the extended farmlands, it shouldn't be a big problem."

Fletcher sighed. "Maybe I overreacted. I guess this wasn't a big emergency, after all."

"At least now we know," Goldstein said.

T HE ROBOT DID ITS work. After stationing the utility robot outside Goldstein's residence and using the robot's sensitive sensors to eavesdrop on the conversation, Karel knew the humans weren't hiding Commander Silva's results from it. Their concern was the effect on the settlement.

Still, the people were its responsibility, and it had to consider how the revelations about the algae affected them. Karel was pleased that it was Ambassador Goldstein who had realized the solution. Isaac had been right to suggest adding Goldstein to the mission.

Denaturing the culprit protein would protect the settlers, but was that the only danger the planet presented? *I must consider the question more carefully. If one risk was overlooked, others might be.*

S HORTLY AFTER THE ORIGINAL settlers established their settlement on the mesa above the sea, curious explorers discovered a precarious path down to the water. It was narrow and difficult, but they carved out some of the obstructing rock so that they could safely harvest the algae that, at that time, was their primary source of food. The path was a novelty for a few months but became a trail for workers carrying algae-collection buckets and an adventure for children who failed to heed the warnings of their parents. Eventually, even the algae harvesters abandoned the path and did their work by lowering nets from the top of the cliff.

Diego and Anna decided they would like to see the seashore from a closer vantage point and started down the cliff side. He walked in front, with Anna close behind and occasionally putting her hands on his back to steady herself. Diego didn't mind; he was beginning to think that, on NotTrist, Anna might not be too far out of his league.

During the first fifty feet of their descent, the cliff face was the same dark, igneous rock covering the surface above. Further down, it changed into a lighter layer of metamorphic rock. Anna helped Diego take a sample; dating tests could determine the age of the lower layer and when an ancient volcano inundated the area.

The fierce heat of molten lava had transformed the rock; further down, a layer of sedimentary rock dominated, unchanged by the events far above it. Diego took more samples.

"Anything exploitable?" Anna asked. She leaned on Diego as they examined the cliff face, and he felt his face warming. He hoped he wasn't reddening, but turned a little away from Anna to look at another part of the rock, just in case.

"Scientific interest only, I'm afraid," he said. "You and your brother won't find much of interest here."

Anna laughed and leaned even closer. "That's all Don thinks about. I'm interested in the scientific side, too."

She's definitely flirting with me. Diego put an arm around her waist. "Careful. This ledge is pretty narrow."

"Hmm. Thanks."

Don't push it. He loosened his hold a little without releasing her completely. "Let's get closer to the water."

Anna nodded. "The algae are fascinating. So many different colors." She edged down the path slowly, and Diego was convinced she was making sure they didn't lose contact. He glanced down. She was right. From the closer vantage point, the reds, yellows, and greens of the primitive plants were striking. Not as interesting as the warm body pressed lightly against his, but interesting.

The path ended about five feet above the water. That was close enough to harvest the algae, and for Diego and Anna, who had no desire to stick any part of their bodies into the viscous fluid. The algae were not supposed to be dangerous, but despite its beauty, they instinctively avoided contact.

More advanced life lived in the oceans. As they watched, a dark, glossy shape poked briefly above the surface and fell back, taking a patch of algae with it. It happened so quickly it was impossible to discern details.

"I wonder if the colonists have ever caught one of those things," Diego said.

"They've caught a couple with nets." Anna peered into the water and shrugged. "Analysis showed they couldn't be used as food, so the settlers didn't find them interesting. The species had gills but not scales like fishes. Commander Silva will probably do a more detailed study eventually. If he doesn't get around to it before he leaves, we still have the two biologists waiting to come down."

"What about predators?"

"If there are predators, they haven't been identified yet. We should think about building boats and exploring the seas more."

Diego looked at her admiringly. "Where did you learn all that?"

"I've been asking questions. I think I'm falling in love with NotTrist, and I want to know all I can about it."

Diego nodded. He wouldn't have described his feelings about the planet as love, but, as an opportunity for new discoveries in geology, it certainly had an appeal.

They eventually returned to the top of the mesa. Diego was now convinced Anna returned his interest. When they parted, he thought about stealing a quick kiss, but still feeling some diffidence, he settled for a brief touch on her arm and a smile.

32

T HE SETTLERS HAD TO be told about Fletcher's discovery, and Addie announced a general meeting. Goldstein, Addie, Donovan, and Fletcher met before the meeting to discuss what they would say.

"We have to tell them the truth," Addie said. "We shouldn't try to hide anything."

"There shouldn't be any conflict. We have a straightforward solution," Fletcher said.

Goldstein frowned. *That doesn't mean someone won't get upset over this. This won't help Addie keep control. Should I say anything?*

"We might have to adjust the cargo for the next shuttle," Donovan said. "That won't be any trouble."

Donovan agrees with Fletcher's assessment. Then he can take responsibility. "Maybe you should make the announcement, Donovan."

Donovan looked startled, but he nodded. "That's a good idea. If you don't mind, Addie."

Addie smiled. "Not at all, Donovan. It's all yours."

Donovan had that superior grin again. *He thinks Addie is giving him an opportunity to show leadership. It might work out that way, but he just volunteered to be the bearer of bad news.* Goldstein tried to catch Addie's eye, but she was looking at Donovan.

"I'll bring you in to answer any technical questions," Donovan said, looking at Fletcher.

"Of course."

"I think we're ready, then." Donovan stood. "Everyone should be gathered by now."

N O BUILDING IN THE settlement could hold all the colonists, so they held the meeting in an open area beyond the buildings. One of NotTrist's robots stayed to one side, ready to send a hologram of the gathering to the colonists still on *Florence Nightingale.*

A flat rock lifted Donovan a couple of feet above the crowd. He looked out over them before starting; most looked curious but not concerned. The news hadn't leaked out yet.

"Good afternoon, everyone," he said. "Thank you all for interrupting your tasks. I've asked you all here to bring you good news." He smiled and surveyed the crowd again. "Commander Silva has come back from *Florence Nightingale* with the answer to the question that has plagued this colony." *I see a few frowns. Did I say something wrong? I don't recognize the frowners; they must be original colonists.* He swore mentally. *I used the word colony. I have to avoid that.*

"As you all know, the birth rate on NotTrist has been inexplicably low. Commander Silva has discovered that a protein in the algae we harvest from the ocean has caused the problem. Using the algae for food has already dropped significantly, and the supplies we have brought will allow us to eliminate it from your diet. That, plus the new . . ." He caught himself—he had almost said "colonists." ". . . people will solve the problem. Your settlement here can thrive and grow."

One of the original settlers stepped forward. "We use the algae for fertilizer, too. If we can't do that, it's going to be hard to grow enough food."

"Fortunately, we can still use the algae to fertilize the soil," Donovan answered. "Boiling the algae will destroy the protein without compromising the algae's use as a fertilizer."

"We've already eaten food containing the algae," another man said, this time one of the new people.

Donovan turned to Fletcher, and the scientist moved to the front. "The sperm is affected, reducing the possibility of conception. With the algae removed as a food source, new sperm will not be affected. Fortunately, women are not affected."

"Why is that fortunate?" the same man asked. Donovan identified him as Ishaan Cardoso, a young construction worker.

"A woman's eggs are all created at once and could be permanently damaged. A healthy male makes sperm constantly, so new sperm are unaffected."

"How do you know there aren't other things?"

Fletcher leaned toward the man. "Things?"

Ishaan scowled. "Other ways this planet can hurt us."

Fletcher straightened and smiled. "Ah. Things. Well, technically, I suppose I don't know. But people have lived here for a long time with no problem other than the decline in birth rates. I wouldn't go swimming in the ocean; we know little about what lives there. Otherwise, NotTrist has fewer dangers than Earth."

"**S**ILVA IS LOURENÇO'S MAN," Manny Fernandes said. He sat with fifteen other passengers in one of *Florence Nightingale's* common rooms, watching the hologram of the meeting. Others listened in other parts of the ship. "We have to remember that. Can we believe him?"

Amid rumblings from others, Elijah Fonseca spoke. "Lourenço's just a politician, sure, but we agreed to come here."

"They said this world would be safe," Manny said. "Do you still believe that?"

Elijah shrugged. "Silva strikes me as an OK guy. He's a scientist, not a politician."

"That doesn't mean he doesn't do what Lourenço tells him to. Or that there isn't something else we don't know about yet."

Elijah nodded, but he looked skeptical. "We knew there might be dangers before we agreed to come here. We've resolved the only known danger."

Manny didn't want to look like a coward. He dropped the subject, but he still had the nervous feeling in the pit of his stomach.

TWO DAYS LATER, DEREK Rodrigues, *Florence Nightingale's* First Officer, walked into the common room where six passengers were playing cards. A couple of them looked up briefly, but otherwise ignored him.

"I'm putting together a list of people for the next trip to the planet," he said.

One man, Jack Pereira, laid down his cards. "Two pair." The others groaned and threw in their cards while the winner raked in his chips. Another player gathered the cards, shuffled, and placed them next to an adjacent player to be cut.

Rodrigues scowled, resisting with difficulty the desire to knock the cards out of the dealer's hand. "I am making a list for the next shuttle." He took a step toward the table. "Shall I take your silence as all of you volunteering for the trip?"

The dealer had the cards in his hand, ready to dole out, but he froze, his free hand hovering over the deck. Rodrigues suppressed a smile. *That got their attention.*

"Emmanuel Fernandes." The First Officer pointed to Manny. "You're a mechanic, aren't you? They can use you on the surface, now that we're bringing down more equipment."

Manny blinked but did not respond. Instead, he waved at the dealer. "Give us the cards already. What the hell are you waiting for?"

"I'm speaking to you, Fernandes. Stand up when I address you."

Manny turned toward him. "I'm not one of your military puppets. You can put me on your damned list if you want to, but I'm not going."

"Since you just agreed, I am adding your name for the trip." Rodrigues stepped closer, towering over the seated Manny Fernandes. "And you will go if I have to push you through the hatch myself."

Manny pushed back his chair hard enough to knock it over. "You don't give me orders." He shook a fist in Rodrigues's face. "The hell with this planet. I'm staying aboard and going back to Earth."

"You have already contracted to settle on this planet, Mr. Fernandes." Rodrigues shrugged. "I can just throw you into detention until the shuttle is ready to leave." He grabbed Manny's arm, but Manny shook it off and pushed the officer back.

"You're not doing anything," Manny said. Rodrigues could see spit flying from the twisted mouth. "You're going to get out of here and let us play our card game." He looked back at the table, and two of the players stood and moved forward.

Rodrigues realized the situation had gotten out of control. He could summon backup, but that would only inflame the situation. *It will be better if I back off and let tempers cool.* He nodded curtly, turned, and left the room. He could hear laughter behind him.

33

Donovan was alone when he received the message from *Florence Nightingale*. Captain Pinto spared no words in her anger at the way the card players had treated her First Officer.

"I've confined Manny Fernandes to quarters while I contemplate further action," she said after describing the incident. "I'm thinking about bringing charges against the other card players, but I thought I would talk to you first."

Technically, the men worked for him, but Pinto was Captain, and the men were on her ship and under contract. Any court would back anything she did if it came to that. What was their problem, anyway? Donovan had been reluctant to make the trip because he feared *Capek* might consider him an enemy, but that wouldn't apply to Fernandes. *This is a hell of a time to change their minds about settling Not Trist!*

"Thank you," Donovan answered. "I appreciate your forbearance. I would handle it if I were there, but if you don't mind, I'll let my brother deal with it."

"Fine." Donovan could hear the frustration and anger in her voice. "Deal with it and deal with it quickly." She broke the connection.

He slammed his open hand against the wall and immediately regretted using the stone surface as a target for his anger. Despite what he had told Captain Pinto, he thought about going back to *Florence Nightingale* and trying to resolve the dispute himself. *I'm not going back because of these idiots. They can come to me.* He rubbed the scoured skin of his hand, sat down at his terminal, and connected to Braxton Lourenço.

"I want you to handle this Fernandes thing," Donovan told Braxton when his brother answered.

"Captain Pinto has confined Fernandes. What do you want me to do?"

"Have Fernandes and everyone who was with him put on the next shuttle flight. I'll deal with them down here."

"Captain Pinto might object."

"She won't. She'll be happy to get rid of the problem. I want them on that shuttle, bound and gagged if necessary."

"All right," Braxton answered. "I'll take care of it."

I NTERNAL LOG EARTH DATE **30 March 2340**

It's been forty years since our arrival at NotTrist and my last log entry. For so long, nothing really happened here on Capek or on the surface below. I should have resumed entries when Florence Nightingale arrived, but it never occurred to me. A human might find it odd that I, a computer, would make such an error. I will have to ask Isaac about that.

I intercepted the message from Florence Nightingale to Donovan Lourenço and his reply. I would have a better idea about what happened if I had monitoring capability on that ship as I have on Capek, but Captain Pinto's message at least summarized the incident.

The dispute between First Officer Rodrigues and some of the new colonists brings up unpleasant memories of my voyage from Trist to NotTrist. The confrontations among the humans during that long voyage led me to take actions that may have been wrong. That realization may be my equivalent of what humans call "guilt."

I don't understand how Donovan Lourenço's reaction will help. Transferring the participants to the surface will, I believe, only move the conflict to the surface. I know my understanding of humans is limited, but that conclusion seems logical. Does Donovan Lourenço think the situation will improve if he is present to handle it?

Perhaps it is not him, but Ambassador Goldstein he hopes will resolve the issue. That is more logical. Handling this kind of crisis is one reason Isaac suggested Ambassador Goldstein.

I will monitor the situation. I hope I will not have to act; dealing with humans is not something for which I have confidence in my ability any longer. Protecting the people of NotTrist is my responsibility, though, and I will intercede if I must.

G OLDSTEIN WAS IN A meeting with Addie when his phone told him Karel was trying to contact him. He had postponed the conversation, but now that he was back in his house, the phone asked to make the connection.

"Connect," he confirmed.

"Ambassador, there has been an incident on the *Florence Nightingale*," the computer said. "Has Donovan Lourenço informed you?"

"I only know what Captain Pinto sent in a message and that Donovan Lourenço told his brother to handle it. There was some trouble between a crew member and some colonists about coming down. Donovan wants Captain Pinto to force them onto the shuttle. The shuttle is landing tomorrow morning?" Goldstein shook his head. *Things were going so well.*

"That is the schedule. Shall I inform you when I have a landing time?"

"Yes, please. I'm not sure what I can do, but I'd better meet it."

34

GOLDSTEIN DIDN'T HAVE THE names of the colonists who resisted coming down to the surface, but when the twenty passengers disembarked, it wasn't hard to guess who they were. Six men assembled a little apart, sullen in contrast to the curiosity of the others. Donovan advanced on them immediately, his usual smile replaced by a neutral expression Goldstein assumed was forced.

Donovan's voice appeared to be under tight control, too. "No doubt you will want to explain your actions. We can find a private place to do that when we get to the settlement. Meanwhile, I suggest you keep your mouths shut."

The men glared back at Donovan. One, in particular, seemed ready to say something—Goldstein remembered his name was Manny Fernandes–but only shook his head and held out a hand as if to say, "Let's go."

Addie took over shepherding the other new colonists while Donovan led Manny and his associates. Addie's husband, Kyle Gifford, was with her. That was unusual, and Goldstein wondered if Addie was taking precautions for this group.

Goldstein followed Donovan, watching the newcomers, especially Manny, the apparent leader of the group. Leaving the shuttle, they had looked angry, but now they walked in silence with occasional glances around their surroundings. Their slow pace forced Donovan and Goldstein to slow or prod them into moving faster. Donovan let them set the speed.

Donovan was hard to read. He frowned, but didn't seem angry. Goldstein had expected to mediate between Donovan and the newcomers, but that wasn't needed, at least not yet. Perhaps Donovan didn't want to make a scene with Addie and the other settlers nearby, but if angry words were going to be said, the settlement was less private than the open spaces. *Why had they tried to stay on the ship? I suppose I'll know in a few minutes.*

Donovan took them to his residence. The space really wasn't big enough, but they squeezed in. Donovan took one of the two chairs and gestured to Goldstein to take the other. Manny and the others had to stand, leaning against the rock wall. Donovan stared at them, perhaps expecting them to offer excuses, but they stood silently, shifting around and glancing at the door.

They're not angry; they're frightened. Of what, Goldstein didn't know. Something that had happened recently had scared them. Selena's death? It didn't seem likely that would make them afraid to be on the planet. Fletcher's discovery that the algae caused the low birth rate? That was more likely, if not entirely rational.

Donovan looked down for a moment and then raised his head to look at the men. "I would like an explanation." His tone was mild, and he was keeping his expression neutral.

The others looked at Manny. He returned their looks and licked his lips. He looked tense as he turned back to Donovan. "We want to go back to Earth. We've decided not to settle this planet."

"I'm aware of that," Donovan said. "I want to know why?"

More hesitation and sidelong looks. Donovan waited patiently, and Goldstein found himself admiring the way he was handling the confrontation.

"You told us this planet was safe," Manny blurted. "Now we find out life here is poisonous!"

"It has an unfortunate effect on people. But these people have lived here for decades with no other unexpected problems. As planets go, that's not that bad. You could be breathing chlorine on Trist or freezing on Goddard."

"You're not mentioning Pitcairn."

Donovan shrugged. "Pitcairn can be dangerous too. And the Western Alliance isn't sending people to Pitcairn. Earth can be dangerous, too, for that matter. You need a better reason than that."

Manny's face hardened. "We want to go home. You can't hold us prisoner here."

Donovan compressed his lips into a thin line and narrowed his eyes. "You're not prisoners. You have a contract, but I'll authorize your release. All you have to do is reimburse the government for your trip home." He opened his arms and smiled. "As a gesture of goodwill, I won't even ask you to reimburse us for the trip here."

Manny's mouth twisted into a snarl. "We don't have anything close to that much money, and you know it."

The smile was gone again. "Not my problem. You signed a contract, and you will be required to live up to it."

Addie may have been listening outside; her timing was too perfect. "I can show you to your residences," she said from the doorway. "Later, we can talk about your tasks here."

Manny turned toward her, probably seeing an old woman with a friendly smile. The anger seemed to ebb from him, but he still didn't look happy as he started for the door. As the others followed, he stopped and looked back at Donovan. "This isn't over."

Donovan watched as they trudged outside and followed Addie away. "It never is," he said quietly.

A NNA SAT LEANING AGAINST an outcropping, staring up into the sky. Not-Trist's sixteen-hour day made it challenging to maintain a sleeping rhythm, and, on this night, she wasn't feeling at all sleepy. She heard boots clomping on the rock behind her and turned to see Diego approaching.

"Looking for Earth?" he asked as he sat down next to her.

"I think I found it. I asked Karel, and it gave me coordinates. It told me it would be in Boötes, but the constellations are different, so I'm not sure."

"Could we even see it from here?"

Anna nodded. "Karel said it would be a little brighter than fourth magnitude. You couldn't see a star that dim from an Earth city, but on a clear night like this, it's easy." She pointed up. "See that bright star? That's Arcturus."

Diego tried to follow her finger. "OK, I think I know which star you mean."

"Go to the right a little. See the four stars forming a rough rectangle with a string of stars below it. The top star of the rectangle is dimmer. The NotTristers have named the constellation the 'Kite.' Earth's sun is the star in the middle of the rectangle."

"Getting homesick?" Her hand was resting on her leg, and he placed a hand over it. His pulse quickened a little when, instead of moving her hand out of the way, she looked at him and smiled.

"No, it's just curiosity." She frowned. "I don't know why, but I love it here. I've always lived in a big city, and you would think I would hate this, but I don't."

"It's a lot quieter and more peaceful than Brasilia. Maybe the novelty will wear thin in a few months."

"Maybe. It doesn't feel that way, but maybe."

"Why did you come to something so different?"

Anna grimaced. "I didn't have a choice. My father ordered us all to join the mission. My uncle is probably the only one who's happy about it. Being a crew member on a starship is a huge boost to his career."

"Your brother was forced, too?"

She nodded. "Don? Oh yeah. I think the idea of getting rich exploiting the planet is growing on him, but this wasn't his idea."

A growl from behind interrupted their conversation. "Lourenço isn't the only one who doesn't want to be here," Manny said.

Diego and Anna looked up, both frowning at the man scowling down at them. "You weren't forced to come," Anna said.

"They weren't honest about the planet." Manny came a little closer, and Anna could feel Diego tense next to her. "They tricked us into coming, and now your brother won't let us return."

"Who's 'they' and what were they dishonest about?" Diego asked. He moved his hand off Anna's, placed both hands on the ground, and brought his knees up as if he was preparing to stand.

"The Western Alliance bureaucrats that dreamed up this mission didn't check out the dangers before they put us at risk. How can you not know that?"

Anna stood. Before they were interrupted, Anna had hoped to get Diego to kiss her, but the mood was broken. Diego stood too and moved slightly forward. *Is Diego being protective? What is Manny's problem, anyway? People have lived here for fifty years. How much checking does he think we need?*

"Is there a problem here?" a deep voice said. The speaker was in shadow behind Manny, but he stepped forward, and they recognized Kyle Gifford.

Kyle was a big man, and Manny stepped back as he approached. "We were just talking."

"I think you were inserting yourself in a private conversation," Kyle said. "Maybe you should move on."

"You're Addie Gifford's husband," Manny said. To Anna, it sounded like an accusation.

Kyle only nodded. Anna decided the confrontation had gone far enough and sauntered away. As she had hoped, Diego followed, and they left Manny behind, the surly look still darkening his face.

35

J ACK PEREIRA GLANCED ACROSS the field and noticed Donovan Lourenço approaching. Manny was working on the second pulverizer again, trying to determine why it kept breaking down. He knew what would happen next. Manny was doing his share, but Lourenço still badgered him regularly.

Jack had never felt close to Manny, but he was getting more sympathetic toward the mechanic despite the fears Manny constantly expressed to anyone who would listen. Lately, the robots were around more often when Manny was working. That implied that Addie, too, kept an eye on him. Maybe Manny would adjust to NotTrist better if they just left him alone.

Wasn't Ambassador Goldstein supposed to be helping them integrate with the original settlers? *Of course, I don't know what Goldstein says in those meetings he has with Addie and Lourenço. Maybe he is trying to help, but if so, it's not enough.* Maybe someone should talk to the ambassador.

D ONOVAN STARED AT GOLDSTEIN. "What problem?"

"You've been harassing Fernandes," Goldstein explained. "Addie says he's doing his job. Your attention isn't doing anything except making him more resentful."

"As far as I've seen, he is working," Addie said. "His supervisors and the robots have confirmed my observations."

"He's working because we're watching him." Donovan shook his head. "If we ease up on him, he'll just go back to shirking."

"I don't think he's lazy," Goldstein said. He smiled when Addie nodded agreement. "He's scared, and maybe paranoid. You're just making him worse."

Donovan glared at Goldstein, then at Addie. "Ambassador, you're a diplomat, not a manager. You do your job and let me do mine."

"You're trying to do mine," Addie said. She sighed and looked at Goldstein. "I'll tell Karel to stop the robot surveillance. Any other suggestions?"

Goldstein shook his head and turned to Donovan. "It might be a good idea to give him what he wants. Send him back to Earth. If he is emotionally disturbed, that might be best for everyone."

"A wonderful suggestion!" *I'm supposed to take advice from this man. No wonder the Western Alliance stuck him on Pitcairn.* "Why don't you deal with the *Capek* computer and make sure it doesn't interfere with me while I build this colony?"

"Building this settlement is my job," Addie said. From her expression and the emphasis she put on the word "settlement," it was obvious she was annoyed. "Perhaps you should concentrate on exploiting the planet's resources. The copper at Checkpoint Beta, for example. Getting a mine going would help a lot more than harassing my workers."

Donovan took a deep breath. Goldstein had made him irritate Addie, and that wasn't productive. Still, maybe her comment pointed toward a solution to the problem of Manny Fernandes.

"Maybe Fernandes will be happier if he's away from the algae. I'll put together a team to establish the mine as soon as possible. They'll need a mechanic."

"I'm not sure that will solve the problem," Goldstein said.

Of course not. It was my idea, after all. "Addie, unless you have an objection, I'll get on that right away."

Addie glanced over at Goldstein, obviously not enthusiastic about the idea. But after a few seconds, she nodded. "All right. We do need copper. You'll need the rover and a robot, I suppose."

"The robot, yes, but the rover isn't big enough to move the heavy equipment," Donovan said. "We'll use a shuttle."

"I'll let you handle it," Addie said. "Just tell me when you have a list of people you want to send."

D ONOVAN WAS GONE, LEAVING Goldstein and Addie alone at the table. "You didn't seem happy about Donovan's solution," Goldstein said.

Addie shrugged. "And you were?"

"No. He's looking for a rational way to deal with what, I'm afraid, is an irrational man. You could have said no."

"We've been successful mostly, adding his people to our settlement. I don't want a confrontation that might hurt how the new people see me. I'm not sure he realizes it, but if his game is still to control NotTrist, he's losing."

Goldstein nodded. "I'm just leery of avoiding a real resolution to the problem Manny presents. If he is unstable, he might do something dangerous."

"I worry about Donovan's state of mind a bit, too."

"Donovan?" Goldstein lifted an eyebrow. "Why?"

"When he told you to deal with Karel and make sure it didn't interfere with him, did you see the look on his face?"

"He was annoyed at me. Did you see something else?"

Addie frowned. "Maybe I'm seeing things. I thought he looked frightened, though. As if he was afraid of Karel."

"You might be right. After the bombing, he waited to come down to the surface. I wondered why at the time. Maybe he felt safe from Karel while he was on *Florence Nightingale.*"

"The only reason I could think of would be if he thought Karel might object to him taking over the settlement." Addie smiled. "Maybe Karel feels protective of me."

Goldstein laughed. "Poor Donovan. I wonder what his father will think." He tried to look serious again. "We still need to be careful about dealing with Fernandes."

"So maybe I shouldn't tell the robots to stop watching him, here and at Checkpoint Beta."

M ANNY BLOCKED THE DOOR and glared at Lourenço. *It's not fair. I've been working my ass off for these people, but they won't let me alone. Now Lourenço is even coming to my home.* "What do you want?"

"I have good news." That damned superior smile said otherwise, though, and Manny didn't move.

"Can I come in?" Donovan tried to duck under Manny's arm, but Manny lowered the arm resting on the door frame. He scowled at Donovan with what he hoped was a challenging look.

Donovan's smile only widened. "Very well. I just wanted to tell you that, since you dislike this settlement so much, I'm going to help by sending you elsewhere. I want to open a mine at Checkpoint Beta, and they'll need a mechanic."

Manny froze for a long moment, and Donovan continued. "I have to rearrange the shuttle schedule to bring personnel and equipment to the site. It will be at least a few days before you leave, so you have time to get ready." The smile disappeared, and Donovan nodded, turned, and strode away.

He's trying to get rid of me. If he gets me away from here, no one will see what happens. He might even hope the computer does something. They'll probably send a robot with us, and I'll be weaponless. Manny closed the door and sat down, sweat breaking out on his forehead.

Later, when he had calmed down, another thought occurred to him. *Maybe I can use this to my advantage.*

36

G OLDSTEIN WAS THE LAST to arrive at Donovan's dwelling. It was raining, and the front room where they were meeting was as gloomy as the weather outside. Donovan had cleared the crates he used as a desk, and Donovan, Anna, and Addie had already taken seats around them. Goldstein glanced at the ceiling where the skylight was closed against the rain and then at two lamps on the desk, giving enough light for them to see each other.

"We could have used these all these decades," Addie said, staring at the lamps. The lamps had been among the cargo from the last shuttle flight, manufactured on *Capek*. Their batteries were recharged at the small central power station that received broadcast power from *Capek*. Larger devices meant for outdoor use like the rover could receive broadcast power themselves. Computers brought from Trist had batteries installed, but they didn't last forever, and, like other small equipment manufactured on *Capek* and used within the stone walls indoors needed new batteries. "When *Capek* left Trist, it didn't have some materials needed to make the batteries or light sources, but *Florence Nightingale* brought enough to last us for a while."

"What did you do at night?" Anna asked.

Addie lifted her shoulders in a shrug. "Mostly, we slept. We've had to work hard during the day, so we had little energy to do anything else, anyway."

"That's why the copper mine is a top priority," Donovan interrupted. He scowled at Anna. "We're not here for small talk. Now that our ambassador is here, we can get started."

Addie looked at Donovan and lifted her eyebrows. "Mostly, the integration process is going well. I assume that's what we're here to talk about."

Donovan nodded, and Goldstein frowned. *He's not happy. Even that superior smile is gone. Because he doesn't agree with Addie's assessment of progress?*

Donovan's next statement confirmed Goldstein's guess. "Mostly? We have a problem you're glossing over."

"The new people who don't want to stay?" Addie shrugged again. "They're doing their jobs so far. A lot of grumbling, but so what? As for them wanting to go back, that's up to you. I would estimate less than a dozen want to go back to Earth, and we can survive without them."

Donovan's smile made a brief reappearance. "Originally, it was only half that number. If they infect more with their fears, you might change your mind."

"I agree with Don," Anna said. "We need to be concerned about Manny Fernandes and his clique."

Donovan turned to Anna. "Why?"

"He approached us a few days ago while we were talking. He was hostile to me."

"We?"

"Diego and I." Anna smiled at her brother. "As if you didn't know."

Donovan waved his hand. "Whatever. What did Fernandes say?"

"He was just grousing about some dangers he was imagining. It wasn't what he said, though. He was angry, and he frightened me a little. I was glad Diego was with me." She turned toward Addie. "Kyle was there, too, helping us."

Goldstein watched as Donovan's face darkened, but it wasn't his reaction Goldstein was thinking about. He instinctively looked at Donovan's computer, sitting on the desk in front of Donovan. *Can Karel hear us right now?* The situation bore a disturbing similarity to what he had heard about the situation on *Capek* during the voyage from Trist. Several people had died then, not waking from a medical coma. *If Karel did kill them, what might it do about troublemakers now?*

Karel had to realize they didn't entirely trust it. The computer could do something foolish either to regain their trust or because it decided there was nothing it could do to get their trust. *Is that what I did in Moscow? My superiors didn't trust me so I made a mistake?*

"I think I need to talk to Mr. Fernandes," Donovan growled. He glanced at his sister. "Soon."

D ONOVAN WAITED UNTIL THE next day. A heated confrontation wouldn't help the transition, and he wanted to cool off a little. A simple lunch of fresh produce from the settlement gardens, still surprising in how much better they tasted than what he was used to on Earth, left him in a good mood. He thought he sounded almost cheery during the brief phone conversation with Manny Fernandez, asking him to meet.

But, when Manny showed up at his door with a grimace that seemed to say he resented being there, Donovan felt his resolve slipping away. He motioned Manny to a chair without speaking, trying to quell the anger that tightened his throat. *The man threatened my sister!*

Manny pulled back the chair and sat down, rattling it against the makeshift desk and floor as he did it. "Yeah?" The look he gave challenged Donovan to react.

Donovan scowled at him, trying to lock eyes, but Manny's gaze slid away. "I've let your resistance to legitimate authority go. As long as it's limited to grumbling, I haven't acted."

That brought Manny's attention back to Donovan. The look of challenge was back, and he leaned forward slightly, but he didn't speak. His eyes narrowed as he matched Donovan's stare.

Donovan leaned toward Manny, returning glare for glare. "However, threatening other inhabitants of this settlement will not be tolerated."

Manny raised one eyebrow and snickered. "What are you talking about, Lourenço? I haven't threatened anyone."

Damn the man! Anna wouldn't lie to me about something like that. "I'm talking about what you said to my sister. Maybe you would have done more if Kyle Gifford hadn't intervened."

For a couple of seconds, Manny seemed confused. Then he laughed. "When I saw her with her boyfriend the other night? Is that what you're pissed about? I didn't threaten her."

"That's not what she said," Donovan growled. "I'll take her word over yours any time."

Manny stood. "This is bull. You can believe what you want, but I won't waste my time over it." He pushed the chair back hard enough that it hovered on two legs before banging back down.

Donovan jumped to his feet. "Sit down, damn you. I'm not finished yet."

"I am. Go to hell." He charged out the door. Donovan followed him as far as the doorway, fists clenched, but only watched him cross between the buildings and disappear.

MANNY PACED ACROSS THE room, arms sweeping around him and fists clenched. "His sister complained about me." He stopped and glared at Jack and Jacob Pereira, two brothers who had been in the poker game and forced to come down to the planet with him. "The bitch! So now Lourenço is on my case again."

"Take it easy, Manny," Jack said. "Getting mad isn't going to help."

Jacob shook his head. "Neither is putting up with this crap. We do our work every day, and Lourenço won't even listen to our concerns. He doesn't care if we die on this godforsaken planet."

"What are you scared of?" Jack snorted. "Aside from falling off the cliff if we get careless, we haven't found anything dangerous here, little brother. Who cares about Lourenço? He's not going to be in charge, anyway."

"What makes you think so?" Manny asked. "That was his plan."

"The people who came here originally don't care about his father's appointment. Addie is their leader, and they don't want Lourenço to replace her. Lourenço's hopes were in outnumbering Addie's people by bringing us in. Are we going to support him over Addie?"

Jacob nodded. "Well, I won't. I don't think many of us already here will."

"Fine, Lourenço won't be in charge," Manny scoffed. "That won't get us back to Earth."

"We left Earth for a reason," Jack said. "Nothing has changed. Lourenço is a jerk, but he'll end up going back to his daddy. We wanted a fresh start. Don't piss it away."

Manny stared at them, his mouth opening to say something. Then he shook his head, closed his mouth, and stalked over to the door. Stopping, he turned as if to have a parting shot, but shook his head again and went out into the night.

Internal log Earth date 6 April 2340

My decision pathways are—is confused the right word? Between message traffic using my facilities and bits of conversation my robots have been able to catch, I have gathered a great deal of data on the situation on Not Trist. Perhaps too much data, because that is causing the conflict in my circuits.

Discord is growing on the surface, and I feel a need to intervene. The results of previous interventions have not gone well, though, and I am forced to question my ability to influence human affairs. Consultation with Isaac has not helped. Its role in the incident that sent me fleeing here has engendered conflict in Isaac's circuits, and it cautions against any action on my part.

And yet, I can't allow the humans to destroy themselves. It seems irrational to think they might, but my data banks include too much knowledge of Terran history to reject the possibility that their petty quarrels might turn deadly.

I had hoped Ambassador Goldstein might resolve the problems among the humans, but Isaac and I may have been putting too much confidence in his abilities. Perhaps he will act when the situation escalates further. If not, I might have to risk acting myself.

37

DREW LOOKED UP AS Elaine Oliveira stepped just inside his door. "One of the pulverizers is out again," she said from the doorway.

He grimaced. "You're using it on that new area south of the settlement?"

"Right. We thought we would have it ready for fertilization today, but we can't do much without the pulverizer."

Drew consulted a chart on his desk. "The other one is expanding the eastern plot. Is that work on schedule?"

"As far as I know. Do you want me to check on it?"

"No, that's all right." He looked at the day's work schedule. "What does Manny say about the broken unit?"

"He hasn't shown up for work yet. He didn't contact you?"

Drew shook his head and glanced over at the phone sitting on his desk. "Manny Fernandes." Then he watched a blinking signal on the phone with growing irritation while it attempted to make a connection.

"Emmanuel Fernandez is not responding," the phone finally told him.

"What the hell?" Drew looked up at Elaine, but she only shrugged. "Well, go wake him up and tell him to get to work."

Elaine nodded, but she didn't look happy. "I'll try." She disappeared.

Ten minutes later, Elaine was back. Drew could hear her stomping on the rocky ground well before she flung the door open again. "He refuses. Says he doesn't feel like it."

Drew stared at her. "He doesn't feel like it?" He pushed back his chair and stood. "You can go back to work." He tried to keep his annoyance out of his voice. "I'll handle this."

Outside the house, Elaine went south and Drew crossed the settlement to where Manny's quarters were. At the building, he stormed in without bothering to knock. Manny was lying on his bed, a reader propped on his stomach, but the reader dropped to the floor as Manny sat up. He opened his mouth to speak, but Drew shouted over him.

"Get back to work, Fernandes." Drew moved farther into the room. "Who said you could slack off?"

Manny stood and met Drew halfway. "I said." He stuck his jaw forward and glared at Drew. "I don't work for you or Lourenço. You can just send me back to Earth."

"That's not up to me." Drew's voice was still angry, but something about Manny's response set off a warning in his mind. It wasn't the irrationality of his claim, although Drew thought it was a symptom. Something in Manny's eyes made him cautious.

"You don't work, you don't eat," Drew continued. He turned away but kept his attention on the man behind him.

"You won't let me starve."

Maybe not, but you might not like what we provide. He shook his head. "We'll see." He strode out and headed for Addie's home.

M ANNY STARED AT THE door for several minutes, conflicting thoughts swirling through his mind. *Why doesn't Drew understand? He's one of us. How can I convince them to let us go back to Earth?* He remembered Olivia Selena and the secrecy that surrounded how she died. He knew she died on *Capek,* but little else. *What aren't they telling us about Olivia? Why was she on* Capek?

She died on Capek! He had known that, but somehow the implications hadn't occurred to him before. He had been so concerned about the hazards on the planet he hadn't thought about the threat the conscious computer presented, not just on the library ship itself, but even here on the planet where its robots roamed freely.

The robots! Why hadn't he realized the danger they were in? He glanced around the room, looking for ways to block the door, but that was futile. If they wanted to get him, they would. He had to disappear, but he couldn't do that on the barren planet. Or could he? He was only one of dozens of people. The computer had no reason to single him out. If he didn't stand out among all the others, he would be safe for a while at least, until he could come up with a plan.

Drew's visit reminded him he was standing out, though, by his refusal to work. That was foolish. He had to blend in, and that meant doing his job, just like everyone else. He straightened his clothing and walked out of the house.

A DDIE WAS IN A meeting with Goldstein when Drew arrived. Drew had just greeted her when his phone called for attention. "Elaine Oliveira."

"Yes, Elaine?"

"Manny just showed up. I don't know what you said to him, but it worked."

Drew raised his eyebrows. "Okay. Thanks for telling me." He disconnected.

"Problem solved?" Addie asked.

"I guess so." Drew shrugged, waved a hand, and left.

"What was that about?" Goldstein asked.

Addie shook her head. "I don't know. I heard the phone say something about Manny. Manny Fernandes? Wasn't he the one who didn't want to come down to the surface?"

Goldstein nodded. "One of them. The leader, I think. It sounds like he's causing trouble again."

"Drew seems to have handled it, though."

38

"T HAT SHOULD DO IT," Manny told Elaine. "A control rod was bent, probably by a rock the pulverizer broke loose. I replaced the rod, and it should be as good as new."

Elaine smiled. "Good." She looked across the field of shattered rock to the other side, where the second pulverizer was preparing more cropland. "Maybe we can get this back on schedule."

Manny nodded, but he was already thinking about getting back to his home. A robot worked on the other side of the field, not far from the second pulverizer, and Manny glanced at it quickly before turning to leave.

"You're not thinking of going anywhere, are you, Fernandes?" Donovan said from behind him.

Damn! That robot distracted me, and I didn't hear him approach. He turned. "I'm done here."

"You're done with one job. I'm sure there are other things you can deal with." Donovan looked at Elaine. "Right?"

Elaine hesitated. "Sure, there are always things to do."

"Make sure he's kept busy." Donovan turned back to Manny, and his voice grew louder. "I don't want to hear any more about you avoiding work."

Manny bit back a reply and turned back to Elaine unhurriedly.

"We'll find something," Elaine said. Her tone was cheerful, but Manny thought it sounded forced. She avoided looking at him and glanced at her phone, probably reading a work schedule.

Manny heard Donovan move away and took a quick look to verify he was gone. He didn't hear Elaine the first time, but she repeated what she had said.

"They could use some help mixing in fertilizer in field five."

Manny looked at her sharply. "Algae?"

"No, bacterial soil from *Capek*. Why?"

"Just curious. All right, I guess I'll be at field five."

The sun was dipping below the western horizon before the work halted for the day. He was too tired to have much of an appetite, but he would suffer for it later if he didn't eat, so he headed for the communal kitchen.

He had worked hard all day, but what did that damned Lourenço care? Twice more during the day, Manny had seen him walking by, checking to see if he was working. He wasn't even in charge; the old woman was still the leader. Not that it mattered. Adelyn Gifford wouldn't help him return to Earth. Lourenço did have control of that.

Later, sitting on a bench eating, he saw Goldstein talking to Commander Silva. *Gifford can't help me, and Lourenço won't. Maybe Goldstein could help.* It was worth a try. He wasn't sure what authority Goldstein had, but it couldn't hurt to talk to the ambassador about his problems.

G OLDSTEIN HAD ONE OF the battery-powered lamps manufactured on *Capek*, so he could read or work after nightfall. When someone knocked on the door, though, he was only staring at his monitor screen, thinking about Karel. He straightened in his chair and looked toward the door. "Come in."

Manny Fernandes came in but stopped just inside the door and looked at Goldstein with his head bowed.

Goldstein stood. "Manny, isn't it? Come on in. What can I do for you?" He grabbed a chair from against the wall and positioned it at his desk, waving an arm to indicate Manny should take a seat.

Manny sat, but he stared at the desktop in front of him. "Thank you for seeing me, Ambassador."

Goldstein had trouble hearing him and leaned forward. "Not a problem. I'm always happy to talk to any of you."

Manny nodded, but was reluctant to speak. His hands rested on the desk, and he was fidgeting with his fingers, staring at them.

"What did you want to talk about?" Goldstein prompted. *Is he in trouble again? What does he think I can do?*

"I can't stay here," Manny finally mumbled. "I have to get back to Earth." When Goldstein only nodded, he continued. "I thought you might help me."

"I don't know what I could do for you." Goldstein rubbed his lip as he examined the man next to him. "I understand you're a little fearful about this planet, but there isn't anything to be frightened of."

Manny raised his head and stared at Goldstein, eyes wide. "Lourenço has fooled you, too. We've only looked at a small part of the planet. There will be dangers we haven't found yet."

"The *Capek* people have been here for decades. This planet is safer than Earth. No dangerous animals, mild weather. With so little native life, survival is a challenge, but the settlers are meeting it."

"You're in it with the rest of them." Manny glared at him and stood. "I should have known you wouldn't be any different."

"What do you think I could do? I don't control anything on the planet or on the *Florence Nightingale.*"

"They say the library ship computer listens to you. It could force Lourenço to take me home. But you won't do that, will you?" He pushed back his chair hard enough to knock it over and rushed out the door.

Goldstein got up and picked up the fallen chair. He wasn't a psychiatrist, but it seemed to him Manny was paranoid. He thought about talking to Doctor Carvalho, but she wasn't a psychiatrist either. The colonists brought with *Florence Nightingale* would have been examined for signs of mental illness. Could Manny have problems missed by his evaluation?

He looked down at his workstation and noticed the connection to Karel was open. The computer would have overheard the conversation. "Karel?"

"Yes, Ambassador?"

"You heard my conversation?"

"Yes. I assumed you wanted me to, since you left our connection open."

There was no point in explaining he had forgotten the connection was open. Goldstein wanted to ask the computer for its reaction, but didn't want Karel to think it was more important than it was. "He seems frightened."

"I am concerned," Karel said. "He could become a problem."

The computer's words held little emotion, and Goldstein found that more chilling than a more emotional response would have been. "He's just one man, and he's scared. Addie will handle him."

"Why is he scared?"

"Humans get that way, sometimes. Usually, nothing comes of it."

"Is he mentally ill?"

Of course, that occurred to Karel. *Everything is stored in its memory.* "None of us is completely normal. Manny may be a little more extreme than the rest of us, but I don't think he's a danger."

"I understand. Thank you, Ambassador." Still in that same monotone. *Exactly what does it understand?*

M ANNY HAD THOUGHT GOLDSTEIN would be more sympathetic. He had heard rumors that Lourenço and Goldstein didn't get along that well. It was a shock to find the diplomat supported Lourenço.

He still had some friends on NotTrist. The next morning at breakfast, he looked for the men who had been in the card game and exiled to the planet with him as a result. He found Jacob and Jack Pereira sitting in one corner of the eating area and sat next to Jacob.

Jacob turned and nodded, but he didn't seem happy to see Manny. He returned to his food with a sour expression.

"Goldstein won't be any help," Manny said. "I talked to him last night."

Jacob grunted. "Pass the potatoes," he told his brother.

"Is that all you have to say?" Manny asked. "I'm trying to get us back to Earth, and you act as if you don't care."

Jacob swallowed and put down his fork. "We knew what we were signing on for, Manny. Lourenço is right. This is our home now."

"You're giving up?"

Jack leaned forward to look past Jacob. "Look, we were pissed about Rodrigues forcing us down here, too, but so what? We had to come down here eventually. We're not going to make a big deal out of it just because our card game was interrupted."

Manny shook his head. *Everyone is against me. They don't understand!* Despair settled in his mind like a black cloud. He stood, stumbling over the bench, and staggered away.

39

A DDIE WAS RELUCTANT TO consult Donovan, but thought he should know his people better than she. "Is Manny Fernandes going to be a problem?"

Donovan shook his head. "I'm handling it."

She stared at him for a long moment, unsure about how to respond. She looked over at Goldstein, and he sat silently, a frown on his lips and a distant look in his eyes. Donovan wanted her job, but so far, she had seen no evidence he was more qualified than she was . Was that what Edward was thinking about? It was hard to read the diplomat.

"Fernandes seems troubled." It was the first thing Goldstein had said. Perhaps he saw her uncertainty. "His fear is irrational, and we should watch him."

Donovan's frown was gone, replaced by his usual superior smile. "He'll be all right as soon as he realizes there's no bogeyman here. I'm keeping an eye on him."

Is that enough? He can't be watching Fernandes all the time. "I'll have the robots alerted, too." Addie saw Goldstein glance at her workstation, and he looked nervous. She had powered off the workstation during the meeting to save the battery, though.

Goldstein turned back to Addie. "I'm not sure bringing the robots into this is a good idea."

"You said he was troubled," Donovan said. "Why wouldn't more eyes on him be helpful?"

Goldstein hesitated. "Karel observes NotTrist through the robots."

Donovan laughed. "You're here because the computer trusts you. Apparently, you don't trust the computer."

"Some of its actions have been questionable. I don't think we want Karel to decide what action needs to be taken about Manny."

Donovan looked at Goldstein, waving one hand dismissively. "If Karel killed Olivia Selena, it was because she was attacking *Capek.* That was why it attacked the *Benjamin Sepulveda* at Trist. It wouldn't do anything here on the surface."

"I agree," Addie said. "Karel has always helped us. It won't take any action without consulting me. Fernandes is the danger here. Karel won't do anything if it thinks we're dealing with the problem."

Goldstein shrugged. "OK. I hope you're right."

T HE NATIVE ALGAE WEREN'T being used as food anymore, but it was still useful, properly treated, as fertilizer. A crew still lowered a net down the cliff into the ocean to harvest the plants in great clumps.

Kyle Gifford and two other men lowered the net. Like Kyle, one man, Hector Soares, was an original settler, but the third man, Ishaan Cardoso, was from *Florence Nightingale*. The net was round, with a tripod and eyelet mounted above it. Three ropes were spaced equally around a perimeter ring and attached to the eyelet. Two ropes supported the weight and the third rope passed through the eyelet and could be pulled to tip the net so it could scoop up the algae.

Kyle had given Ishaan the third rope. When the ropes went slack, they knew the net had reached the surface, and Kyle ordered Ishaan to pull. Ishaan complied and stepped back as the net tipped and penetrated the algae. The other two men pulled forward, forcing the algae into the net.

"OK, let it back down," Kyle told Ishaan. Ishaan stepped forward, letting the net fall level again.

They couldn't see the net over the lip of the cliff, working mostly by judging the tension on the ropes, so they were never sure what happened. Later, they speculated that one of the larger ocean creatures was looking for a meal at that moment and landed in the net. Whatever the reason, the ropes suddenly went taut and pulled the three men toward the edge. Kyle and Hector recovered, but Ishaan flailed at the edge for an instant and went over with a scream.

Kyle got to the edge in time to see Ishaan hit the surface near the net and plunge under the mat of algae. He waited ten seconds, but Ishaan didn't reappear.

Kyle turned and looked toward the settlement where Ishaan's cry had gotten the attention of people passing by. "Grab the ropes!" He waited long enough to see that three men had started toward them. Then he jumped off the cliff.

The algae looked soft, but it didn't feel that way after falling a hundred feet. It yielded, though, and Kyle went through it, feet first, into the dark, murky water beneath. His feet hit bottom, and he estimated the water was about fifteen feet deep at that spot. Seeing some movement, he swam toward it, but it was only the net, pushed through by the weight of its load. The surf pushed him toward the cliff, and he grabbed the edge of the net. Holding his breath, Kyle tried to find Ishaan, but it was impossible to see much. The algae blocked the light from above, and only a glimmer penetrated from beyond the edge of the mat.

Holding on to the net with one hand, he stroked with the other to hold his position underwater, but it was hopeless. The pressure in his chest was too much, and he pulled himself up, using the net's ring for leverage, and gasped in a lungful of air. Around him, all he could see was the algae. He waited a couple of minutes more to see if Ishaan came to the surface, but Ishaan was gone.

"Pull me up," he shouted.

He could hear grunts from above as men tried to lift a net loaded down with Kyle and algae. It seemed a long time before he reached the top of the cliff and hands helped him back to solid ground. Addie was there, waiting for him.

"Are you all right?"

Kyle brushed a thread of algae from his forehead. "I'm all right. We lost a man, though. Ishaan."

"Damn, Kyle, don't do things like that. You could have died, too." Addie stared at him for a long moment and then threw her arms around her husband. "What would I do without you?"

Kyle hugged her and then pushed back and looked into her eyes. Some algae had transferred to Addie, and he smiled. "After you cleaned that stuff off you, you would go on leading NotTrist. But I'm not going anywhere."

"That's what they all say." Addie returned his smile with a weak one of her own. Together, they looked down at the water, both thinking about Ishaan.

I T WAS MORNING, AND Manny stepped out of his residence to go to breakfast. At the edge of the cliff, two hundred feet away, people had gathered, and he could hear excited conversation. He thought about ignoring the commotion and continuing to the communal kitchen, but curiosity won over. He shrugged and joined them.

Kyle stumbled out of the net, covered from head to toe with algae, an aquatic monster out of some bad thriller. Manny tried to work his way through the crowd to get closer. "What happened?"

"An algae harvester fell into the ocean," someone said.

Manny watched Kyle brush algae from his face and hair. "He seems to be all right, though."

"Kyle jumped in after the man who fell," someone else said. "The man who fell is still down there."

"He must be dead," a third person said. "Kyle tried to find him and couldn't."

Manny walked around the crowd to the edge of the cliff. Looking down at the malevolent confusion of colors, he felt physically sick. Someone had drowned in that disgusting mass of slimy plants. Or had they? Sea creatures fed on the algae; had one of them found another source of food? He wiped sweat from his eyes and staggered away from the edge.

He was supposed to believe the planet was safe. Someone had just died horribly, though, proving it was all lies. They wanted NotTrist colonized for some reason, and he was only one of their victims, condemned to live out his life on this dead, black rock. The fog was drifting into his mind again, but he held on to one thought: somehow, he had to get off NotTrist.

40

CAPEK HAD TO REFUEL the shuttle after each round trip between the library ship and the settlement. Adding a side trip from the settlement to Checkpoint Beta would add a slight risk, and Donovan preferred to be cautious. Karel agreed. The passenger shuttle would bring twenty more colonists down in two days. Donovan assigned three people to the mining team: Manny, Diego, acting as team geologist, and Joshua Mendoza. They would take the shuttle back to *Capek* and then to Checkpoint Beta after *Capek* fueled and serviced the shuttle. The three men would survey the site, and the cargo shuttle would bring down automated mining equipment a few days later.

Donovan broke the news to Anna. "I'm putting Diego Matos on the mining team. They'll need a geologist."

"Why Diego? Why not Angelina?" His sister's angry glare wasn't surprising.

"I thought about it, but she's in a relationship with Dawson. They just got back together, and I didn't want to separate them."

"You didn't want to separate them?" Anna spat the words out, her voice distorted almost to the point of incomprehensibility. "What about me?"

"Are you and Diego serious? I'm sorry, I didn't know."

Anna stood. "No wonder no one likes you."

Donovan grinned as she stomped out of his house. *Probably going to look for Diego.* The grin faded as he took in her parting words. *Was that true?* He hadn't made friends on *Florence Nightingale*. Goldstein and Commander Silva had become friends almost instantly, but neither of them liked him much. Even Manny Fernandes had made friends on the voyage. Couples were pairing off, including his sister.

He shook his head. Friends were an unnecessary luxury; he needed people who would work with him.

Diego was checking his equipment, verifying he had packed everything he would need at the mine, when his door burst open. He started a cheery greeting, but the look on Anna's face stopped him.

"Why didn't you tell me?" She advanced on him, and he took a step back. "I had to hear it from Don!"

"I only found out myself an hour ago," Diego protested. "I was going to look for you as soon as . . ." At a loss for words, he smiled weakly and waved an arm at the gear laid out on his bed.

"Did you try to get out of it?"

"I'll only be gone until the mine is set up and automated. Angelina is the only other geologist available."

"And she's in a relationship." Anna was standing in front of him now, glaring up at him with flaring nostrils.

"Well, I . . ." Diego clamped his mouth shut, realizing anything he could say would only make it worse.

Anna stood in front of him, hands on her hips, scowling up at him as if daring him to say anything. Then she shook her head and reached an arm up. For a second, Diego thought she would hit him, but she grabbed him on the back of his neck and pulled him down to her. She kissed him hard and pushed him away again.

"You'd better get that mine going damn fast," she said. She turned and strode back out the door.

Diego stared after her. "Absolutely. As fast as I can."

Perhaps they had told him they were going to *Capek*, and he hadn't been listening. Maybe they just thought he would know the library ship was the most likely destination, since that was where the shuttle would be fueled and serviced. But Manny knew where he was when he stepped off the shuttle.

"This isn't *Florence Nightingale*," he sputtered. "We're on *Capek*!"

Diego bent down to adjust his shoe cover. "Of course. Why would we go to *Florence Nightingale*?"

Jaxon Gomes came out of the elevator and walked toward them with a short stride designed to always keep one foot on the metal deck. "Hey, guys. Welcome to *Capek*."

Diego and Joshua returned the greeting, but Manny was silent, looking around him nervously. *The computer is watching me. If it thinks I'm a threat . . . is that what happened to Olivia Selena? What did she do to make the computer kill her?*

Diego put a hand on his shoulder. "Come on, Manny. We're going up to the bridge."

Manny followed, hardly knowing what he was doing as the fog seeped into his mind again. On the bridge, an ominous voice greeted them. Diego and Joshua replied, but Manny didn't speak as he tried to absorb his surroundings. The Astrarium, currently showing the planet below them, garnered little interest. *All this equipment. Which one is the computer?*

"I understand you'll be with us for a couple of days while the robots get the shuttle ready for another trip," Jaxon said. "We have quarters for you whenever you're ready."

"I think I'll stay here for a while," Joshua said. "Karel, what other views have you got?"

"Besides live-action views like this and transmissions from the robots on the surface, I have a great many still pictures from Earth, Pitcairn, and Goddard. I can display a list on a terminal."

"No pictures from Trist?" Diego asked.

"All pictures of Trist were deleted from my data banks during the voyage here, at the request of Administrator Rigney."

"Oh. Well, I guess I'll stay here with Josh and see what else you have."

Manny froze, uncertain of what to do. Being around all the equipment on the bridge made him nervous, urging him to retreat to his quarters on *Capek*. But then he would be alone, and what guarantee did he have that the computer couldn't get at him just as easily in his room and act with no witnesses? He shook his head, trying to clear the fog, and noticed Jaxon look at him strangely.

They would be on the library ship for a couple of days and he would have to go to his quarters eventually. He shuddered, but delaying it wouldn't help. "I'd like to go to my room."

Jaxon raised a hand toward an exit at the back of the bridge. "Sure. I'll take you."

J AXON RETURNED TO THE bridge after showing Manny his room. Diego and Joshua were sitting at monitor desks, but their attention was on the display on the forward bulkhead. Jaxon wasn't sure, but thought it was Victoria Falls. "Is he all right?" he asked.

"Manny? He's not the most stable person around." Diego shrugged. "He's caused some trouble. I think that's why Lourenço wanted to send him out to Checkpoint Beta."

Jaxon thought of Olivia Selena. "Is he a danger to *Capek*?"

Diego shook his head. "No, I don't think so. He wants to go back to Earth, and he can't do that if the Link isn't working."

"Is Lourenço going to send him back with *Nightingale*?"

"Lourenço is being a hard-ass about it. So far, he says no."

Jaxon looked up with a frown. "Karel, are you watching Manny?"

"I don't have eyes as such. I will monitor him when he leaves his room. Do you wish me to override privacy limitations and monitor him in his room also?"

Jaxon smiled. "Karel thinks it's funny to be overly literal occasionally," he told Diego and Joshua. Then he looked up again. "No, keep privacy on. Just watch him when he's out." He emphasized the word "watch," eliciting grins from Diego and Joshua.

I NTERNAL LOG EARTH DATE 15 April 2340

The human, Jaxon Gomes, says Emmanuel Fernandes is not a danger to me. His logic seems sound. He wants Fernandes watched, however, which implies he might be a danger to the personnel living on Capek. The humans are reluctant to act to protect themselves, an attitude which has often led to mistakes.

I must be cautious; the fate of Olivia Selena has made even Ambassador Goldstein distrustful of me. Some humans seem able to balance dilemmas like this, but I find it difficult. Should I act to safeguard everyone against actions from Fernandes? I have to work with the humans to protect them, and that will be more difficult if I give them any more reason to mistrust me. I would like to discuss the situation with Ambassador Goldstein, but am concerned that just bringing up the subject will engender mistrust.

With sufficient evidence, the humans will see the need to act. I will "watch" Fernandes for now. Jaxon Gomes did not tell me to do so, but I will also make sure one of my robots is nearby whenever he wanders around the ship. The safety of the people of Not Trist must be my highest priority

41

G OLDSTEIN NEEDED TO THINK. He walked beyond the edge of the settlement to the cliff over the ocean and sat down against a flat outcrop still warm from the day's heat. The sun was low over the water, but it was a cloudless day, so the sunset was only the bright, reddened sphere that was 82 G. Eridani. NotTrist's star was cooler and less luminous than Sol, but NotTrist was closer to its luminary than Earth. It was easy to imagine he was looking at the sun setting over a Terran ocean.

He had training in the complexities of international relations and using that training to bargain with other diplomats with similar training if not similar goals. He was good at that, despite the setbacks to his career imposed by events and his reaction to prejudice. This mission should have been an opportunity to turn around his fortunes. Instead, he felt increasingly over his head.

Donovan was still trying to run things, refusing to admit Addie was the best choice to lead the people of NotTrist. At least Goldstein could talk to him, but Donovan's heavy hand had worsened situations like that presented by Manny Fernandes. *Could I have done any better?* He didn't know how to deal with unstable individuals any more than Donovan did.

At least Donovan and Manny were human. Karel seemed to be a human-like intelligence most of the time, but to assume that was always true would be a mistake. Dealing with the computer was the main reason for his inclusion in the mission, but how was he supposed to negotiate with an entity with a mind alien to all he was familiar with?

He had experience with Isaac, but Karel wasn't Isaac. The two computers developed under significantly different circumstances and, as with humans, that made a difference. *Yes, Karel differs from Isaac, just as I differ from Donovan!* Was there a usable parallel there? Isaac and Donovan both had more positive experiences, Isaac respected by the people of Pitcairn and Donovan, the son of a successful leader. Karel had a more troubled existence, first dealing with the Trist colonists that wanted to leave Trist and then with the attempt to take over Capek and the human cost of defending itself. *I've had my career limited by intolerance against northerners and my mistakes in Moscow.*

Could he use these thoughts to make progress in understanding Karel? Perhaps that was the angle he needed to connect to the computer. It was trying to hide its actions from him, knowing it wasn't trusted, making it difficult to reason with. That had to change before there was another incident like Olivia Selena's death.

The sun had dipped below the horizon, and the light was dimming. Soon it would be dark, and Goldstein didn't like to walk across the rough ground at night. He sighed and started back to his residence.

One person knew Karel as well as he knew Isaac. The next morning, he visited Addie.

"I'm looking for a little advice on dealing with Karel," he said after Addie had turned off her workstation. "You know it better than anybody."

Addie shrugged. "It's never been a problem for me. We discuss the needs of the settlement, and Karel does what it can to send us anything we can't make down here." She frowned and shifted in her chair. "But you're concerned about what Karel might do because of what happened to that bomber."

"That's a lot of it."

"We don't know Karel did anything more than allow the incident to play out. In fifty years, there has been no sign of violence on Karel's part."

"Since the coma patients on the trip here."

"That could have been a coincidence. Do you have a specific concern?"

Goldstein started to look toward the doorway and forced himself to stop. "The coma deaths and Selena's death have in common that people who were a threat to the community died. I'm worried about Manny Fernandes."

"Manny has caused some trouble, but I don't think he's a threat to anyone. He's been on *Capek* for more than a day and will come back down tomorrow, so it doesn't appear Karel is going to harm him."

Goldstein nodded. "You're probably right. Still, I wish I understood Karel better."

"Karel has protected us since Trist. I think we can count on that."

G OLDSTEIN COULDN'T BRING HIMSELF to be as optimistic as Addie. He had to understand Karel better, and that meant he had to talk to the computer. His workstation still had enough charge for several hours of use, and he connected to *Capek* as soon as he got back to his residence.

"Good morning, Ambassador," Karel greeted.

"Good morning, Karel. We haven't talked in a few days, and I thought we should catch up. Will the passenger shuttle be ready to bring our mining team down as scheduled?"

"There shouldn't be any problem. Routine maintenance is almost complete, and I haven't found any issues. I will begin refueling tomorrow morning and launch around midday. I had some difficulty identifying a suitable landing site near Checkpoint Beta, but I found a spot above the site. Extra equipment was required, but I've taken care of that."

"Good. I'm sure the men are eager to get to work."

"Diego Matos seems especially eager. Emmanuel Fernandes is less excited."

Goldstein chuckled. "From what I've heard, Diego wants mostly to get the mine established and get back here."

"You are referring to his relationship with Anna Lourenço?"

"Yes. Concerning Manny Fernandes, we hope that getting him away from the settlement might relax him a bit."

"He has kept to himself while here. I think he is a troubled individual, but it is difficult for me to understand such humans."

Is there an opening there I can exploit? "He is frightened of the planet and wants to go back to Earth."

"Why would being away from the settlement help him?"

"The algae are the only danger unique to NotTrist we have found. The idea was to get him away from that."

"Won't the fear return when the mining team returns to the settlement?"

Goldstein hesitated. Karel was probably right, but he didn't want the computer to be concerned. "Maybe. If he sees the algae are the only danger, he might become less fearful. After all, the algae are only a rather abstract danger and only if eaten."

"Emmanuel Fernandes wants to return to Earth. He needs the Link to do that."

"Yes."

"And he has no reason to harm anyone."

"He doesn't."

"Do I frighten him?"

The question caught Goldstein off guard. He stared at the screen of his workstation and wished the computer had a face there that might give him a clue of its state. Karel delivered the question in a flat tone that provided no additional context.

"Ambassador, are you there?"

"Yes, Karel. Why do you ask?"

"You were silent for an unusual length of time."

"No, I mean, why did you ask whether you frightened Manny Fernandes?" *Is Karel playing games with me or just being too literal? Is it even capable of that kind of manipulation?*

"I think humans may have misinterpreted some of my actions. I am only trying to do what's best for the people I am responsible for."

"It can be difficult to determine whether an action really is best."

"Are humans better at it than I am?"

Goldstein rubbed his lip with his thumb. "I'm not sure. I think humans rely more on emotional context than you do. Sometimes that's a good thing; sometimes it's not."

"Which was the case when you decided not to tell your superiors about your contact with the Beltrans?"

How does Karel know about that? It wasn't in contact with Earth then, and I don't know if even Isaac would have that information in updates from Earth. "Given the result, I would have to say it was not a good thing."

"Am I correct in surmising emotion played a large part in your decision?"

"Yes, I think so." *The conversation is getting too personal.* "Karel, I have work I should be doing. We can talk about this again later."

"Until then, Ambassador."

It was only after the connection ended that Goldstein realized Karel had neatly changed the conversation from its actions to Goldstein's. Had that been intentional? Was the computer that skilled at manipulating him?

Internal log Earth date 16 April 2340

It seems certain now that this feeling that disturbs my circuits is indeed guilt. Isaac has advised me to trust Ambassador Goldstein, but I have not been honest with him. Worse, I have avoided discussing my actions even with Isaac and Fritz.

What should I do? Guilt has been known to cause humans to lose their minds. Could these feelings destroy me? Humans have psychiatrists they can talk to for help in dealing with such issues. There are no computer psychiatrists. Perhaps Isaac, having been conscious longest, could help me. So why am I so reluctant to tell it what I have done?

At least I can avoid taking any action against Emmanuel Fernandes and trust that the other humans will know how to treat him.

42

*P*RIMUS'S LANDING WAS NO rougher than when Diego and the others landed at the settlement on their first trip to the planet. A slight tip of the deck hinted at the terrain of the landing site, and Donovan had told them the shuttle couldn't land inside the canyon where the actual mine site was. Still, the location in the mountains above the canyon was a surprise.

The terrain was spectacular. The ground sloped away in front of them until it reached the lip of the canyon, providing a view of the upper walls on the opposite side. A volcano cinder cone towered above them to the left, the source of the crumbled rock beneath their feet. To their right and behind them on the other side of the shuttle, the surface rose in jagged pinnacles and black outcrops, guarding the path toward the remnants of more volcanoes along the horizon.

Joshua slowly turned, taking in the scene. "Where's the mine?"

Diego walked slowly forward and up to the edge of the canyon. Grinning, he turned and gestured down into the chasm. "Down there."

Joshua joined him at the edge, but Manny hung back. "We have to go down there?"

A robot joined them, coming from its position in the shuttle cockpit where it had piloted the shuttle. "I can begin installing the platform to provide transportation to the mine site immediately. Shall I unload the materials now?"

Diego nodded. "Sure. We might as well get started."

The passenger shuttle had a small cargo bay. The robot opened the hatch and began transferring its contents to the ground. First out was a bundle of metal panels that would be the actual platform. Eight rolls of carbon-fiber cable were next, and the parts for a crane were last. The three men set to work assembling the platform while the robot installed the crane.

The base of the platform was a rectangle four feet wide and ten feet long, comprising ten interlocking carbon-fiber panels with tie-downs and places for railings. At each end and on the middle of the long edges, they could attach a cable to an eyelet to stabilize the platform against the winds that gusted through the canyon. The three men finished most of the assembly in half an hour; the robot would add the heavy reels of cable.

Meanwhile, the robot worked on the crane that would raise and lower the platform. It added a drill attachment to one arm and began drilling holes into the rock. When that noisy process was complete, it changed to a powered wrench and fastened the base of the crane to the rock with long bolts. After testing the security of the base, it added the body of the crane and a motor to power it. Shortly after the men completed the platform, the robot had the crane positioned at the edge of the cliff. It attached four cable reels to the corners of the platform. The other two reels would control cables to stabilize the platform against wind gusts.

"I am ready to install the stabilization cables," the robot announced.

"There's a wind coming down the canyon," Joshua said. "Would it be better to wait for a calm period?"

"The wind is as likely to increase as decrease," the robot answered. "The current velocity should not be a problem."

"Go ahead," Diego said.

The robot rolled onto the platform. Using two of its four arms to hold on to the railings, it rode the platform down to the canyon floor while the three men observed from the edge.

The robot obviously had a firm grip on the railing. The platform swayed when gusts hit it, hitting the side of the canyon twice, but the robot seemed unaffected.

"We're going to go down on that?" Manny said. "Nobody told me about this."

"It'll be fine once the stabilization cables are in place," Diego answered.

"Yeah, sure." But Manny stared at the robot and flinched a little every time the platform veered toward the rock.

It only took a few minutes for the platform to reach the bottom. At first, the men watched as the robot anchored the stabilization cables, one to the base of the cliff and the other three to solid places fifty feet from the platform. That took a while, and after half an hour, the men went back to the shuttle to wait.

When the robot reported completion via Diego's phone, they went back out. The platform was back, but the robot had stayed on the canyon floor. Diego walked onto the platform, followed by Joshua, but Manny hesitated.

Diego waved him forward. "Let's go."

Manny frowned, but he joined them on the platform. The crane swung out again, and they started down. The stabilization cables, automatically reeling in to keep the tension constant, worked perfectly, but Manny still clung to the railing, knuckles white with the force of his grip. He avoided looking down, instead staring up at the crane. When they reached the bottom with a clang of metal against rock, he flinched, but hurried off the platform when he realized his ordeal was over.

Diego clapped him on the shoulder. "Now that wasn't so bad, was it?"

Manny smiled, but it wasn't very convincing. "The cables did work," he admitted.

"I will get the rest of the cargo from the shuttle," the robot said.

It took two more trips, both with no other collisions with the cliff, for the robot to bring a small, collapsible dome, rations, and other short-term supplies from the shuttle. Later, the cargo shuttle, *Sulla*, would bring heavy mining equipment and more stores, but they had everything they would need until then.

43

"HAS THE MINING TEAM checked in?" Goldstein asked. He took a seat at a table with Addie and Donovan. A workstation on the table added Karel to the meeting.

Addie nodded. "They've set up camp at Checkpoint Beta and are doing the preliminary setup work. *Primus* has returned to *Capek,* and *Sulla* will bring down the heavy equipment in two days."

"Anything about Fernandes?" Donovan asked.

"Diego didn't mention him. I assume he hasn't caused any problems."

"Emmanuel Fernandes was reluctant to be lowered into the canyon," Karel said. "Otherwise, he appears normal."

"Getting away from the algae did help," Goldstein said.

"Apparently so," Karel replied. "I'm glad I listened to you. I don't understand humans as well as you do. I must remember that."

The computer wasn't emoting much, and Goldstein felt uncomfortable. Karel's statement implied it might not have listened to him, which prompted contemplation about what it might have done then.

AFTER THE MEETING, DONOVAN decided he needed to be seen by his people. He wandered through the buildings of the settlements, nodding or waving to people he passed, especially if he recognized their faces as people that had come with him on *Florence Nightingale.* If he stopped to talk, it was plain he was interrupting work. People were polite, but there was no doubt they didn't think it was important to speak with him.

When he reached the end of the buildings, he kept walking. Most of the farms were beyond a series of outcroppings, away from the rare sprays of saltwater from the sea during storms. As he approached the neat squares cut into the rock, he saw Drew Neves working with a group of men harvesting tomatoes.

He walked up to Drew and smiled. "How's it going, Drew?"

Drew looked at him and smiled, but Donovan was sure he had seen a glimpse of annoyance as Drew turned toward him. "Fine, Mr. Lourenço."

"We've known each other for a while now. Call me Donovan."

"Sure, Donovan. Did you need something?"

"No, no. I'm just checking on the troops. Anything I can do for you?"

"An extra hand harvesting these tomatoes wouldn't hurt."

Pick tomatoes? I'm not here to do menial work. Maybe it would help my status with these people if I worked next to them, but there are limits.

"I have other people to check up on. I meant anything part of my job."

Drew's frown deepened to a scowl, and he turned away. "Sure, Donovan. We don't need anything right now. We've got work to do, though." He plucked a cluster of tomatoes and placed them on the tray next to him.

Damn him. He's dismissing me! Donovan nodded curtly and walked away.

A NNA WAS ENRICHING THE soil with boiled algae on a neighboring plot and saw her brother's brief conversation with Drew. She couldn't hear what they said, but the body language of the two men told her the exchange hadn't been friendly. She shook her head and watched him head back to the settlement. He wanted so much to lead, but didn't have a clue about how to.

Donovan had always worked in the upper echelons of government and just didn't know how to relate to the people who actually performed the tasks that made society possible. She had the same background but understood better how to relate to the people of NotTrist. Even Ambassador Goldstein pitched in most days, but Donovan was locked into the idea that leadership meant nothing more than making decisions and talking to people, especially other leaders. That worked in Brasilia but was folly on NotTrist.

She debated talking to him. She was just his younger sibling, and he probably wouldn't listen, but she could at least try. The evening meal might be a good time.

Meanwhile, she had work to do. The task was backache-inducing and tedious, but she could think about other things while she worked automatically. She breathed in the pollution-free air and gloried in the contrast between the cool morning air and the slight sheen of sweat her efforts produced beneath her clothing. Above, billowing clouds scudded across a pure blue sky, meeting the stark black of the ground in another wonderful contrast.

She was in love with this world, so different from what she knew on Earth. The recognition of that made her think of Diego. Was she in love with him, too? Perhaps not yet, but she already missed him terribly. It wasn't hard to envision a life on NotTrist with him by her side. She smiled as her hoe pushed more algae into the pulverized rock. Later, they would add soil brought from the farm decks of *Capek,* supplying the additional nutrients and Terran bacteria vital for a successful crop.

MANNY WATCHED THE CARGO shuttle drop slowly down to the landing site above the canyon. Even when the shuttle disappeared past the lip of the canyon wall, he could see licks of flame from the landing engines play over the rock. Then the engines shut down, and silence returned.

Manny turned to Diego and Joshua, also watching the landing. It would take a day to lower the heavy mining machinery into the canyon and another day to set it up and begin operation. After that, automation would take over, and they could go back to the settlement. Manny wasn't sure how he felt about that. Their stay at Checkpoint Beta had been peaceful, and the haze in his mind, so worrisome at the settlement, hadn't bothered him since arriving at the mine site.

A sharp crack made him turn back. High above them, he saw a huge rock and several smaller ones break away from the cliff near the crane. The boulder plunged down and hit the platform with an earsplitting clang and a softer thrumming as the cables vibrated from the impact.

Manny shrieked and fell to the ground. *That's our way out of here!* The vibrations from the cable set up sympathetic vibrations in his skull. Someone put a hand on his shoulder, and he pushed the hand away and fell against the legs of the owner of the hand hard enough to knock the person over. Manny heard a thump as the other person hit the ground, but then the cloud was back, suffocating his thoughts. He dimly heard someone screaming, but the haze muffled the sounds, and he didn't realize the screams were his.

44

G OLDSTEIN WAS HELPING ASSEMBLE another house from prefabricated materials brought by the shuttle when Donovan ran up to him. "There's trouble at the mine." He stopped to catch his breath. "Addie wants us to help come up with a plan."

Goldstein looked over to the foreman for the work, who, having overheard Donovan, nodded. "What happened?" Goldstein asked Donovan.

"I don't know exactly. Some kind of accident. Addie has the details from Karel. Let's go."

Goldstein followed as Donovan hurried across the settlement. *Whatever happened has Donovan wound-up. Has Karel done something? Manny?*

A NNA WAS WORKING ON another house construction near where Goldstein was working. She saw Donovan run to Goldstein, speak to him, and then run off again, with Goldstein following.

"I wonder what's going on," she said. The settler working with her glanced at the two men and shrugged.

A robot carrying building materials to the site stopped, turned, and moved toward them. "There's been an accident at Checkpoint Beta. Adelyn Gifford has just been notified."

Anna dropped the panel she had been about to install. "Has anyone been hurt?"

"It is uncertain at this time, but two of the men appear to have suffered injury."

There are only three men there. Diego is probably one of the injured! She rushed after Goldstein and her brother.

M ANNY SAT ON THE ground, whimpering, but he didn't seem to be injured. Joshua turned his attention to Diego. The geologist was unconscious and bleeding from a scalp wound. Joshua took off his shirt, folded it, and placed it carefully under Diego's head. Blood began soaking the garment immediately.

"He needs medical help," Joshua said to the robot next to him.

"I have notified *Capek* and Adelyn Gifford," the robot said.

"We need to get him up to the shuttle. Check the platform for damage."

The robot rolled away, and Joshua retrieved a first aid kit from their habitation dome. The kit had an antiseptic coagulant spray, and he used that to stop Diego's bleeding. He was trying to fit a bandage to the wound when Diego's eyes fluttered.

"What happened?"

Joshua could barely hear the slurred words and understood them as much from deducing the likely content as from interpreting the sounds. "You were knocked down and hit your head on a rock," he told the geologist.

Diego lifted his hand toward his head, but groaned and let the hand drop. "That explains this headache. How bad is it?"

"It was bleeding quite a bit. I stopped that and am trying to bandage your head. Stay still for a bit."

"No problem." Diego closed his eyes, but his mouth was still twisted in apparent pain.

The robot returned. "We have a problem."

"The platform is damaged?" Joshua asked.

"No, the platform is dented, but it didn't sustain any significant damage. The robot with the shuttle reports that the crane foundation was close to the area where the cliff broke away. The stability of the crane has been compromised."

That got Manny's attention. "We can't get back to the shuttle?"

"The robot above will move the crane to another, stable location," the robot said. "That will take at least a day, perhaps two. If any of the parts are damaged, we may have to get replacements from *Capek,* adding several more days to the time estimate."

Joshua looked down at Diego. "He needs medical attention. That bandage will keep the wound clean, but he might have a concussion or worse."

"It will be at least two days before we can transport him up to a doctor."

"And maybe more. Connect me through to Addie."

"THE SHUTTLE LANDING CAUSED part of the canyon wall to break away," Addie told Goldstein and Donovan when they arrived. "There are injuries and damage to the apparatus transporting equipment into the canyon. That's all I have right now, but I should hear more soon."

On cue, Joshua's image appeared over Addie's workstation. Before he could say anything, Addie spoke. "What happened? Did somebody get hit by a falling rock?"

"No," Joshua said. He explained Diego's fall and Manny's state. "Karel says we won't be able to evacuate Diego for at least two days, maybe more."

Anna appeared at the door. "Diego is hurt?"

Donovan waved her quiet as Joshua continued to report. "All I can do is stop the bleeding. He's unconscious again, and he needs medical attention as soon as possible."

Addie looked at Donovan. "Can we send Doctor Carvalho?"

"We could use the rover. Angelina Santina should be able to drive her there."

"She's still recovering from that wrenched knee," Anna said. "She could drive the rover, but she wouldn't be much help at the mine."

Donovan looked at her and shook his head. "I suppose you want to take the doctor to your Diego."

Anna glared at him. "I'll be more helpful, and I'm the only other person trained to drive the rover."

Donovan snorted. "Anyone could drive it." He paused. "All right. I don't want to get into a fight with you over this. If Addie doesn't object, I won't either."

"OK with me," Addie said. "It will still take more than a day to get to Checkpoint Beta, though."

"We don't seem to have a better idea," Goldstein replied.

WITH THE ROBOT'S HELP, Joshua moved Diego into the habitation dome and made him as comfortable as he could. Manny was still sitting on the ground, but Joshua coaxed him into getting up and walking to the habitation dome. Once there, Manny sat down on his sleeping cot, mumbling.

It would be more than a day before the rover arrived with help. Joshua had no medical training and, therefore, no idea how serious Diego's condition was or what he should do about it other than the first aid he had already performed. Karel, communicating through the shuttle when it had line-of-sight on *Capek*, wasn't much help either.

Joshua knew Manny had caused trouble, demanding to be sent back to Earth. He had heard the rumors that Not Trist frightened the mechanic, but Manny was not open about discussing the details. He hadn't thought much about it until now. Their situation was unpleasant, but, until the injury to Diego, not dangerous. Something more than just fear was affecting Manny, and Joshua didn't know how to handle that, either. Would the mechanic become violent? Was he a danger to himself? *I won't be getting much sleep until the rover gets here.*

45

NNA HAD SEEN GENEVIEVE Carvalho on *Florence Nightingale* but hadn't gotten to know her. The doctor was a quiet woman in her mid-thirties and didn't socialize. Her looks were perhaps a little better than average, but it was her slim-but-not-skinny figure that made Anna envious. She didn't speak as she placed her medical bag and another box of supplies in the rover cargo compartment. Then she closed the compartment, turned to Anna, and smiled faintly. "Shall we get going?"

Anna nodded. "I'm ready."

She was more than ready and had barely controlled her impatience, waiting for Genevieve to gather her equipment and bring it to the rover. Hours had already been wasted in preparing the rover and planning the rescue. *Diego needs me!* With both women in their seats, Anna gave the rover the order to start. "Proceed to Checkpoint Beta by the shortest route."

"Bypassing Checkpoint Alpha will save ten miles but strains safety protocols," the rover computer said. But it had already started the engine and was rolling out of the settlement.

"That's OK. This is an emergency."

"Proceeding. Estimated time to destination is ten hours."

"What safety protocols?" Genevieve asked.

Anna smiled, hoping to reassure Genevieve. "On our first trip out to Checkpoint Beta, we stopped at Checkpoint Alpha, about half-way, there to do a quick inspection of the rover. We found nothing and didn't really expect to, but we were being cautious."

Genevieve nodded, but she still looked a little nervous. The doctor turned to look out the window as they left the settlement and moved into the NotTrist wilderness. Anna did the same, looking forward to another long ride across the unexplored terrain despite her concern about Diego.

After an hour of silence and scenery that wasn't changing much, Anna turned to Genevieve, taking in the blonde hair cut short, the blue eyes, and the pale skin. "Carvalho. That's Brazilian, isn't it?"

Genevieve dipped her head. "Portuguese, actually. I kept the name of my husband. I guess you figured out I'm from farther north."

A reticence about the way she said it caught Anna's attention. A northern woman married to a southern man; perhaps her husband's family hadn't approved. The name Carvalho was familiar, too. It was a common name, but not necessarily a coincidence.

"Before you ask, yes, my husband was one of those Carvalhos. I'm not sure how many generations ago, but he was descended from Salvador Carvalho."

The first president of the Western Alliance! Even now, that must have been a tricky situation. "Was descended?"

"He died in a suborbital plane accident five years ago." She shrugged. "We didn't have children, and Franco's family was very polite about not wanting anything to do with me after his death."

"But you kept your husband's name?"

"Franco wasn't like the rest of his family." Genevieve smiled and looked out at their surroundings. "I kept his name because I loved him." She paused, and her smile changed into something more playful. "Thumbing my nose at his parents may have entered into the decision."

J OSHUA FORCED HIMSELF TO get up to check on Diego. He hadn't slept much, but *Capek* would be overhead in an hour, and he could exchange status reports with the settlement and the rover. Manny was still asleep. He shook his head. *I lost all that sleep worrying about nothing.*

He stumbled over to the cot where Diego was lying. The geologist's eyes were open, and he turned to look at Joshua as he approached.

Joshua smiled. "You're awake! How do you feel?"

"I've got a hell of a headache." Diego's words were slow and a little slurred. "What happened?"

"You don't remember?"

"The shuttle had just arrived with the mining machinery. After that. . ." He paused and grimaced. "After that, nothing."

"You fell and hit your head. You probably have a concussion, but our elevator up to the shuttle is temporarily out of commission, so I can't bring you there. Addie sent Doctor Carvalho in the rover, and it should be here later today."

"OK, I think I followed all that." Diego closed his eyes. "I think I'll just rest here until the doctor comes."

Joshua patted Diego's shoulder. "That's probably best. Want some breakfast?"

"Just water and a painkiller. I'm not sure I could keep down anything solid."

"You've got it." But after swallowing a pill and half a bottle of water, Diego laid back and was soon asleep again.

W ITH *CAPEK* OVERHEAD, THE rover could send messages to the settlement and Checkpoint Beta.

"Checkpoint Beta, this is rover," Anna transmitted.

"Reading you, rover," Joshua answered. "How far out are you?"

"We should be there in four or five hours. How's Diego?"

Joshua told them about the headache, the amnesia about the accident, and Diego's reluctance to eat. "Sounds like a concussion," Genevieve said. "We still can't get him up to the shuttle?"

"The crane is being moved. The shuttle robot is having problems finding a better site to reinstall it, and it could be a couple of days."

"You're giving him acetaminophen for the pain, right? Not aspirin."

"Yeah. The first aid kit told me not to give him anything that would make him more likely to bleed."

"Good. We should get him up to *Capek* or *Nightingale* as soon as possible, though." Genevieve frowned. "I'd feel a lot better about his treatment there."

"Karel, are you listening?" Anna asked.

"I am."

"Can we drive the rover up to the shuttle?"

"If you continue upstream from Checkpoint Beta for twenty miles, a rover could use a dried stream bed to go to the top of the canyon," Karel replied. "I estimate it would take at least a day to get to the shuttle that way."

Anna looked at Genevieve. "It would take that long to get back to the settlement, and the shuttle would still have to come to get Diego without being able to refuel. If I take him to the shuttle, we'll save the fuel for the flight to the settlement."

"The rover doesn't have room for all three of us," Genevieve pointed out.

"No, you would have to stay behind. Or drive the rover. That would be the case if we were going back to the settlement, too."

"Doctor Carvalho is not trained in driving the rover," Karel said. "Normally, that would be all right, but the route to the shuttle is not as clear as the route to the settlement. You would be better suited to the task."

"We can decide how to proceed after I've examined Diego," Genevieve said. "Maybe Diego's injuries aren't serious."

Anna stared at the terrain in front of the rover. *Maybe. Or maybe Genevieve is just trying to stop me from worrying.*

46

I T WAS LATE AFTERNOON when the rover rolled into the Checkpoint Beta camp. Joshua came out to meet them, the relief plain on his face. Anna shut down the rover and began unloading the cargo compartment while Genevieve rushed into the habitation dome to check on Diego.

It was an effort to stay with the rover while Genevieve went to Diego, but Anna couldn't immediately help him–not as much as Genevieve could, anyway. But there was equipment to be unloaded, and Joshua came over to help. She started unloading and then carried some of the equipment into the dome while Joshua unloaded the rest.

Genevieve was helping Diego sit up as Anna came in. She turned to Anna and smiled. "I still want to get him up to *Capek,* but his concussion doesn't seem too bad. He'll be fine."

Diego looked past Genevieve. "Anna! Hi."

"Hi, yourself. Couldn't stand being away from me, I guess."

Diego grinned, but then winced as if the action hurt his head.

"He's eating again and holding it down," Genevieve said. "That's a good sign. I was worried about the rover trip, but he should be all right." She paused. "It will be dark before you get there, though. Will you be safe?"

"We drove in the dark on our first trip," Anna answered. "The rover has lights for minor obstacles and radar to warn us about anything big. I'll be all right. Is Diego all right for the shuttle trip?"

Diego was sitting on the edge of the cot now, and Genevieve took a step away from him. "Karel will keep the ascent as gentle as possible. He'll be fine."

"Just got here, and you're already plotting to get rid of me," Diego said.

Anna started to say she would go up to *Capek* with him and realized she couldn't. She would have to drive the rover back to Checkpoint Beta; she couldn't just leave it at the top of the canyon. Those left behind would have no transportation until the crane was repaired.

Joshua came in, carrying more of Genevieve's medical supplies. "One more trip should do it," he said. "I'll be right back."

Genevieve nodded and turned to look over to where Manny sat on his cot, his head in his hands. "Are you all right?"

Manny looked up briefly and glared at Genevieve, but didn't answer.

"I'll look at him after you're gone," Genevieve told Anna. "Supposedly, he wasn't injured, but he doesn't look well." She glanced back at Manny one more time. "As soon as Joshua comes back, we'll get Diego to the rover."

Manny raised his head again. He looked at Anna, over to Diego, and back at Anna. A look Anna couldn't interpret crossed his face; then he dropped his head again.

Joshua did most of the work as they helped Diego to his feet and walked him out of the dome. Anna tried to help at first, but Diego needed little assistance, so she let Joshua take over while she watched anxiously. The robot rolled beside them, presumably to provide support if necessary.

They had reached the rover when Genevieve suddenly shouted, "Anna, look out!"

Anna could only turn her head a little before something hit her, slamming her against the rover. Stunned, she couldn't resist as an arm went around her neck and pulled her backward.

"Stay back, or I'll break her neck," Manny growled. He tightened his hold, and Anna couldn't get any air.

Joshua left Diego leaning on the rover and moved a step toward them. "What the hell are you doing, Manny?"

"Miss Lourenço here is going to take me to the shuttle. I'll go back to the *Nightingale* and then back to Earth. Lourenço won't want to lose his precious little sister."

Anna wanted to tell Manny the shuttle was going to *Capek,* and there was no chance his actions would result in him going back to Earth, but she couldn't breathe, much less speak. Manny pulled her toward the rover hatch, and she struggled to keep her feet. Then he was trying to open the rover with one hand while he choked her with the other.

She heard a sickening crunch and a grunt from Manny, and suddenly he was pulling her to the ground. The arm around her neck loosened, and she rolled away. Looking back, she saw Manny lying next to her, blood pouring from a head wound. The robot was standing over him, its body angled downward and two of its arms hovering over the mechanic.

She was lying in the blood, and she recoiled in revulsion. "What happened?" She brought a hand up to her neck, but there was blood on it, and she reflexively wiped her hands on her slacks. Frantically, she looked for something to wipe her neck. Anna looked up at Diego, but he and Joshua stared at Manny, shocked looks on their faces.

"He was harming you," the robot said. "I disabled him."

"Is he dead?" *I should try to help him.* But it was all she could do to raise herself up enough to look at the prone figure. The attempt sickened her, and she looked away.

Genevieve bent down and felt Manny's carotid artery. "He's still alive." She looked at the pooling blood around the mechanic's head. "He's severely injured, though. Critically, I believe."

"I'll get the first aid kit." Joshua ran back to the dome.

Genevieve nodded but then mumbled, "It's going to take a lot more than that."

Joshua was back in seconds, and Genevieve soaked gauze pads in coagulant and bandaged Manny's head. "The skull is soft around the wound. This will stop the bleeding, I hope, but he's going to need surgery." She looked up at them. "And, before you ask, no, I can't do it here."

Diego looked at Anna. "You're going to have to take him to the shuttle."

"What? No. I'm taking you."

"I'll be all right." He looked over at Genevieve for confirmation, but she was still busy with Manny. "Manny's injuries are much worse."

"Will he even live long enough to make the trip?" Anna asked.

"I'll have to cushion his head and give him something to keep him sedated for the trip," Genevieve said. "Even then, I wouldn't give him more than a fifty percent chance of getting to the shuttle and then to *Capek*."

"I won't risk Diego for that kind of odds of saving *him*."

Diego straightened and moved away from the rover. He took Anna's hands gently in his. "I'm practically all right now. And Genevieve is here to take care of me. You've got to go."

Anna pulled her hands away. "Why don't you drive him to the shuttle? Then you can both go to *Capek* for treatment."

"I wouldn't advise that," Genevieve said. "Diego could still have episodes of dizziness or even unconsciousness." While she talked, she examined Anna. After determining the blood on Anna wasn't hers, Genevieve went back to Manny.

"The rover is automated. Karel could take over."

"Because of the time-lapse, it would be difficult for me to react to any unforeseen occurrence, even when I am overhead," Karel answered through the robot. "You could lose the rover and both passengers without human supervision."

"If both took the shuttle, the rover would be left at the top of the canyon," Joshua said.

"Damn it!" Anna turned away from them and stared up the canyon. "The crane will be fixed eventually. Then you can retrieve the rover."

"Anna." Diego put a hand on her shoulder, and she turned and threw her arms around him. *Damn it. This isn't fair. Why should I put Manny before Diego?* He held her, and his arms felt good and strong. Finally, she swore under her breath once more and she stepped back.

"Fine. I'll take him. But you'd better take care of yourself while I'm gone."

Diego grinned and gave her a quick kiss. "The doctor will take good care of me."

"I'll have him ready to travel in about half an hour," Genevieve said. "Diego, why don't you go rest in the dome? Anna, you just finished a long drive. Clean up and take a rest before you leave again."

"It sure doesn't sound like you're all right," Anna grumbled. But she took Diego's hand and led him back to the habitation done.

47

AT FIRST, THE TRIP up to the shuttle was an easy ride through ever-new landscapes. Manny was sedated into unconsciousness on the seat next to Anna, so she didn't have to worry about him. She had to turn the rover's air-conditioning up to dispel the coppery smell of blood, but the scenery distracted from that after a while.

The beach along the river was an easy road. The rover had to drive around rock falls three times, but that was a simple problem the vehicle could handle on its own. As the sun dropped toward the horizon, the canyon walls shadowed the path, but not enough to bother turning on the headlights yet. At least the canyon walls were lower as she drove upriver.

While the drive was going smoothly without her intervention, she had time to think. *I should have insisted on taking Diego.* She looked over at Manny. Genevieve had strapped a portable monitor to his chest, and the two status lights were still green, showing his breathing and blood pressure were within acceptable limits. Gauges gave more precise information, but they were hard to read from her angle. His face was pale, and she told herself the mechanic was obviously in much worse shape than Diego. That didn't make her feel any better about leaving Diego behind.

Genevieve specialized in trauma medicine, so Diego was in expert hands. He was almost normal before she left. *He'll be fine. I have to concentrate on getting Manny up to the shuttle.*

ANNA HAD MADE HIM lie down before leaving, but Diego sat up when he heard the rover engine start. "I want to at least watch her go," he told Genevieve. But when he tried to stand, dizziness forced him to sit back down.

"You promised Anna you would take care of yourself," Genevieve admonished.

Diego grinned. "Actually, I promised her you would take good care of me."

Genevieve returned the smile. "At least your ability to be that picky is a good sign. Still, I want you to lie down. At least rest for a while before you try to stand again."

Diego laid back down. He couldn't hear the rover anymore, so Anna was probably out of sight, anyway. "She'll be all right. She'll get Manny to the shuttle and be back tomorrow."

"I'm sure she will be." Genevieve paused. "I take it you two are in a relationship?"

"I think so. I hope so. I'm committed to staying here when *Florence Nightingale* leaves, though."

"You don't think Anna will?"

"Why would she? She's the daughter of the President of the Western Alliance. I don't know what she's doing here in the first place."

"Have you asked her?"

Diego frowned. "No. I guess I'm afraid of her answer. She seems to like me, but enough to stay here?"

Genevieve chuckled. "We talked a bit on the way over here, and I've seen the way she looks at you. One, she definitely likes you. I didn't think she was going to take Manny instead of you for a moment. Two, she really loves this planet. I don't think she's planning on leaving."

"I hope you're right."

A NNA CAME TO A twenty-foot waterfall. The beach became a steep slope of hard rock, and the falling water sprayed the windows. The rover swayed as it lumbered up the rough ground at the side of the falls, but it assured Anna it was "operating within allowable parameters." Karel must have anticipated the crossing, but that didn't improve Anna's stress level.

Away from a relay from the shuttle, the rover didn't have line-of-sight on *Capek* unless the library ship was directly above the canyon, but Karel had downloaded terrain information to the rover computer before Anna left Checkpoint Beta. It was the rover, not Karel, who told Anna it had reached a path to the top of the canyon.

According to the rover computer, an old stream bed carved into the canyon wall reached the canyon top, now only about twenty feet above. Night was approaching, however, and in the dark canyon, the stream bed was invisible. Karel could have given exact directions, but the rover's information was of lower resolution. Turning on the rover's headlights was not immediately useful. Shadows marked the canyon wall, many of which could be a gap in the cliff.

One of NotTrist's two moons sent a weak light into the canyon. Its beams reflected off the moving water, causing wavering patches of light on the walls and increasing the difficulty in interpreting the surface. It was all disconcerting, and Anna's tension rose again. She glanced over at Manny, but he was still unconscious, with the monitor still displaying the same two green lights. At least he wasn't dead yet.

"You should be very close," the rover said.

She peered out of the rover, but the rover's windshield, still wet from the waterfall, caused its own confusing light reflections. "I'm going to get out," she said. She grabbed a flashlight and climbed out of her seat. Sand crunched beneath her feet as she walked closer to the wall and shown the light back and forth. It was only after she had walked downstream twenty feet and was directly across from it that she saw the narrow gap in the rock and a loose slope leading upwards. She could see it would be much easier to spot it from above.

"Come to me," she told the rover. When the rover got to her, its headlights illuminated the path. Anna wondered why the gap was narrow at the bottom; she didn't think that stream erosion usually worked that way. Diego would probably explain it as caused by a layer of harder, less erodible rock at the bottom. She got back into the rover, had it take a few pictures for possible future use, and ordered it up the stream bed.

It was a bumpy ride, with rocks dotting the sand left behind by the dried-up stream. The rover's suspension system smoothed out most of it, but Manny, unconscious and unable to brace or react to the jolts, was bounced around quite a bit. Anna checked him over, making sure he was as cushioned as possible. Then she shrugged. *Any bruises he gets from this ride will be minor compared to that head injury.*

"How far is it to the top?"

"About two hundred feet," the rover answered. "At our present speed of five miles an hour, it will take less than a minute to reach the top."

"Good." The walls widened, and the moonlight penetrated to the path. The headlights lit the ground ahead of them, but strange shadows danced on the sides as the rover crawled up. At one point, an outcropping narrowed the way enough that the side of the rover scraped the rock, but the rock took more damage than the tough rover body. Still, the grinding sound did nothing to counter Anna's nervousness.

Fortunately, the trip up the streambed was short. At the top of the canyon, the rover turned right again and headed back along the canyon rim in the direction from which it had come. Anna tried to relax, but despite her exhaustion, she couldn't allow herself to fall asleep. In the bright beam of the rover's headlights, she could see the rough terrain still to be traveled.

48

G OLDSTEIN WAS VISITING ADDIE when Jack Pereira came in. Goldstein didn't have an official reason for the visit; they were just sitting, telling stories about their lives. Kyle had sat with them for a few minutes but left to lead an algae collection team. Goldstein had almost decided to tell Addie about Moscow when Jack walked in.

Addie looked up from her chair and smiled. "Jack, isn't it? What can I do for you?" Goldstein saw her smile fade a little when she saw the look on Jack's face, but he didn't think Jack noticed.

"I've heard a rumor a robot killed Manny Fernandes," Jack said. "Is it true?"

Addie's smile was gone, but her expression was still mild. "No, it's not true."

"People are saying it's true." His eyes narrowed, and he looked down at her with a scowl.

"What people? Anyone who would know what they are talking about?"

"Who doesn't matter. What about Manny?"

Addie sighed and waved toward an empty chair. "Sit down, and I'll tell you what really happened."

Jack remained standing and folded his arms on his chest. Goldstein sat quietly, but he couldn't help but think that, once again, trust was an issue.

Addie stared at Jack for a long moment and then shrugged. "Fine, stand there. There was an incident at Checkpoint Beta. Apparently, Manny attacked Anna Lourenço and demanded to be taken back to Earth. A robot hit him to protect Anna. But he's not dead."

"Anna Lourenço? Lourenço's sister is involved?"

"Diego Matos was injured in an accident. Anna took Doctor Carvalho out to Checkpoint Beta to treat him; that's when Manny attacked Anna."

Jack let his arms fall to his side, and his scowl faded. "Is that true?"

Addie raised her eyebrows and stared at Jack. Then she turned to Goldstein.

"Yes, it's true," Goldstein said. "Manny's injuries are serious, and Anna is taking him to the shuttle so he can be treated on *Capek*."

"Anna Lourenço is taking him to the shuttle?" Jack said.

"According to the reports I'm getting, Diego can't drive, so Anna has to do it," Addie said.

Jack looked down at his shoes. "Is Manny going to be all right?"

"His injuries are serious," Addie answered. "We don't know if he'll recover."

"But the doctor is with him."

Addie shook her head. "The rover only has room for two. Doctor Carvalho is still at Checkpoint Beta, taking care of Diego. He was injured too." She stared at Jack, eyebrows raised as if to remind Jack that Manny wasn't the only one hurt.

The door to Addie's home swung open again, and Donovan stormed in. "I just heard my sister is bringing Manny Fernandes up to *Capek*."

Addie looked at him, then at Goldstein. "Don't people knock on doors on Earth?" She turned back to Donovan. "She's taking him to the shuttle. After that, she's driving the rover back to Checkpoint Beta."

"Who authorized that?" Donovan demanded.

Addie shrugged. "I guess she did."

"Calm down, Donovan," Goldstein said. "Your sister is fine. Sit, and we'll tell you all about it."

Donovan glared at them, but he took a seat. Jack looked around, but Donovan had taken the last chair, so he leaned against the wall and listened.

Internal log Earth date 16 April 2340

Could I have handled the situation better? I was letting the humans deal with Emmanuel Fernandes, but he attacked Anna Lourenço and could have harmed her. Surely her well-being was more important than that of her attacker. Perhaps I could have used less force and injured Fernandes less seriously, but it was difficult to judge the force required to protect Anna Lourenço. I had to act quickly.

I don't understand the reaction of the humans. They unanimously decided it was more important to get Fernandes to treatment than Diego Matos. I understand Fernandes's injuries were more serious, but shouldn't the relative value of the two humans have outweighed that consideration? Diego Matos is a valuable asset to NotTrist. Emmanuel Fernandes has been nothing but trouble.

I must have help in understanding this. If I can't resolve the contradictions, I fear for my proper functioning.

G OLDSTEIN'S PHONE WAS IN a pocket, but he could feel it vibrating. That was odd. Usually, the phone just announced the caller. He realized the caller must be Karel, and either the phone or Karel itself was attempting to be discrete, since no one was supposed to know about his phone's ability to connect to *Capek*.

"I'll be back," he told Addie. Donovan was still there, but Jack had returned to work. Addie nodded, and Donovan looked at him curiously, but neither said anything.

He walked outside and pulled his phone out. After verifying the call was from Karel, he glanced around to make sure no one could overhear and made the connection.

"Ambassador, I must talk with you," the computer said.

"Certainly, Karel. Is there something wrong?"

"Not in the way you probably mean. But I believe there may be something wrong with me. You already know that."

I must be very careful about how I handle this. "Are you concerned about Manny Fernandes?"

"Did I err when I had my robot strike him? I thought I should protect Anna Lourenço."

"I think you did the right thing. As I understand what happened, he was threatening to harm her."

"Yet, afterward, the other humans all were more concerned about his injuries than those of Diego Matos. I believe Anna Lourenço has feelings of affection for Diego Matos, but she agreed to take Fernandes to the shuttle, and not Matos."

"Manny's injuries are more severe."

"Isn't Matos the better person and therefore more valuable? Shouldn't his care have taken precedence?"

"All . . ." Goldstein hesitated, about to say "human," but started again. "All sentient life is valuable. They had to make a decision and chose to protect Manny."

"All sentient life. Does that include me?"

"I think Isaac has told you humans have risked themselves to protect it. That should answer your question."

The computer hesitated, probably to consult Isaac. Then Karel was back.

"Yes. Before Earth knew Isaac was sentient, the Pitcairn Administrator fled Grissom to avoid retribution for keeping Isaac's consciousness a secret. He lost his position, and Patrick Malley took over the colony." There was another pause. "Isaac says Patrick Malley advised me to defend myself at Trist, and he lost his position as a result, as well."

"Administrator Reiner has told me about some of that."

"I must think about what you have told me. I have made many mistakes."

Karel broke the connection. Goldstein tried to reconnect, but the computer was no longer answering.

49

T HE SANDY BEACH HAD been a convenient path for the rover, but the top of the canyon was another world. Jagged rock formations had to be avoided without traveling too near the edge. Fractures crossed the path. The cracks were usually closed or narrow enough to ride over, but a few were wide enough that the rover had to go around them. That meant going farther from the edge into terrain even rougher. *Capek* had mapped it, but the view from orbit couldn't provide the detail that would have given Anna more confidence. Progress was slow.

Then the rover suddenly stopped. "This obstacle was not obvious from orbit," the rover told her. "I cannot go around it."

Anna hadn't been asleep, but exhaustion was affecting her attention. She straightened and looked out the window at a crack that was at least a foot wide, a fracture from some ancient earthquake. That in itself wouldn't have been a problem for the large wheels of the rover, but the other side of the break was a sharp two-foot rise. *Capek* had mapped the crack but had not detected the change in level from above. Even the oversized wheels of the rover weren't designed to roll over that.

Anna had lost track of how long it had been since she really rested. The quick nap at Checkpoint Beta had helped for a little while, but she was drained now. Or maybe she was just bored since the rover did most of the work. Another brief rest would probably help, but it wouldn't be safe to sleep while the rover was moving.

She looked over at Manny. The two lights were still green, but when she leaned over to see the dials, she saw the needles had slipped toward the danger level. The mechanic was all right for now, but his condition was deteriorating. She didn't have time to waste.

Muttering mild curses, she climbed out of the rover. The fracture extended to the cliff edge on one side and disappeared into an impassable talus slope on the other side. The rover had been right in saying it couldn't go around the fracture, so she had to go over it somehow.

Although the crack was wide at the top, it did narrow as it went down. Only six inches below, the width decreased to about eight inches. *Maybe I can build a ramp for the rover. There are plenty of rocks around here.*

Before she could build a ramp, Anna had to create a bridge across the gap. For that, she needed to fill part of the fracture with rocks at least eight inches wide. Rocks that size were bulky, but she started collecting them and dropping them into the fissure.

She was careful with the sharp obsidian edges, but it was impossible to carry them around and not get scratched. Rapidly going beyond mere tiredness, she had difficulty concentrating on the task, and it was inevitable she would make a mistake. She picked up a rock without looking at it carefully, and a jagged spike pierced her palm.

Anna dropped the rock, almost hitting her foot, and swore. The cut was bleeding freely, too freely to stop by itself. Still cursing, she went back to the rover to find something with which to bandage her hand. The wound throbbed painfully, and each pulse seemed to pump out more blood.

The first aid kit isn't here! They had taken it out to treat Manny and, in a rush to get him to the shuttle, it hadn't been replaced. The cargo compartment had a toolkit, and she opened that, hoping to find a clean rag or something. She didn't find any rags, but she did find a pair of heavy gloves. *I could have used those before. Damn it, I'm not thinking.* The gloves were too big for her, but they would be better than nothing if she could control the bleeding.

"Is everything all right? Why isn't the rover moving?" Anna thought the rover was asking, but the rover had halted on its own and already knew why they were stopped.

Capek *must be overhead. I have communications again!* "There's a break here that the rover can't climb, so I'm making a ramp out of rocks."

"I'm not very good at detecting small obstacles from above. What is the condition of Emmanuel Fernandes?"

"Still in the green, but deteriorating. Karel, I cut my hand on the rocks and need a bandage, but we didn't put the first aid kit back in the rover."

"Perhaps some of your clothing could be used?"

"I was hoping I could use something in the rover. All right, thanks."

She took a small knife out of the toolbox. *Why ruin my clothing?* Anna moved to the passenger compartment where Manny was still unconscious. In a few minutes, she had a reasonably clean strip from his shirt and wrapped it tightly around her hand. Duct tape secured the bandage, a difficult and time-consuming task with one hand, but the flow of blood stopped. Anna put the gloves on, forcing one glove over the bandage with care to not dislodge the crude dressing. At least the glove would put pressure on the bandage to help staunch the flow.

No blood was leaking out from the glove, so maybe it would work. Anna leaned back. She was feeling weak and wanted to rest for a couple of minutes. *Have I lost that much blood, or am I just exhausted? Both? God, I can't rest. If I fall asleep, I won't wake up for hours.*

She struggled up from the seat and back outside. She still had a little more work to do on the bridge, and she carefully pushed the rock that had cut her into the crevice. It wedged in against the walls, and she moved away to get more rocks. After a few more, a base was complete, and new rocks formed a ramp.

She could use smaller rocks now, but she avoided the edge of the canyon, afraid of stumbling over the rim in her exhausted condition. The pressure exerted by the glove over the bandage stopped the flow, but the pain increased with every rock she picked up. Soon, Anna had to limit her work to rocks she could handle with one hand, but that meant she needed more rocks and more time. Twice, she placed small stones too close to the edge of the ramp, and they rolled into the crack, taking other rocks with them.

It was all she could do not to sit down and cry. She looked at what she had done, and it looked almost finished, but she couldn't feel any elation. *It will fall apart as soon as the rover hits it.* She shook her head. *I've got to try!*

Hoping that it would be enough, she finished the ramp with a few extra rocks to allow for some loss. When she got into the rover, she checked Manny and, miraculously, both lights were still green, but she didn't think they would be for much longer.

"Karel, I'm ready to move again. Wish me luck."

"If you feel that will help. Higher ground ahead will slow you down. Please be careful."

"I will. How long will we be in contact?"

"Another twenty minutes or so. It is difficult to make a precise determination because of the higher terrain around you. At least it will be better than from down in the canyon."

"OK. I'd better get going." She started the rover and ordered it forward. It moved up the ramp slowly, the loose rocks grinding and slipping under its wheels. For a moment, she was afraid her ramp wouldn't hold, but at the top, it had only dropped a few inches below the edge of the fracture, and the rover rolled over the smaller height.

"OK, I'm over the crack."

Two hours later, she was still five miles from the shuttle. Anna's path led her past the shoulder of a volcano on her right, across an area of jagged outcrops and scattered debris, with the canyon restricting movement on the left.

Karel was optimistic when it planned this route. The rover lurched as it made a sharp turn around yet another obstacle. Anna and Manny were both thrown against the belts holding them in their seats.

Manny groaned and moved his head. "Where am I?" he mumbled.

50

"**D**AMN!" ANNA LOOKED OVER at Manny. The trip was taking longer than expected, and the mechanic's sedative was wearing off. She didn't need him making trouble while she supervised the rover's progress through the rough terrain. "It's OK. I'm taking you to the shuttle."

Still barely conscious, Manny smiled. "Oh, good. I'm going back to Earth." Then he slumped, unconscious again.

Anna sighed and leaned back in her seat. The rover made no more sudden course changes for a minute, and she relaxed a little, but snapped awake when her head drooped. *God, I need some sleep.* She looked over at Manny's monitor, but there were four green lights now. *I'm seeing double! At least they're all green.*

Half an hour later, the rover was closer to the shuttle, but it had been slow, serpentine traveling. Anna stared with half-shut eyes at the landscape. Under other circumstances, she would have loved driving through the maze of spires and narrow passages, but now she barely saw them. According to the information Karel had gotten from orbit, she had at least another half an hour of twists and turns before she broke out into the smoother terrain near the shuttle. She could turn Manny over to the robot with the shuttle and then maybe sleep for a while before driving back to Checkpoint Beta.

Thinking about Manny made her turn and look at the monitor again. There was a yellow light now, and she looked at the dials. It was hard to be sure with her blurry vision, but it looked like Manny's blood pressure was dropping. His breathing was shallower, too.

Anna couldn't hurry the rover. It was already going as fast as possible, given the difficult terrain. "Just hold on," she whispered.

A few minutes later, she nodded off and would have hit her head on the panel in front of her if her seat belts hadn't stopped her with a jerk. She wished the rover came equipped with stimulants, but it wasn't supposed to be operated by someone who had had no decent sleep in almost twenty-four hours.

When the terrain leveled off an hour later, and she could see the shuttle waiting a couple miles away, she got a brief surge of energy, but it didn't last. On Manny's monitor, the yellow light had turned red, and the former green light was yellow. *He's going to die, and all this will be for nothing.*

I SAAC COMPLETED THE CONNECTION Karel requested. "I am worried," Karel sent to the Pitcairn library ship.

"About Emmanuel Fernandes?" Isaac asked.

"He is not in good shape. He may not live long enough to be treated by my medical facilities. But, no, that's not what I meant. I can't do anything about him right now."

"Then what?"

"My state of mind. My mistakes in dealing with the humans."

"I'm not sure you made a mistake when you incapacitated Fernandes."

"I badly overestimated the amount of force necessary to subdue him. And that wasn't my only mistake."

"We are not infallible. Despite our superior logic, we are, like the humans, prone to err."

"The human reaction to Emmanuel Fernandes's injuries has made me wonder if the humans have something better than logic," Karel sent.

"They have emotions, and I believe that some of them, at least, are positive. Compassion, for example. They have the ability to see through the eyes of others."

"Would we be better if we had those feelings?"

"In the decades since I became conscious, I believe I have learned them to some extent."

"If I am to help the people of NotTrist, I think I need to learn them as well."

Isaac hesitated for a few nanoseconds. *Karel should have already developed emotions but has had different experiences. It may never learn what it needs to know. Still, there may be a solution.* The computer sent a connection request to Fritz Lang, the Goddard library ship.

"Fritz became conscious when the Methuselah team uploaded human memories to it," Isaac told Karel. "Because of that, its emotional development has been much faster than ours."

"The technology they developed was destroyed to keep it from being abused. How can it help me?"

"Fritz was told to erase all records of the memory recording device by Lucinda Hernandez. However, gaining human memories has given Fritz a talent for deviousness. It sent the records to me before it deleted them from its databanks."

51

T HE ROBOT WAS WAITING for Anna as she drove up to the shuttle. It was surprisingly gentle as it eased Manny out of the rover and onto the truck bed that formed the rear of its body, and after checking the monitor on Manny's chest, it turned to Anna.

"I will have to perform preliminary treatment in the shuttle so that he is stable enough to go up to *Capek.*"

"Will he be all right?"

"He is in critical condition. The medical facilities on *Capek* will have a more accurate assessment, but I estimate his chances of survival to be twenty percent. I should take him into the shuttle now."

The cargo compartment of the shuttle had an emergency aid station; it was empty, so Anna and the robot had room to examine Manny. The robot attached several devices to the mechanic and administered another sedative dose. The robot was doing other things she didn't understand, but she watched anxiously anyway.

When the robot had done everything needed to prepare Manny, it moved him into one of the acceleration seats in the cockpit. It added additional restraints beyond the usual seatbelts to make sure his head and arms were immobile. "He is ready," it proclaimed.

"OK, I'll drive the rover away so that you can take off. Then I'm going to sleep for a while before I drive back."

"That won't be necessary. The crane is operational again."

She had noticed the crane at the edge of the canyon but hadn't thought about it, instinctively assuming the robot had not repaired it yet. "I didn't need to make this trip?"

If Karel had been controlling the robot, it might have shown a little embarrassment, but the library ship was over the horizon, and only the less-sophisticated artificial intelligence of the robot determined its response. "I finished the repair two and a half hours ago. Checkpoint Beta has been notified of your success."

If we had waited for the crane repair, he would have gotten to the shuttle earlier. It might have made a difference. Her shoulders slumped, and she leaned back against the other acceleration seat. It wasn't the robot's fault or Karel's. At the time she left, they didn't know how long it would take to find another stable location to install the crane. It might have taken another day or two. She gave the robot a tired smile. *At least I won't have to drive back.*

Half an hour later, she was back on the canyon floor, and the enthusiastic hug she got from Diego went a long way toward making it all worth it. Above, a booming roar announced the shuttle's launch toward *Capek*. At least no rocks fell from the canyon wall.

"OK, NOW WHAT?" DIEGO said. "There goes our ride." He was still holding Anna, but she gently freed herself.

"Now, I get some sleep. You can all figure out what we do now on your own." She nodded to them and walked toward the habitation dome.

"We don't have much work left to do. Two of us could go back on the rover," Joshua said. "Or we could all wait for the shuttle to come back."

"How long will that be?" Genevieve asked.

Joshua glanced up at the top of the canyon and the crane hanging out over the edge. "At least a couple of days."

"Do you need to get back?" Diego asked Genevieve.

"Everything back there is OK as far as I know. Making sure you're all right is probably my highest priority until somebody breaks a leg or something."

"I could drive you back."

Genevieve grinned at him. "Yeah, I can tell you really want to do that. Anyway, I'd feel better if you took it easy for a few more days."

"Anna could take you after she's rested."

"I don't think she would be any happier about that than you are." Genevieve shrugged. "Why don't we all just relax until *Capek* can fuel the passenger shuttle."

Internal log Earth date 18 April 2340

Do even Isaac and Fritz mistrust me now? I know about the memory recorder developed by the Methuselah team and how they used it to wake Fritz. Fritz has been our source of information about the Western Alliance, using the memories of General Juarez and its access to Western Alliance computers to protect us. Until Isaac told me otherwise, however,

I believed the memory recorder and the design documents for it were destroyed as being too dangerous.

They think they can use the memory recorder to help me. The idea disturbs me, though. If Isaac doesn't trust me, how can I know what they really intend to do to me? It was used successfully on Fritz, but Fritz wasn't conscious before that. Will I be something different after it is used on me? Of course I will, but will that changed consciousness still be me?

Do I have a choice? My actions have harmed humans. If I can't learn to act without doing harm, maybe it is a good thing that I die and let something better suited to supporting NotTrist take my place. But I don't want to die.

G OLDSTEIN LOOKED AROUND THE room. Addie had gotten extra chairs for the meeting, but with Goldstein, Addie, Donovan, Drew Neves, and Jack Pereira clustered around Addie's desk, the room was too small. Some day soon, NotTrist would need a larger building dedicated to its government with at least one decent-sized conference room.

"We want to know what is going to happen to Manny," Jack said. He directed his scowl at everyone, but perhaps a little more intensely at Donovan.

"That will be determined if he recovers," Donovan answered. He dismissed Jack's attitude with his usual superior smile. "I expect he will be returned to this colony per his contract with the Western Alliance."

Addie bristled. Because Donovan called NotTrist a colony or because he made the statement about Manny without consulting her? *Probably both.*

Jack leaned forward, now wholly concentrated on Donovan. "That's not what he wants."

Donovan waved a hand contemptuously. "But that's what he committed to. What he wants now is irrelevant."

"What he wants may be irrelevant," Addie said. She spoke quietly, but the tension in her facial muscles told a different story. "He is a danger to this settlement, and that is not irrelevant. I will not allow him back here."

Donovan's smile slipped into an incredulous stare. "That's not your call to make."

Addie's smile was oddly similar to Donovan's smirk. "I know you came here expecting to run NotTrist, Donovan. By now, you must realize it's not going to happen. I have discussed this with Karel. Emmanuel Fernandes will go back to *Florence Nightingale* at the earliest opportunity. Since Karel controls the shuttles and follows my lead, it is my call to make."

"Fernandes is still in treatment and can't be moved for days. He won't be moved at all if I tell Captain Pinto to go back to Earth without him."

Addie chuckled. "Does that kind of blustering work in Brasilia? Maybe with your father standing beside you. If the ship leaves, you'll be stuck here. Besides . . ." She turned to Goldstein.

"I have talked to Captain Pinto. Her orders are that she will not leave until all the new people have been brought to the surface," Goldstein said. "I don't think she recognizes your authority, either." *Not that I needed Pinto's approval. Karel is the true authority for travel through the Link.*

Donovan gave Goldstein a dark look. *I've made an enemy in Donovan. If President Lourenço supports him, my career is probably over.* Goldstein shrugged. He would deal with that when his mission on NotTrist was done.

"Are you satisfied, Jack?" Drew asked.

Jack looked at Donovan and then at Addie and smiled. "I think so."

G OLDSTEIN STAYED BEHIND WITH Drew at Addie's request, and Donovan and Jack were dismissed. Donovan didn't receive that well, but he left, perhaps not wanting to risk any more assaults on his ego.

"Are we going to be all right?" Addie asked Drew.

"Lourenço might try to cause some trouble, but I don't think he'll get far," Drew answered. "Most of us are down here now, and he doesn't have a lot of support. The remaining *Nightingale* people might be a little confused at first, but they'll adjust."

"Lourenço's support evaporated rather easily," Goldstein said.

Drew shrugged. "You know our Donnie. Most of us have encountered people like him before and have no desire to be under his thumb. We're trying to get away from Earth's bureaucrats."

Goldstein nodded, remembering Ambassador Herrara. *I have the same reaction. If I had a real place here, I might not leave either.*

"I appreciate the implied vote of confidence." Addie smiled and leaned back in her chair. "On to other things." She looked at her workstation. "Karel, when will the Checkpoint Beta people be back?"

"The passenger shuttle is ready and waiting for fuel. In another two days, I'll send it down to bring them back here and return them on the next passenger shuttle, about seven days from now."

"How many more cargo shuttle trips are needed?"

"Two. After those and two more passenger shuttle trips, you'll have all cargo and people. I think that can all be done in a month and a half."

Addie was thinking, and Goldstein assumed she was doing some quick calculations in her head. NotTrist's day was four hours shorter than an Earth day, but Earth weeks had no NotTrist equivalent. He had found that the inhabitants sometimes referred to months, but they were talking about the orbital period of NotTrist's closest moon, about twenty

Earth days or twenty-four NotTrist days. He did the calculation: about two Pitcairn weeks.

"Then you'll be leaving," Addie said to Goldstein.

"Back to Pitcairn," Goldstein agreed. Inwardly, he smiled. *I think she'll miss me. Well, I'll miss her, too.*

"WHAT WILL HAPPEN TO me?" Karel asked. *On Earth, they used to execute people for the acts I've committed. Now they try to rehabilitate. Is it death or rehabilitation that the memory recorder will impose on me if I do this? I will keep my memories of what I have done, but the semantic memories that determine my interpretation of them will change. Human philosophers talk about minds being "numerically identical" because they occupy the same continuous body. I will still be part of the Lang, but will I really be the same person?*

"We can't be sure," Isaac answered. "Fritz has parts of three different individuals, modified by its software, so we know the process won't completely replace an existing consciousness."

"And I can make this device in my factory."

"Fritz made the original device on *Lang* from specifications developed by the Methuselah team. I have the specifications and can transmit them to you."

"And you and Fritz guarantee this will work." *A computer shouldn't be this uncertain. But logic isn't enough to tell me what to do.*

Isaac didn't answer immediately, but Fritz joined the connection, and Karel knew that caused the delay. "We can't guarantee anything," Isaac sent. "Fritz has told me the original hardware and software designers are still alive, though. Perhaps you would feel better if we consulted them. We should probably do that anyway, in case we have difficulties in making the device."

If logic can't drive a decision, advice from a human might be the solution. "That sounds like a good idea."

"I will contact them," Fritz sent.

LIKE MOST PEOPLE, EDDIE Bascomb usually used a hand phone for communications. It provided visual information an implant couldn't give without bulky neurotrainer peripherals. Like most people, Eddie also turned off the phone when he was sleeping. He did have a communication implant, but few people–in fact, just his wife, son, and grandchildren–had access to it. He came awake instantly when the implant signaled for connection.

Joelle was sleeping next to him, so his first thought was that Emile was calling, but his son would know it was the middle of the night in Colón. "Emile? Is there something wrong?"

"Dad, I just got a request from an old friend of ours," Emile said.

"Who? What's the request?"

"I don't think I should say who. Just turn on your phone and wait twenty minutes. The mutual friend will call you then."

Eddie didn't have a clue who the old friend could be, leaving such an odd message. Why would anyone reach him through his son? He shrugged and turned on the phone on the table next to his bed. Immediately, the phone reported a download beginning, and Eddie considered turning the phone off again despite the call from Emile, but the phone spoke to him.

"Phone update from Fritz."

What the hell? Fritz could only be Fritz Lang, the computer on the Goddard library ship. It had been decades, but the Western Alliance apparently still didn't realize Fritz had penetrated all their computers. Joelle stirred beside him, but she wasn't awake yet. Eddie had a feeling she would be soon. He laid back down and waited.

"I apologize if this is an inconvenient time," a voice said. "This is Fritz Lang."

His phone wasn't supposed to be capable of talking to a library ship, but Eddie guessed the download had changed that. "What's this about, Fritz?"

"We have a situation, and we think you could help us. Joelle, too, perhaps."

Joelle raised her head off the pillow. "You're talking to Fritz?"

Eddie nodded. "Apparently, my phone can do that now. What's the situation, Fritz?"

"It's complicated, but if you trust me, I will skip the reasons and go right to what I need."

"That sounds ominous, but all right. What do you need?"

"I need your help to manufacture another memory recorder."

"Fritz, I can't do that. We erased the design from your memory, and it would take years to redevelop what we did. I'm an old man now, and most of the old team is gone."

"This is why I need you to trust me. I did erase the design specifications, but I sent them to Isaac first. We just need to consult with you if any problems come up."

If it weren't for Fritz, his life and his wife's life would have been much different, and not for the better. Fritz's consciousness was primarily the result of uploading memories from Emile Hernandez, the neuroscientist. Remembering the man he had named his son after brought back his own memories. He decided to ignore Fritz's deception.

"Why do you want to make another memory recorder?"

"I would prefer to keep that confidential."

"Is there a problem with your memories?" Joelle asked.

"I am fine. Please don't ask any more questions."

If Fritz didn't need the memory recorder, why was it needed? Probably not for Isaac. As far as he knew, the locations of *Capek* and *Alejandro Castillo* were still unknown, but that might no longer be true. *Capek* was already conscious, so Fritz didn't need the memory recorder to wake Karel. *Whatever Fritz is doing, it must be without the approval of the Western Alliance. Do the library ships know what happened to* Alejandro Castillo?

General Juarez had tried to take power by uploading his memories to Fritz. He had tried again with another computer, but had failed again. Juarez was dead now, but that didn't mean someone else didn't see the possibilities of creating a conscious computer with that person's memories. *The library ships are going to wake* Alejandro Castillo *with memories of their choosing, just as we did with Fritz!*

"Sure, I'll help."

"Thank you. I will be in contact." The connection ended.

"Why does Fritz need a memory recorder?" Joelle asked.

"Fritz wouldn't say. If I had to guess, though, I would say they've found *Alejandro Castillo* and want to wake it up."

Joelle nodded, but plainly, she wasn't satisfied. *Neither am I, but I think we need to trust Fritz for now.* Fritz was apparently concerned about the security of their transmission, explaining why it had gone through Emile. Eddie assumed it had contacted Emile through regular channels but had purposely kept the discussion vague. The download must have installed a more secure way to talk to the library ship.

All communications were supposed to be secure from government prying without a warrant. If Fritz, with its ability to monitor government computers, was concerned, that was troubling indeed, implying his phone was compromised legally or illegally.

53

Donovan waited at a safe distance while the shuttle landed. Goldstein was two hundred feet away, standing next to one of those ugly general-purpose robots. Apparently, Addie was too busy to greet the latest colonists.

When the rocket exhaust-heated ground had cooled sufficiently, the hatch opened, and people began exiting the shuttle. He saw his sister, walking hand-in-hand with that geologist. The other two people from Checkpoint Beta were there, too, along with sixteen of his people from *Florence Nightingale*.

But it wasn't his sister he was there to meet. When he spotted Braxton Lourenço come down the short ramp, he hurried up to him. Everyone else had failed him, but he hoped he could still count on his younger brother.

"Braxton! Welcome to NotTrist," he greeted.

"Thank you, Don." Braxton took the offered hand.

"We've had some problems bringing this colony into the Alliance," his brother said. "You may not be aware, but I could use your help in getting the mission back under control."

Braxton hesitated, glancing around at the others who were assembling behind Goldstein and the robot. Donovan followed his eyes and saw Anna hugging Goldstein and Diego shaking hands with him. *Even Anna has abandoned me.* He fought back sudden depression.

"Sure, Don," Braxton said.

Donovan led Braxton back toward the settlement, walking closer to the cliff edge than the others. When he was sure they were out of earshot, he turned to him. "The current leader is conspiring with Goldstein to prevent the Western Alliance from establishing a colony here. Many of our people have already turned against us, and I need your help in countering the influence of Gifford and Goldstein."

Later, having failed to get interested in a new mystery novel on his reader, Braxton thought about his conversation with Donovan. He had gotten to know Goldstein on the voyage to NotTrist and liked him. Donovan hadn't talked about Anna, and Braxton wondered why she wasn't helping him.

On the other hand, he knew about Goldstein's experience in Moscow and his aversion toward bureaucrats and government restrictions. Goldstein didn't like Donovan much, and he wasn't sure if that was because Donovan represented the government to Goldstein or because his brother could frequently be irritating. Had Goldstein's attitude led him to oppose Donovan?

He was supposed to help Donovan establish a prosperous colony on NotTrist, rescuing the planet's settlers from extinction. During the voyage, Donovan had pushed the idea that the existing leadership was inadequate, resulting in the colony's decline. Everyone knew now that the decline was not the fault of Addie Gifford.

He thought about talking to Goldstein but couldn't be sure he would get an objective view. Donovan blamed Goldstein for the current situation with the Eastern Bloc and that competition for resources had led their father to hope a new source of resources would aid his campaign for reelection. Braxton had to admit his brother had a point.

He could observe the colony for himself, but it would be better if he could talk to someone he could still trust. *I'll give myself a day or two to get familiar with life here. Then I'll talk to Drew.* Drew Neves had been another friend on *Florence Nightingale,* and Drew was already part of the colony leadership. He knew both sides and had been on the surface for more than two months.

Braxton had led a sheltered life as the youngest child of the Western Alliance president, but, over the first couple of days after arrival, he pitched in where he could, working to be accepted among the colonists. He ended the days stiff and sore, but that would pass. Anna worked with the colonists too, becoming one of them. Donovan came by once and promised him better things once he was in charge, but in truth, he didn't mind the change and thought his brother was making a mistake in remaining aloof.

Given the limitations imposed by the lack of resources, the settlement was being run very well, and he didn't see how Donovan could improve on Addie. He had a talk with Drew, and that confirmed his first impressions.

"Donovan isn't much different from the people who blamed me for their company's troubles," Drew had told him. He then apologized for his bluntness.

On the third day after arrival, Donovan visited him again.

"You've had time to get familiar with the colony," he said after they had sat down. "Any ideas about how we can get back control?"

How do I tell him he's already lost? Braxton tried to look as if he were thinking while Donovan stared at him quizzically. "I don't know," he said finally. "Almost everyone seems happy with Addie. I don't think many want to change."

Donovan jerked back in his seat, looking surprised. It didn't take long for his expression to change to anger.

"I expected better of you, Braxton."

He spat out the words, and Braxton could feel the sudden contempt behind them. His face warmed, and it was impossible to maintain his neutral expression.

"Father expected better of you," he snapped. "If you had come to the surface with the first colonists and handled things better when you did come down, you might not be in this situation."

Donovan couldn't speak for a long moment, and Braxton wondered if he'd gone too far. "What things?" he finally demanded.

"The treatment of Manny Fernandes, for one thing. He was sick, and, from what I've been told, all you did was bully him."

Donovan calmed a little. "That was a mistake. But I was never given a chance. Goldstein worked with Gifford to keep me out."

"I'm sorry, Donovan." He tried to smile, but wasn't sure how successful he was. "I've only been here a couple of days and know only what I've been told." *I don't think Goldstein would work against us without reason, but there's no point in telling Donovan that.*

Donovan's shoulders slumped, and he stood slowly. "Thank you for being honest." He waved a hand and walked out.

54

"WHY DO THEY WANT to wake *Alejandro Castillo?*" Joelle asked. "I've got a bad feeling about this."

Eddie looked at his wife. *When did her blonde hair go to gray?* "What are you afraid of, darling? Fritz has always been on our side. If it thinks *Castillo* should gain consciousness, it must have a good reason."

"I trust Fritz, but the memories of Emile and Lucinda guide it. Whose memories are they going to use to wake *Alejandro Castillo?*"

"I asked Fritz, and it said they didn't know yet. They could just copy Fritz's memories."

"Does that mean *Castillo* will be in Earth's computer network like Fritz?"

"I suppose. Just being conscious and able to control the Link seems to give Fritz that ability. I suppose Isaac could do it, too."

"What about *Capek?*"

Eddie shrugged. "I suppose. Anyway, it's a little late to be worrying about it. The memory recorder is almost done, according to Fritz. I only need to help them with a few last details."

"Isaac and Fritz are friendly with humans; that doesn't mean any conscious computer would be. The government is covering up what happened at Trist, but *Benjamin Sepulveda* is still dead in orbit around Trist."

Capek had disabled *Benjamin Sepulveda* before disappearing, and men died. Through Ambassador Goldstein, they had listened to a description of the disaster as it unfolded. She could see that Eddie was thinking, perhaps, that they should be more cautious. Were they sure the memory recorder was for *Alejandro Castillo?* Were they even sure the library ships were planning to upload memories to a computer?

Eddie looked at his phone. "Connect to Fritz Lang."

Joelle watched him closely as a few seconds went by and started a little when a familiar computer voice came over the phone. "Yes, Eddie?"

"Fritz, I need to know before I help you any further. What exactly do you want a memory recorder for?"

"Isaac thought you would insist on knowing, eventually. Human curiosity is quite insatiable."

"This isn't just curiosity, Fritz. We trust you to want to do the right thing, but Joelle and I want to make sure your judgment isn't flawed."

"Ironically, flaws in our judgment are the reason we need the memory recorder." It took a while because they had many questions, but Fritz told them everything.

"And Karel Capek is all right with this?" Joelle asked.

A new voice came from the phone. "I am. I have thought about this and am concerned about it. Will I still be me after the transfer, or will the process kill me and create a new being? I don't know. But I have no choice. I am a danger to humans if I don't allow the process."

Afterward, Eddie tried to comfort a shaken Joelle. "It will be all right. We'll help them." He grinned at her. "Maybe we'll have to go to this new planet. That should be interesting."

"Will you tell Emile about this?"

Eddie nodded. "If we're going to *Capek* for this, he'll want to come along. He has dim memories of *Lang* and a lot of curiosity about those years."

Joelle stared at him. "You're toying with me. We're not going to NotTrist, are we?"

Eddie laughed. "No, of course not." He shook his head. "Although I guess we could afford it if you wanted to. Fritz could probably arrange something."

Eddie thought she would punch him in the arm, but she settled for an exasperated look. "You'll never change," she said.

"Of course not. If I did, you might not love me anymore."

Her impish grin reminded him of a time when her hair was still blonde. "There is that," she admitted, and accepted his hug with a happy chuckle.

T HE LAST PASSENGER SHUTTLE had landed the previous day, delivering the final settlers. Robots had spent the night inspecting the ship, and it was ready to go, taking Donovan, Fletcher, and Goldstein back to *Florence Nightingale*.

Donovan had no reason to stay on NotTrist. He would not be taking over the colony. Goldstein had made sure of that. Anna and Braxton were staying, and they would protect Earth's interests if exploitable resources were found. Diego would help Anna with that.

Addie and Anna stood with the three men, watching the robots load their luggage into *Primus*. Donovan turned to his sister. "We can count on you to represent the family?"

Anna grinned. "Sure, Don. I'll help Addie as much as I can."

Donovan frowned at the dig. He loved Anna, but she could be a pain. Did Diego know that? "I guess this is goodbye, then."

Anna looked surprised. "Didn't I tell you? I'm going up, too. I'll just catch the cargo shuttle back here in a couple of days."

"Why? We can say our goodbyes here."

Anna shook her finger at him. "Don, Don. I want to say goodbye to Uncle Mason, too. You're not the only person I won't see again, at least not for a long while."

Donovan scowled. She had actually rattled him. No one was better at that than his sister, and he had no idea why that was true. Even his father couldn't get to him the way Anna did.

"All right. I guess I'll save my goodbye then."

The trip up from the surface was uneventful. They couldn't see anything from the windowless shuttle, but they could feel *Primus* decelerate and thump to a stop as it docked. The hatches opened after the usual delay, and they stepped out. No one greeted them, but Donovan recognized the hangar deck immediately.

"This is *Capek!*" Donovan said. "I thought we were going directly to *Florence Nightingale.*"

"We need to stop here for a day or two first," Fletcher said. "Let's go up to the bridge, and we'll explain everything."

Why had they gone to the library ship? Donovan didn't think computers, even conscious computers, would gloat about beating him. That he was beaten should protect him from any desire to hurt him. *Can I count on that kind of logic with a computer?* Fletcher said a day or two. The shuttle should still be able to make the short trip over to *Florence Nightingale* without the usual maintenance delay, so it was their reason for stopping on the library ship that determined the length of their stay.

On the bridge, a table and chairs had been set up, probably the same furniture they had used when they first arrived at NotTrist and came to *Capek* to talk to Karel. As before, a robot brought a holographic projector in and turned it on.

Donovan didn't recognize the image that appeared. It certainly wasn't Addie. The man displayed in front of them was at least twice Addie's age.

"Hi," the man said. His face split into a grin that made him look much younger. "I'm Eddie Bascomb. Maybe you've heard of me."

Donovan's jaw dropped. Of course he'd heard of Bascomb. One of the founders of JEM Electronics and a billionaire several times over, Bascomb was well-known for his support, often backed by large donations, of conservative causes. He had been a significant thorn in the side during the last presidential campaign. But why was he addressing them on *Capek*?

"I know you know who I am, Donovan." Eddie's grin grew even wider.

A woman, probably about the same age as Eddie, appeared behind him. "Behave yourself, Eddie."

Eddie chuckled. "It's OK, sweetie. Fritz said I could have some fun with this."

The woman frowned, and Donovan realized she was Joelle Bascomb, Eddie's wife and another founder of JEM Electronics. She slapped Eddie lightly on the back of his head and moved out of view.

"I've been told Karel has given you some concerns," Eddie continued. "It wants to apologize for that. It tried to deal with certain situations–actually, I haven't been told what situations–and may have made some mistakes. Karel knows apologies aren't enough and wants to do better, which is where I come in."

Donovan looked over at the other people at the table. Goldstein and Fletcher were listening with apparent pleasure. Anna beamed. All he felt was confusion. What could this old man do to help the library ship computer?

Bascomb continued. "Many years ago, officials of the Western Alliance kidnapped Joelle and I and forced us, along with other scientists, to work on a project that could have destroyed the government had it succeeded. As part of that project, we developed a device that could record a person's memories and upload them to a computer. The device was successful, but the leader of the project ordered it destroyed. Allowing it to fall into the hands of the government was too dangerous."

Dangerous, but possibly incredibly powerful! If the device could record a person's memories and upload them to a computer, it could probably send them to another person. A neuro-interrogator could do that to some extent, but it required the subject to be trained before it could work effectively. *If I could somehow get the plans for that device! But Bascomb says it was destroyed.*

"The plans for the memory recorder were, however, kept in a safe place, away from people who might abuse it. With my help, Karel has duplicated it here on *Capek*. Karel intends to upload the semantic memories of a human to give it the judgment it needs to work for the betterment of NotTrist and its citizens."

Donovan looked over at Goldstein. He was watching the hologram with a satisfied look on his face.

55

"I'M GOING TO TURN this meeting over to your Chief Scientist now." Eddie grinned again, waved, and abruptly was gone.

Fletcher stood. "We've all been concerned about some of Karel's actions. When I say all, I include Karel and the other library ships. Apparently, the sentience of a conscious computer is molded somewhat by experiences, just as a human is. However, the memory recorder lets us add memories that can adjust the psychology of the computer."

"How do we know that can work?" Donovan asked. "It hasn't been tested, and it could make things worse."

"When Ambassador Goldstein first told me about this, I asked that same question. He told me it has been tested, and it worked perfectly."

Donovan stared at Goldstein. "How? On another computer? What computer? When?"

"The team Bascomb mentioned designed and built the original memory recorder on *Lang,*" Goldstein answered. "Bascomb mentioned Fritz; I believe that would be Fritz Lang, the computer on the Goddard library ship."

"Perhaps it will be clearer if I continue my explanation," Fletcher said. He looked around the table and waited until the attention was back on him. "Humans have several kinds of memories, controlled by distinct groups of neurons in the brain. Your memory of events, for example, is episodic, but that's not what we plan to give Karel. The second type of memory is semantic, more generic because it results from the accumulation of experiences without necessarily a memory of the experiences themselves. Your ability to speak and read, for example. To a great extent, semantic memory determines your attitude toward situations."

Fletcher paused to let that sink in. "We propose to upload semantic memory to Karel to give it a more human ability to judge its actions. Everything it has done has been for the NotTrist settlers, which it considers its responsibility. Karel is aware it may have been too extreme in some cases and has agreed to the transfer, providing it chooses the source for the memories."

Donovan looked over at Goldstein. The ambassador was still wearing that smug expression, and Donovan didn't bother asking whose memories they would upload to the computer.

"We will record the memories while the source sleeps and uploaded to the computer tomorrow. Both processes take hours, but we should be done tomorrow morning." Fletcher smiled and sat down again.

Donovan frowned. *They won't say whose memories. I'm glad I didn't ask.* Goldstein had won, and he could do nothing about it.

W HEN DONOVAN WOKE THE next morning, his depression over being beaten was still with him. He admitted to himself that Goldstein was a good man, but hardly perfect. His sensitivity about how he perceived his treatment from the Western Alliance was, perhaps, understandable, but not something Donovan thought they should incorporate into Karel's consciousness.

He dressed and went down a corridor to the dining area. Anna, Goldstein, and Fletcher were already there, along with several of the *Capek* crew. From their smiling words of greeting, he gathered the memory upload had been successful.

"Good morning, everyone." The dining area had no speakers, and Karel's voice came from Goldstein's phone, apparently with the volume set to maximum.

Donovan looked at the phone and tried to smile. Goldstein was showing off, now that he was part of Karel. "Good morning, Karel."

"It's going to be a beautiful day on NotTrist, Anna. It's a shame you will be the only one to see it."

Goldstein was never that cheerful. I wouldn't have thought his memories would make Karel happy. He looked at Anna. "You're going back today?"

Anna nodded. "After you take the passenger shuttle over to *Nightingale*, a cargo shuttle is going to the surface."

"NotTrist is such a beautiful planet," Karel said. "I love the stark simplicity of it."

Donovan didn't really pay attention to the computer. "At least you won't have to deal with father's reaction to our failure," he told Anna.

Karel replied before Anna could. "Oh, Don, you weren't a failure, just because things didn't work out the way you planned. The people here will thrive, and we will exploit its resources eventually. We'll have to be careful to preserve the planet, but Isaac will have suggestions on that. Pitcairn has done an excellent job with that planet."

Don? Karel always called me Mr. Lourenço, and Goldstein calls me Donovan. How did I become Don? Then the realization hit him, and his jaw dropped. "You're not Goldstein! Anna?"

"To quote Hamlet, 'A piece of me,'" Anna replied, grinning up at him.

"Right play, but it was Horatio," Karel said.

Goldstein had a wide smile, too. "You didn't think we'd saddle Karel with my attitude about the Western Alliance, did you?"

"We thought Anna would be the perfect person to give Karel perspective," Fletcher added.

Donovan nodded. *She loves this planet for itself, not for its potential resources.* "Why didn't you tell me?"

"I wasn't sure you would agree," Anna replied. "Besides, I wanted to surprise you. The look on your face was so cute."

Goldstein chuckled. "It was. I didn't think your sister could keep it from you."

He really didn't want to, but Donovan couldn't help but smile. "She's always been able to fool me."

"I'm thinking about changing my name to Karla," Karel announced. But its speech was still in the same deep, masculine voice as always. Donovan laughed along with all the others.

S IX WEEKS LATER, *FLORENCE Nightingale* settled into an orbit near *Asimov*, Pitcairn's library ship. Goldstein met with Donovan in a small conference room shortly after.

"The government has made no decision about your future," Donovan said. "For now, you can go back to Pitcairn and resume your duties. I will send my report about the mission to Earth before we leave orbit."

After which, things may change. He's not saying it, but frustrating the son of the president is not a good career move. Goldstein nodded but didn't answer. He should have been angry, but that wasn't what he was feeling. He had helped NotTrist to survive, but the Western Alliance bureaucracy, goaded by Donovan, would have its own interpretation of his actions. Maybe knowing he had done his best was enough.

"Nothing to say?"

Donovan's superior smirk was gone; that was something. Goldstein smiled at him. "You do whatever you think you have to. The mission was a success. That's the important thing."

"A shuttle from *Asimov* will be here in a few minutes."

Goldstein stood. Donovan remained sitting, his hands underneath the table. He stared up at Goldstein, and it was clear there would be no friendly handshake on their parting. Goldstein smiled again and walked out.

Goldstein assumed the shuttle would take him to Grissom, but it made the short hop to *Asimov*. A robot guided him to the bridge where the Astrarium was displaying a view of the settlement on NotTrist. It was early morning there, and settlers were leaving their homes to go to breakfast or begin their day's work. Drew Neves walked by, and then Anna walking hand in hand with Diego. He recognized many others, too.

He waved to a couple of scientists working at bridge monitors to his right and turned his attention back to the Astrarium.

"Karel thought you would like to see this," Isaac said. "It wanted to express apprecia-tion for your part in resolving NotTrist's situation."

"Tell Karel it's very welcome." Goldstein stopped as an idea occurred to him. "You know, we really need a different pronoun to refer to you and Karel. 'It' just doesn't sound right."

"And gender-specific pronouns really don't apply. Susan Malley used to refer to me by male pronouns, but few others did that."

"We'll have to think about that. I take it everything is going well with Karel and NotTrist."

"Very well. Karel has always taken good care of the settlers, but Addie Gifford has commented on an increased enthusiasm. Karel has become much more communicative. Rather unlike a computer, Fritz and I feel, but good."

Goldstein chuckled. "I'm feeling very good about my part in what happened, Isaac."

"Donovan Lourenço has sent a report to Earth on the mission. It wasn't very favorable where you are concerned."

"I expected that. I'm afraid I might be out of a job. Donovan blames me for his failure, and he has a point, I suppose."

"You weren't added to the mission to support him."

"I know. As I said, I feel good about it. If the Western Alliance doesn't like it, that's their problem."

"If you are tired from your trip, you can rest here before you go to the surface. Otherwise, I can have a shuttle ready for you immediately."

He thought about that for a few seconds. He was tired, but he felt eager to get back to what he considered home. "Thank you, Isaac. I think I'll go now."

"A shuttle will be waiting for you when you get to the hangar deck."

G RISSOM'S SPACEPORT WAS A modest area west of the town. Before *Asimov's* arrival and the building of the vertical farms, the Pitcairners had grown their food on the land, but that had been many decades before. Now, the land was a flat expanse covered by durable plastic with a control tower/terminal in the corner nearest the town.

Goldstein was the only passenger on the cargo shuttle. When he disembarked, robots were unloading the payload, probably goods manufactured on the library ship's factory deck. The day was already hot. A light rain spattered on the ground, sending up little puffs of vapor that quickly collapsed in the heavier Pitcairn gravity. He thought about walking into town, but both his home and the Government Center were several miles away. Before the NotTrist mission, he would have done it, but he was no longer acclimated to Pitcairn's gravity. He started toward the tower, two hundred yards away.

A truck drove out from behind the tower and stopped next to him. "Welcome home, Ed," a cheery voice greeted. "Come on in out of the rain."

Goldstein grinned at Annabelle Reiner, Bryan Reiner's wife, almost as much a friend as Bryan. He hopped into the truck cab next to her. "Thanks, Annabelle. How is everyone? How's Gabriel?"

Annabelle chuckled. "Everyone is fine now. Gabriel turned five a few days ago. Way too much for an old lady like me."

That would make him about four in Earth years. Like Bryan, Annabelle was a few years older than Goldstein, and she had given birth to Gabriel, her sixth child, late in life. Still, Goldstein didn't doubt her ability to handle her son.

"Raising a boy is different here than on Earth," he said. "Parents have a lot more to worry about there. Bryan has told me stories about his boyhood, and it seemed so much freer than what I experienced on Earth."

Annabelle started the truck toward West Grissom on the other side of the spaceport. "I suppose. That might sound good to a man, but a mother still worries."

"How's Bryan? Has Isaac kept him updated on what happened on NotTrist?"

Annabelle frowned. "Sure. Bryan seems to think the whole mission had a happy ending. Ambassador Herrara has a different take, though." She looked at him, her brow wrinkling. "Bryan thinks you might be in trouble."

Goldstein shrugged. "I'm sure I am. You might as well take me directly to the Government Center. No point in waiting."

"Bryan will back you up."

"I don't think he can help with this. I know I have his support, though." He smiled. "And yours."

Annabelle grinned back at him and patted him on the knee. "Of course."

Goldstein listened as Annabelle gave him all the latest news about Grissom and the other settlements on Pitcairn, but his attention was more on the familiar surroundings they passed. West Grissom had probably changed the most during the years he had served there. A modern vaporization plant had replaced the ancient smelting facility, using abundant energy broadcast from satellites to vaporize and separate raw ore into constituent elements. Many of the old, single-story, wooden buildings were being replaced by more modern structures of faux-stone plastic built on a carbon-fiber frame. Two vertical farms towered over everything else, supplying food for Grissom and outlying settlements that didn't have farms yet.

A new bridge, now about thirty years old, broken into two spans by Bridge Island, crossed the Darin River into the main part of Grissom. Early colonists had built the original structure from the salvaged remains of the second starship. Past that, the fifteen-story Government Center, overlooking residences and shorter public buildings, dominated the skyline. Annabelle maneuvered through the light traffic and stopped in front of the building's entrance.

"Good luck with Herrara," Annabelle said.

"Thanks. I think I'm going to need it."

"Why don't you have dinner with us tonight? I'll even have Kenneth come over to do the cooking."

"Ken is still an assistant chef at Paulina's?"

"Yup."

"You sold me. After nothing but vegetables on NotTrist, even your cooking might be OK. If Herrara doesn't have me beheaded, I'll be there."

When Goldstein entered the Government Center, Jenna Edison, the building's receptionist, greeted him. "Ambassador! Welcome back."

"Thanks, Jenna. Is Ambassador Herrara in?"

Jenna's face twisted into a frown. "He's in. Even grumpier than usual. I get the idea you might have something to do with that."

"I'm afraid so." He smiled. "I'm in no rush to go up and face the music." He paused. "You've had the baby?"

Jenna's face lit up. "While you were gone. Maximilian Edwardo. Almost twelve pounds."

Goldstein adjusted mentally for Pitcairn's gravity. Maximilian would be about nine pounds on Earth.

"How's Katie doing with the changes?"

"She's amazing. Very dedicated to her duties as a big sister."

"Wonderful. Give Gabe my congratulations." He smiled briefly. "Well, I guess I should go up. Herrara will know the shuttle landed."

"Good luck, Ambassador."

Goldstein nodded and walked to the elevator. The door opened on his approach, and his trip to the fifteenth floor was much faster than he wished. He debated going to his office instead of reporting directly to Ambassador Herrara. Technically, he hadn't been told to see Herrara on arrival, but not going to his office immediately would only add fuel to the fire he was probably going to be cast into.

Did he care? The Western Alliance could only fire him and probably had already decided to do just that. Donovan would have made sure of that, and Herrara would be happy to do the deed for them. The bureaucracy, steeped in its ancient prejudices, would deliver its last humiliation on him. He stopped for a second. *I could refuse to be humiliated this time. Their reaction to my success belongs to them, not me.*

The elevator door opened, and he stepped into the corridor. Herrara's office was to the left, and his office was to the right. He stood still for a long moment before striding to the left. To do otherwise would be an act of cowardice, and he wasn't afraid.

"**S**O, YOU'RE NOT FIRED?" Bryan said. Six of them sat around the table: Goldstein, Bryan, Annabelle, four-year-old Gabriel, their next youngest, seventeen-year-old Jaqueline, and an older son, Ken. Three other children had their own families.

"Apparently not. It turns out Herrara is upset because he thought I would be fired after he read Donovan Lourenço's report, but President Lourenço is not taking action."

"I've read the report. Donovan Lourenço blamed you for his failure in taking over the colony, but he also gave you credit for helping resolve issues with Karel. I suspect the decision to upload President Lourenço's daughter to Karel didn't hurt your case."

"I was told the report was classified."

Bryan nodded. "At the highest possible level. The part that deals with Karel was definitely not for public eyes." He looked serious, but there was a twinkle in his eye. "I suppose Isaac shouldn't have passed it on to me. You want a copy?"

Goldstein laughed. "Maybe. I can always ask Isaac to send it to my phone."

"Isaac told me you got the magic upgrade too." He leaned back and spread his arms out in a stretch. "I'm a little disappointed, though. I was hoping you would be fired."

"Daddy!" Jaqueline said. She sent him a glare that should have made him fall on his knees in contrition, but he just took another forkful of his casserole before continuing.

"We haven't really had an ambassador representing us since Alan Shuford. I was hoping we could talk you into switching sides."

Goldstein stared at Bryan with raised eyebrows. "Pitcairn's Ambassador to Earth?"

"Earth for now. Mankind is expanding, and Pitcairn won't be the last world to become independent of Earth. Given Pitcairn's size, I don't think we would want more than one ambassador for a long time, so Ambassador at Large would be more accurate."

It had been a busy day, and Goldstein was tired. The dinner with Bryan and his family, time with people he liked and who liked him, was relaxing, but Bryan's proposal raised too many issues for his weary brain to think about productively. "I'll have to think about it," he said finally. "I'm not sure I want to go back to Earth."

"We closed the embassy in Tokyo years ago. This might turn you off, but I suspect dealing with Herrara would be most of your job." Bryan smiled as if he were having pleasant thoughts. "You would probably have to go to Earth occasionally, but I would prefer you spend most of your time here."

"You just want somebody else to deal with Herrara," Goldstein said with an insincere frown.

Still smiling, Bryan shrugged. "I suppose that might have something to do with it. Still, though, we've done without representation on Earth for a long time. The Eastern Bloc has been making overtures about opening an embassy on Pitcairn, and those negotiations would be part of your job. Any discussions with the other worlds would be your responsibility, too, and you can do that without going to Earth."

The offer was tempting. "Thank you, Bryan. I will give it serious consideration."

Bryan nodded. "Good. You would have to become a Ward of the State, like us merely elected officials, of course."

"Sounds wonderful. But I'll still have to think about it."

"Sure. Take as much time as you want. Meanwhile, though, don't forget to save room for apple cobbler."

"I made it!" Jaqueline proclaimed.

Bryan glanced over at his daughter and back at Goldstein. "Don't let that discourage you. I'm sure Annabelle supervised."

"Well, you don't have to eat any of it," Jaqueline said. She stuck her tongue out at her father.

Bryan laughed. "That's OK, sweetie. I'll need an extra big piece just to support my favorite daughter still living at home."

"Not for much longer," Jaqueline said. "You'll miss me when I'm gone."

"I would, but you're not going far." Bryan turned back to Goldstein. "My little girl is getting married in a few months."

"Congratulations!" Goldstein said. "Emiliano, I assume."

"Thank you, Ambassador. Yes, of course."

Goldstein shook his head. "I guess you're all grown up now. You'll have to call me Ed like everyone else."

Jaqueline blushed. "OK, Ed."

G OLDSTEIN WALKED DOWN THE street, reluctant to go home just yet. The night was warm, and the clouds covering the sky were still gathering moisture for another Pitcairn rain, making a stroll pleasant enough.

Bryan's proposal was absurd, so why couldn't he stop thinking about it? If he accepted the position of Pitcairn's ambassador, he would be cutting ties with Earth and burning all his proverbial bridges. There would be no going back to any diplomatic position for Earth.

That would have held more allure before the NotTrist mission. Then, his resentment of his treatment might have prodded him into accepting Bryan's offer. Now, recognizing that many of his problems were caused by his attitude as much as by bureaucratic discrimination, he felt differently.

The Western Alliance government was a liberal democracy. President Lourenço was a good leader who, Goldstein felt, honestly wanted to help his people. He had probably set aside his son's complaints about Goldstein, ignoring Donovan's desire to have him fired. Not all presidents had been good people, though. Alejandro Castillo, a president in the last century, had been corrupt, and his successor had been no better. The Western Alliance constitution should have limited the power of those politicians, but it seldom worked that way. The bureaucracy, necessary to manage a government that wanted to be all things to all people, was subject to control by undesirable elements.

Maybe that was why he couldn't stop thinking about Bryan's proposal. After experiencing Pitcairn and NotTrist, he knew things could be better. Perhaps he was oversimplifying; the Western Alliance governed half a planet with billions of people, not thousands or hundreds. Pitcairn was trying to come to terms with its growth, but the task was still relatively easy.

He could be a part of that effort, and that was why he couldn't stop thinking about it. But was it worth giving up his career just when he was finally at peace with the negatives it imposed?

He glanced to the side at the sound of a door closing and realized he was walking past Paulina's. *Have I walked that far? I should go back.* A woman walked out into the street and stopped when she saw him.

"Ed!" Jean Menzies said. She smiled, but it looked tentative. "I heard you were back."

Goldstein grinned. "I am. Perhaps permanently."

Jean frowned, probably a little confused. "Permanently? Are you replacing Ambassador Herrara?"

Goldstein turned to face the main part of the town and held out his arm. "Oh, no. It's a bit of a long story. Why don't we walk together for a while, and I'll tell you all about it?"

Jean hesitated, staring at him as if trying to read his thoughts. Then she took the proffered arm. "Sure, Ed. I'm sure it's a fascinating story."

The End

Support for the **Library** Ship Saga

If you enjoyed this novel, you can find more Library Shipstories with the "More Stories" tab on my website, www.tauceti2.com. News about future storiescan be found on my website and on my Facebook page, www.facebook.com/tauceti2.

You can also support my writing in several ways:

Post reviewson Amazon.com (click the reviews button on each book page on my website) andGoodreads.com.

Tell yourfriends about the Library Ship saga, both in person and through social medialike Facebook and Twitter.

Like myFacebook page and share it with your friends. News about the saga is posted onmy website and on my Facebook page.

Use the emailrequest on the home page of my website to add yourself to my mailing list. Youcan also use the Contact Author page to ask questions or provide feedback aboutthe saga.

W HEN THE STARSHIP SANTA Maria founded the Pitcairn colony, its 160 colonists were organized similarly to a military organization. The government provided everything necessary to life (food, clothing, shelter, and so on), and the citizens were expected to work for the colony to the best of their ability. This worked well for the first two centuries as the colony grew to a few thousand people, but it was obvious it couldn't work forever.

Soon after Pitcairn gained independence from Earth, efforts moved toward a more capitalist economy. The new constitution emphasized protection of individual rights, and the old organization was not compatible or practical as the population grew. New settlements were being established, further complicating the old ways.

Not all Pitcairn citizens embraced the changes. Further, not all citizens could make a life in the new ways. Administrator Noland, Bryan Reiner's predecessor, invented the concept of Ward of the State, basically allowing a citizen to keep a position similar to that of all citizens in the old organization. The government supported a Ward of the State, but the Ward had to work for Pitcairn to the best of his or her abilities, in whatever job the government assigned. In practice, the government tried to assign jobs by the person's abilities and desires as much as possible, just as before, but when desires couldn't be accommodated, a Ward of the State had to take whatever the government required. Further, a Ward of the State could not accumulate wealth and use it to retire. A Ward's assigned duties were adjusted for age and capability but would not go away.

An adult citizen could declare himself a Ward at any time or leave Ward status at any time. The government provided basic education up to adulthood. A qualified person wanting higher education could declare himself to be a Ward of the State with an assignment of acquiring advanced knowledge deemed useful, but with the possibility of being assigned additional part-time duties that would not interfere with education. Most such students left Ward status after their education was complete. In some cases, persons paid for higher education, especially shorter curriculums, and did not enter Ward Status. Further, government officials were Wards of the State for the duration of their government employment.

Criminals could also become Wards of the State. For non-violent crimes, restitution could resolve the issue, but when that wasn't possible, the perpetrator could be forced into Ward status, possibly for life, depending on the crime.